ZUNU SCRUBS

and

The Odd Excursion

Series by
M.S. Friko

Illustration *by* **M.S. Friko**

CONTENT

To every Zunu Scrubs and Danh Nguyen that resides in us.

With open eyes I often dreamt of a world. Another universe…

A home…

Far away from this home… a special connection.

I am grateful for the lawn that needs mowing, windows that need cleaning, and floors that need waxing because it means I have a home.

– Anonymous

Below is a free book mark for the reader of the book.
How do readers use it?
INSTRUCTIONS ON NEXT PAGE.

Ask any Print shop/Xerox shop to print the image over a thick paper like a photo paper. (Take the 'paperback' book along.)

It can be printed over a cheap paper too. If the paper is low quality, you can stick the image over cardboard, punch a hole in the center given. (You maybe having at home some useless carton box, pizza cover box or a used note book whose card board can be used.)

Push a string or ribbon through the given hole and tie both ends of the string. (Laminate the book mark for longevity.)

Also, you can simply take a print of the image on A4 paper. Then fold the sides of the remaining paper behind the image and glue behind neatly. Crop or fold remaining top and bottom paper such that only the image is seen. Laminate it.

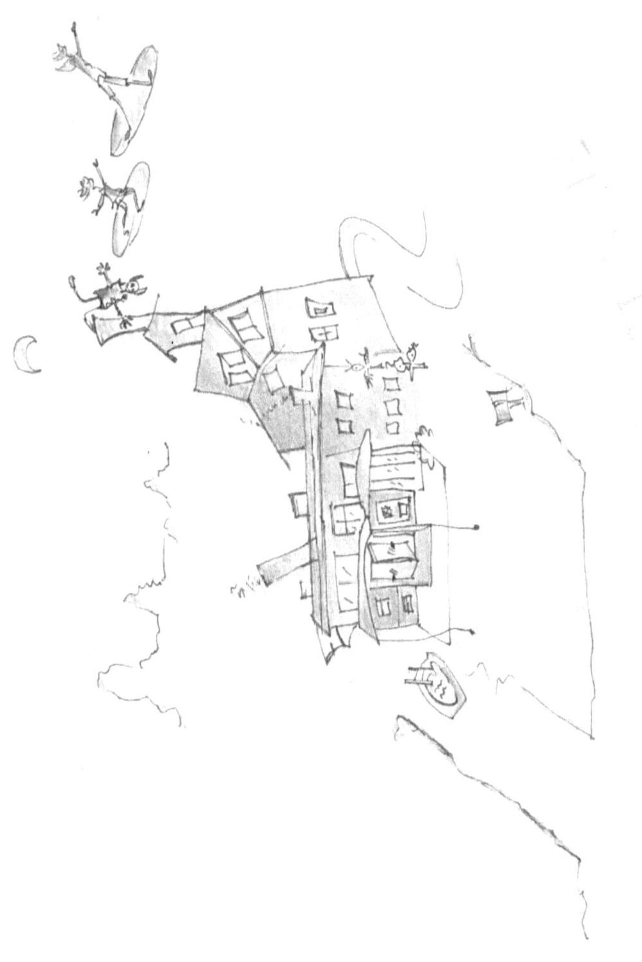

CHAPTER ONE

Moo the Spoiler

In a far far universe in its own, planets had their tiny thrilling moments. Some shifted smoothly, others clashed, banged and knocked each other out while the notorious stars watched the soccer game without a blink and as much a squint. They gruffly grinned, clapped, waved and then dozed off.

In between the tiny social wars stood a 3,000 km rectangular biscuit. A blue crumbly puny little biscuit. That's how we humans would define it over seeing it through a telescope. Some enthusiast called it a three layered biscuit, as though it had cream filling inside it. Few intelligent laboratories in the 17th century referred it as a pure isolated square land though it was a rectangle. Some nerdy scientist even believed it was a messed up piece of earth that flew off to another universe.

They nudged their telescopes, they poked their lenses. In the 18th century they drew earth maps without a rectangle for a while. But none of the beliefs had any impact.

Galaxy 1x with life in it was far by unimaginable. As the word went by the brighter and 'trendy' of humans hadn't acknowledged it as yet, leave aside coined a name for it. The fashionable and the classy circuit were just not in the mood for another planet. Not yet. They were busy and obsessed with the usual chores; dabbing lipsticks, finding the best loose finishing powder to apply over their cheeks, different shades of rose compact that made their skin a salmon pink, and which metal suited the necklines and ears the best. The silver mirror polish also needed to be changed to gold keeping in taste of the elite club. Each disclosure was prized and granted with bunches of cash.

"Today you are the toast of the town. Every woman cherishes the glitteri. You shall have a house over moonhills with bricks of platinum." Clever women clapped and extolled the chosen genius.

People going against the government were deemed silly, pea brains; some rebuffed too for perfidy, underhandedness and punished harshly.

"Grab the invent and drown it in the seas. Place him in the dungeons and lock him with chains till he learns to call the cat a rodent."

So the piece of flat 'dough' in the sky remained so as one of the 'unnamed' biscuits and not on our mission. Human seasoned study charts skipped them. Life continued for us and way beyond us. The tiny planet still kept breathing far away, undisturbed.

Obere Tuftra, Plot no 12, Pinea town.
Year 2019 –

Galaxy 1x. The dim porch light was on. A quiet silent night. Blue light was flooding the entire space. Eleven year old Zunu was talking to his friend over planet Earth. He lay on his front, with his back to the dark steely unswerving skies. A slender bamboo torch hung from his neck silhouetted by the dim light. The light shone upon him outlining a shadowy average built body that was now rolled onto its four's.

Zunu looked quite like one of us. Black hair, dark black eyes that pierced you with honesty, sensitivity & a deeply inquisitive nature.

'We don't have any animals, birds, flowers out here. The mono season is on,' said Zunu with disappointment.

'Once in a while we have plant Cactus growing in. My ancestors got it from some galaxy. Sometimes it gives yellow flowers too. The plant has very sharp spines and no leaves. I don't like it.'

'Some are slim and extremely tall, and others are short and round like a ball… a very spiky ball. There are even desert floras that resemble hedgehogs and some that resemble ping pong paddles.'

'I had it too. It was a Saguaro, but it threw the bucket soon,' Danh was quick to add.

'Oh. Why did it die?' Zunu valued plants very much. Galaxy 1x had its limited periods of flora and fauna.

'I gave it a lot of water each day. I thought all plants need water,' Danh pressed his lips inwards and chuckled with his hand squeezing his mouth.

'That isn't funny. What did happen?' said Zunu. He was a very responsible boy when it came to protecting the 'Greens'.

'If it didn't like the water, is that my slip up?' Danh quietly murmured with downcast eyes. He suddenly flattened himself onto the floor and covered his notorious face with his arm.

'Oho. Nice act by our drama queen,' said Zunu ironically.

'I didn't drown it.'… hiding his head still lower.

'Oh, I see. So that was it. You did drown it by your own admission,' Zunu pulled his leg further.

'.. Accidentally,' Danh said twitching his face over to one side, still covering it.

'I punish you, you will grow another one.'

'He he, I already did so Zunu,' Danh turned around and burst into laughter.

Danh Nguyen was a lovely Vietnamese boy all of ten. Very friendly, easy-going, wore an easy smile, playful and adventurous. He and Zunu had been friends since Danh intercepted his coded messages via a twig. Zunu was looking for friends over Earth and both hit off very well.

Danh had a diligent patient listener in Zunu. Chubby chinky eyed, Danh was quite a chatterbox. There was no need for television, as alone he could make up for all the diversion for people even outside his window. The sharp crisp grass outside his tiny window was now a brown bald patch with a few signs of grim pale tufts still left to see. It lay very flat and always busy with small pair of bare springy feet. Wherever a little grass found its way it was soon squashed and beaten down. Children climbed over each other and peeped in his modest wooden window with noiseless giggles.

– 'Danhi, the ice cream truck is waiting for you.'

'Just turn around, it's inside your room. Vonk Vonk.'

Someone'd let go a 'crazy' horn blaster.

The taunt had rattled him and ruffled him endlessly, innumerable and untold times. His tiny eye balls would be as big as the biggest cufflink black button ever seen and cheeks a hot scarlet red. One thing he hated was being called fat. (A little over weight was more apt.)

When Danh was five, he never knew Cactus should not be watered much. Otherwise he was quite a wise little man. One day to make the cactus grow faster and bigger, he chose it needed a lot more water just like his paddy fields do.

He planted it in a bright and new terracotta plant pot. He poured jugs of water till water reached the rim of the mud pot. One fine day when Danh showed up the cactus appeared simply too soggy and lost its hold. It lay upside down like a plumpy well fed green Zucchini ready to be plucked from soil.

'I like all plants without a doubt and take good care of them. No ifs or buts in it. I give just enough water. Nothing for you to get stressed about,' clarified Danh knowing Zunu's anxiety for greens.

'Glad to hear it. Me too,' replied Zunu.

The breeze rubbed his freckled nose daintily and flew over his velvety thick hair.

'Not Bambi! My neighbor's goat hates hedgehog. Every morning she'd come around the wooden fence lined with morning glory, moon flower, sweet pea and rose creepers... she loves to smell the blooming roses. But then the hedgehog started sprawling all over.'

'One day she got a very bad prick and had to be taken to vet. We tried to pull it out with tweezers, but it was painful for her. Since then she keeps a good distance,' remarked Danh.

'We have many plants, animals, flowers, and trees everywhere. I wish to travel to wildlife sanctuary, but we don't have the money. I hear Africa has the best animals. I don't have internet, otherwise I would show you my favorite animals,' Danh added excitedly.

'Interesting!' replied Zunu. 'I wonder why my galaxy has nothing except sand dunes in this season.'

'Wildebeest, giraffe, gazelle, big cats, elephant, zebra, eland, topi, kongoni! they all stay in Serengeti national park. It's their home. I told dad that we must build a home for them right here in Vietnam!' Danh chattered away while Zunu appeared deeply engrossed in his conversation.

'My dad says wildlife safari is one of the biggest charms of any African experience and Tanzania is perhaps the best country for adventure into the wild. One day he will take me there. I look forward to it,' he said dreamily.

'Oh! Just wait a second,' said Zunu picking up the book

lying next to him. 'I am beaming you our "Guide Map Book". Just lookout towards the floor for a beam.'

Zunu drew out the light bamboo torch hanging in his neck by a thin belt. He flashed the silver sage torch over the book. The torchlight hit the book, and the tutti frutti colored beams that looked like tiny flying butterflies enveloped the book in seconds. In another instance the zig zag beams had travelled timelessly to fall right out of the empty space into the Nguyen home. The floor was illuminated with a tutti frutti rectangular pattern bursting with energy. The abstract butterfly mesh then bloomed steadily into a sturdy structure almost in a snap. The spectacular sight left Danh's eyes rolling and mouth wide open.

'You should see it now. Just open the second slot of the book.'

'Now can you show me where Serengeti Park is?' Zunu's square charming face was lit up with curiosity.

Danh fumbled through the Earth map with his jaw still dropped. It was too big. So many countries and galaxies.

'I need some time,' said Danh.

Meanwhile Zunu's dad called out for him.

'See you tomorrow, I need to go. Bed time. Dad is screaming,' Zunu ran off.

Danh went through the guide map and decided morning would be a better time to explore. The map was just too big. He placed the book upon his window ledge and fell asleep.

The colossal trees swung in the breeze, with a welcoming hello. Life was just starting to move for remote village Na Rang in Vietnam. The grass was as green as it could be, slope tops and the valley beneath were showered in yolk yellow light. All of a sudden, the fierce tiny sun in the sky becomes huge in the measure.

Milk vendor and newspaper delivery men were heard calling their exchange every step of the way of the road. The newspaper guy scudded the newspaper in the empty verandahs, tossed it over the sloping roofs and slammed it over and into the windows as he stopped his cycle door to door and pedaled away.

The otherwise lazy and slack colony did have two baggy feet scurry out of their homes for the new stories in the newspapers. Hands scooted out of the windows and swept back in with the newspapers. People sat in the dank reedy verandahs goggling the news with big eyes and plummeting glass frames. The busy eyes ignored the buzzing red fruit flies and for once they weren't crushed. As the yellow sun got higher in the cloudless sky, the day's action starts and so our story moves.

The tan shaded savvy farmer agriculturist in his familiar white checked shirt drove alongside his tractor on the worn out street. Sun kissed women started to come to work with a tired and languid face. The grouchy kids got up towards the beginning of the day and begin to play uninhibitedly close to the waterway. The muggy morning appeared to be rather self quieting with bumble bees getting charged by the colorful tangled flowers.

Not long after the lively summer beams had started to warm the day, there was a peculiarly long and shrill siren, a whistle, and Danh's mom jumped up quicker than a cat! The ear splitting siren was blowing hard enough to alert even the blocked ears of the incurious and the indifferent.

It was the milkman, and if she was not quick enough the huge line up would wind around the compound leaving her with an empty can. Mrs. Nguyen stood in the long queue of ladies with mini cans, half asleep, half swaying like a pendulum. Body as square and featureless as a crate box, people refused to believe pudgy podgy Danh was her little boy.

In any case, after a gentle and refreshing sleep, Danh believed the beginning of the day would go as per his plan. There was the usual consoling metallic sound of clanging pans, dishes, crashing skillets and the spluttering of water. The smell of jackfruit stewed in coconut milk filled the small kitchen and the hungry by lanes. Breakfast was all ready, just a brisk splash of banana jam on top of some bread (Danh's favorite fruit jam), and with it Mrs. Nguyen was calling out to them –

'Danh! Wake your dad up. Tea is ready. Don't make it too Long— I always have to reheat the tea, both son and dad are so lazy!' Mrs. Nguyen shouted from the kitchen. Well, they were used to it.

Danh had been waiting for the morning for so long after a late night; he barely believed his eyes, when he saw no sharp sooty shadows in his window cast on religiously by the tall lamp post. They were diluted by the onset of morning light. He rubbed his small beady eyes and knew he was a bit late to get up, but he'd waited for the day so long. He was so excited to see the foreign guide map and what was out there!

He reached out for the window. He quickly felt for the book and his hands grabbed empty air. He felt nervous.

'Go ahead. Close your eyes. 'His mind said it should be found with closed eyes too!

Now re-imagine the window sill Danh. Stress your mind. You did place it right there Danh!

Bet you're picturing this…

There was no wind at night. The book was too heavy to fall off the window ledge. So whatever happened?

The ten year responsible grownup inside him had a lot of explaining to do. Zunu sure would be so angry. He decided to go book hunting.

He placed the first query at neighbor's door. His curious snoopy friends might have deeper insights. Ah! The mystery was solved sooner than a fleeting sneeze.

It appears so that it had caught the attention of a pregnant cow. Call it hormonal changes, but the cow was smitten by the book's smell...

And he always believed cows loved only green pastures and not dead books. 'Guess, I was wrong,' Danh told himself. But I am just a kid. Maybe cows eat ice creams too.

Next time I have to stay wary while eating ice creams.

– It took a cow to ruin his day.

'Still, would it eat the book? With so many green fields – unlikely. It must have just carried it off somewhere?'

"She was pregnant —" said Scotty.

"I saw her, Eat itt. I swear— !" the tittle tattle circulated-from one to another, back to Danh.

The disappearance act "whodunit" unraveled in no time, as word passed from ear to ear.

He searched by the fields and finally zeroed in on the cow that fit the description. The mother to be was restless and all odd behavior. Suddenly it gave a traditional donkey kick. One leg back and up towards the sky,

He saw the book covered with mud slip into the river.

..

'How many times have you heard, 'Will you be able to put those blossoms on the window ledge?'

– ALERT issued by Danh. Don't do it anymore!

… 'Someone needs to clean off the window sill because it's getting grimy?' Alert! You now have cows to lick off the dirt too. Mooooooo! Please come eat up everything.

'Cows grazing on lush green pastures is a pleasant picture for farmers and people driving through the countryside and an integral part of many livestock farms. However, grazing livestock with unrestricted access to our books becoming fodder? is not funny!'

"Stop it Danh!"

'It's just a poor animal,' Zunu had just got in touch with Danh.

Danh was very apologetic about the episode.

'I hope it wasn't all that important. I can buy a map guidebook and replace your loss ?'

'We will sort it out later, my dad will do something about it,' Zunu reverted back.

'I cannot swim. I couldn't help,' Danh face shrunk.

'God knows where the book is! Please help us god,' Danh pleadingly looks towards the sky. His mom had said - God answers every prayer in time.

'It's ok Danh. I understand. You go now and freshen up. Have a nice hot cup of tea.'

'I will solve the issue.'

'Just one more question, Zuny.'

'How did you beam, I want to beam too.'

'Simple physics. Magnets. We have these advanced "black magnets" created technically for superior printing and beaming too. They have customs and convertible magnetic fields. Black magnets are not the same as your standard magnet that have a basic North pole on one side and South on the other. They have customizable patterns that can be designed and created in minutes. They can print on a scope of different adaptable materials like your floor for instance, as well as any other standard substance.'

'Apart from printing, they also have the ability to adjust to the strength of the pull of any other gravity force and thus beam to and fro as needed. They attract, repel, or collectively stay together as the need goes without physically touching any source.'

'It's used to stop and regulate storms too, impacts the atmosphere - is all I know.'

'Now Mr. curious, go and have your tea.'

Zunu was about to disconnect.

'Give the final high five,' Danh reminded him.

Both guys leapt up to their feet, bent low to their knees - cheeks blown outwards with mouth full of air, shook their hips silly and muttered their play slogan as a chorus, their hands and palms raised,

"A little bit crazy,

A little bit fat,

A little bit of us,

A little bit mad!"

Danh frisked over one foot and ran off giving a big high five with his left hand up in the air. Zunu disconnected.

Behind in cosmic Galaxy 1x, stood the ornery tall black rectangular tower with periwinkle blue luminous paint. It stood black in the noon but the luminescence flitted like a trail of running ants when it was dark and the tower glowered. The tower rose so high, it broke through the fluffy snowy clouds into the unknown. The murky dark skies dreaded its neon lights and the timid clouds draped its electricity as it sharpened its claws.

It had a fantastic cryptic spread of very fine seventeen micrometer nickel nails dispersed around its base that looked fairly like a whirl pool - a gigantic swaggering ring. It made these "crash" THUD sounds, nothing unusual about it. Once in a while Galaxy 1x heard it.

Nobody visited the desolate tower, entry was forbidden to maintain security. Its bright blinking light at top of the tower paused the otherwise light blue monochromatic screen of peaceful galaxy 1x with little twinkles every now and then; a place where there was no sun, no moon and no water.

Zunu lifted his index finger and quickly switched off the third button fitted in the wall switch board, used specifically to beam. If left on, it activated the multipurpose torch to be used as beams, which otherwise gave normal light.

CHAPTER TWO

A Messy Start

Zunu Scrubs in his collared white shirt and elasticated shorts, pulled away his pleated grid duvet and jumped out of bed. The 'twig signal' had been going 'croak croak' and vibrating intensely with a large frequency 'bzz bzzzz' since Danh had wished to speak with him. No alarm clock had to whoop out any sound to wake him up that day.

He opened the stuck up washroom door knob with a gentle clockwise push; A board enclosed in a black frame hung quietly from a coir twine, nailed wisely to the fronts of the polished door. It jovially greeted his entry with:

A reminder to the 'Bathroom Rules

–'HANG UP your TOWEL'
~ 'put the seat down' ~ 'wash your hands'
– 'turn off the water and lights'
~ 'floss and flush' ~ 'be Neat & tidy'
– BRUSH your teeth.

Zunu quickly picked up his soft bristled toothbrush, and squeezed a bit of peppermint toothpaste over it, as he held his rinse cup in the other hand. Every drop of water mattered, water was imported to galaxy 1x which never had rivers or streams or a potential source of permanent reliability in the 'mono' season.

He rinsed his mouth, and spit into the round marble wash basin – the water gurgled down the sink hole spirally. He splashed some water over his face, dabbed with a gentle towel and stared into the wide metal frame mirror all refreshened. He ran a comb through the hair to partition it, set it flat with a touch, and stretched his mouth to check all his teeth. All ok.

Zunu then rushed out of his upper storeyed bedroom to speak with dad, and suddenly froze midway; his jaw dropped out, mouth opened and shut, at the sight of the living room as he stood at the top landing edge of the traditional staircase runner, that graced the natural stone travertine stairs to the bottom…

Layers of Sand were covering and choking the entire room including the stairs up to the top level!… Eighty feet mountain of tiny gem like sand. The sand stood there motionless like proud priceless monuments of Egypt. He pressed a button to call 'Plastica' urgently. Left aghast–

Plastica walked in, climbed up the sand towards Zunu and awaited his instructions.

'Please clean up the sandy mess and get the room neat,' said Zunu.

'Yes, I will, but please don't create such a mess again,' Plastica replied. Zunu's dad had him tutored very well not to over pamper Zunu, some discipline was of utmost importance in bringing up kids correctly, and instil a sense of responsibility.

Plastica assessed the room with one round gaze, then got a shovel and **a very big** wheelbarrow, a "300 **liter capacity**" from the garden area. It appeared bigger than Plastica himself! It was Ginormous and Elephantine. It was a delight to watch the tiny man work, Plastica wore a red orange cap that read 'I help', and was battery operated. Of course, he talked as well.

His face was a light grey television box, big round eyes that resembled a swimming pool; one slightly bigger than the other and just beneath it, a straight mouth that ran from one end to another. He had curvy funny lips that took pretty much any shape. His four feet long segmented hands hung larger than his five feet pewter body. His ankles were round balls. His ears looked like two stamping seals stuck over a box. His chest had a blue trapezoid plate that looked like cold artic ice.

Plastica streaked in, zoomed out and then did a double back like a jagged bolt of lightening with a duster and dust picker. He scurried around zap zip with a dry spin mop. He scrambled up and down with a tiny bucket in his hand with the speed a fireball. In no time the empty wheel barrow dump cart was full up to the rim.

The light yellow feathered microfiber duster trapped the dust, cleared all tight corners in the stairs and cleaned up the glazing bars of the window sheets without any nasty chemicals. Plastica looked so assuaged. He used a round big hand lens to check all corners for any sand dust specks and grains.

With a button, he swiped and slid open the special wide plank floor panel over to one side, exposing the huge rectangular storage tank just beneath it. He then started shoving and collecting the sand right into the perfectly shaded ashy crude oak flooring of the empty tank. It took merely thirty minutes with his speed.

Zunu sat patiently over the pale grey eight seater sofa in front of the subtly patterned wallpaper - focal point of the room. A large window opposite it maximized the light and increased the sense of space. Zunu stretched over the chaise end, quite uncomfortably with crossed arms and crossed legs. He tapped continuously, twiddling his thumbs and chewing his nails in between.

With elbow sunk in the soft grey cushion, he lay down on one side, knuckles pressing his cheek and watched Plastica work, 'What madness really! What a dismay! All my fault. First the book episode and now this silly drama. Plastica will fill up dad's ear and he won't be pleased. Not really the right time to go and meet dad.'

At night Zunu had climbed out of the casement window onto the porch to chat with Danh. He forgot to shut back the window and an unpredictable sand storm engulfed the entire room. *Does dad know it...*' he wondered.

After collecting the sand in the tank, and cleaning up the room with a hand duster and mop… Plastica threw the rug mat at Zunu. He caught it swiftly, startled.

'You wash it. I will not,' Plastica said rudely.

'Strange, this one rug is always left for me to wash,' observed Zunu. 'This is the tenth time the sand has set in, and each time I was made to wash the mat. I am just eleven, ten times is not a bad record for any mess up. It could be passed off unapologetically as just once a year,' thought Zunu unabashedly.

'hmm, maybe it has allergy towards cats, the mat smelled of it or possibly my dad told him to leave some work for me too… possibly to teach me a lesson?'

Plastica slid open the flat panel in the ceiling positioned just above the tank. The ceiling lowered the huge three flat blade, high powered pearl white rotating exhaust fan that whirled, whisked, and swallowed away the sand instantly into its own metallic storage tube. The sand moved through it like some fat caterpillar in a cocoon, to be swapped into a thinner aluminum pipe up the chimney route.

One Push– Another fat push (just like Leclerc, a third generation battle tank discharging smoky grenade **balls**.)

… Out Out it moved...

….to be blown back into the air. The panel shut without a noise.

Zunu jumped up from the sofa, and ran out of the main hallway door, to see the grain splash in the sky. There it was! Layers of sand grains screeching against the blue line horizon, sprinkling and splitting the sky with abstract visuals of bird form, rabbit, heart, stallion, cloud shapes and open mouth. It all looked like pretty fireworks and within seconds, 'Plop' the rubble fell flat as though it never existed.

But wait a minute, it never does REALLY disappear!

The adjacent neighbor's door opened and Zunu grit his teeth with 'eeks', tongue sticking out. He sprinted and darted on his back foot, back inside home, his hands over his head.

You see… All seemed ok… but…

Only there was a fault in the system. It always did land on sixty five year old Mrs. Twiny Jansen's roof. Her straight roof had to be switched to complete temporary slant mode to dispel the thick sand layer off and she'd be so angry always. Zunu's dad had made countless efforts to get it rectified, many complains but the galaxy management couldn't find an apt solution - the houses were closely set and they don't control the winds.

'We don't have a solution for this as yet Mr. Antorio, maybe you could shift elsewhere.' The three official men said looking over the top of their glasses as they communicated their lasting verdict. Zunu deplored the grand suggestion. Indeed - 'That's no solution.' Even a child would know it.

There were two loud knocks at the door - no ring and Zunu knew who it was. He ran up the staircase, shut the room door behind him and stood still - rapid quick breathing, clammy palms flat against the door, call it *"Palmar Hyperhidrosis".*

'Plastica… where is Zunu?' the grey haired granny inquired furiously, bunned hair stuck at best, a midriff belt around her over bulging dress. She barged the hallway searching vehemently.

'I am not programmed to give location,' Plastica opened his mouth to make a suitably cutting retort.

'Where is his father?' her voice now raised. 'Both son and dad have made my life so miserable, I am so old,' her vintage dark colored round eyeglasses were halfway off the nose bridge as she pushes them back and raises her index finger sharply.

'Sorry again. I am not programmed to sneak or spy,' Plastica countered and that left her all the more annoyed.

-'Plastica does sneak on me at least, won't be long before dad knows,' Zunu told himself tilting his head yet closer to the door sharply.

'The entire family is one and the same clan, where is the respect towards neighbors or elderly,' her eyes appeared misty, on the lookout for comfort as she struggled to find her polka hanky.

'Why did I ever shift here,' her thick squirry fake eyelash

extensions carried stress and heaviness. It looked like the eyelashes would have her eyes droop to the floor any moment. She scrunched her nose, and went off shouting, seething and stamping her feet, the door slammed behind her.

Zunu could still hear Plastica faintly rattling: 'Sorry, not customized in that area.'

Mrs. Twiny Jansen was completely frustrated…

UH OH! The door *reopened.*

She'd had heard Plastica answering her back …

BLAST!

Irate granny headed like a 'bull' in full power for Plastica. Her thick painted starry nails held around his meager flimsy one inch neck tightly and firmly.

'YOU –DO NOT ANSWER – BEHIND MY BACK.'

'GET THAT? STRAIGHT UH?'

Her huge almond eyes pierced through him as she scoffed. Her heart shaped lips primed and rosy face trembled.

'You cannot murder me. I am qualified to generate opinions mathematically,' Plastica made a terrible face.

Outrage droned through Mrs. Twiny Jansen blue veins.

'NOTT OVER R–ME… you heard dat?'

'NO Opinion over mee— !'

She snapped sternly, her nostrils flared further like a rhino.

'Why not? If you could explain?' Plastica chided further.

'You behave well featherhead —I need not explain a thing.'

' — Crooked Dump!'

Her cheeks were shining red as she yelled and frowned.

'Hu.' Plastica ribbed.

'Icky dump. No one challenges me. You ...you understand.'

She stuttered and swelled into a big balloon sharpening her attack.

'Icky dump challenged and won. The old one is iffy,' Plastica riposted.

'Old? ME? How dare you.. How-w dareee you? Mrs. Twiny pressed his neck harder burrowing her long nails further. The tip of her button nose was a cherry red and about to burst.

'Granny is attempting to break me. Call 8211x... call 8211x...' Plastica made ugly revolting faces, lips jerked like a snake.

'How dare you insult me… you plastic ignorant. I will – BLOW YOU OFF,' she quivered. She snapped at him with her finger, eyes blazing her upper whites.

Plastica now stood still, quiet and almost subdued. Eyes wide open, shifting left - right. He tried to utter something.

'WILL YOU DINGBAT — STAY SILENT ! – I SAID QUIET.'

Plastica froze and solidified. He hurled a silent murmur 'Help me SOS.'

'You substandard, second rate, low grade, low-quality of a fool. Keep shut-t!' she let go of her octopussy hold.

Mrs. Twiny was breathless now, she took a deep breath and inhaled still deeper as she was practically sweating with outrage. She placed her hands over her hips, wiped the sweat off with her hand. It dripped to the floor as tiny droplets along with some of her drool that fell with a spat. She adjusted her lower belt and her dress as a statement of her awesome finale triumph and with firm pleased haughty strides, head held high - strolled off adjusting her specs backwards over her big fat nose.

– SLAMM M

The door shut.

Zunu heaved a sigh of relief. Plastica broke into a two second jig rather quickly.

'Goodness! But she isn't too bad, past eleven episodes assert it.' Zunu plunged into his calligraphy print filled bean bag, and recalled how every time she yelled, she got a pizza for him the following day, saying she simply had an uncontrolled temper and he was only a kid. Thankfully she is still sane.

'Her house is just adjacent. I cannot fight with her... She takes good care of my cat. My imported cat from planet Earth, granny's home is second home to her. She gifted my cat a bow and my cat refused to come back till I enticed her with a bigger bow. It's a complicated relationship,' Zunu thought to himself.

He drifted into the past. Once granny was so annoyed that eggs were thrown through his bathroom window. Next day a 'sponsored' pizza showed up at the door.

"It was summers…"

Subway tile and classic white sash windows was always dad's clean modern bathroom idea for the newly renovated home and I was sitting in my tub just opposite it enjoying my new interiors. The double hung window was open. Granny actually climbed her toilet seat and threw eggs at me.

Can anyone believe that… Her aim is quite good, she knows how to spin well and land things right over your head, without hitting the exterior awning!

I could hear her child like giggles, as she quickly shut her frosted opaque special glass window of the bathroom. Now what's so peculiar about these windows… opaque glasses are not even permitted in galaxy 1x!! It's banned.

Really! Who is the bigger kid, me or her?

Dad just laughs it off and says: 'She is old.'

…I am sure Danh will be a perfect match for her.

Say Danh is nice… he will be nicer.

Say he is bad he will be worst.

She is always paying fine each year for misuse of light, 'well not exactly electricity.'

And that's altogether another story as to why she pays those fines and breaks galaxy rules. She is a bit quirky.

You see, we galaxites have the 'Monochromatic/Taxing' season for seven months. That is, we see only monochromatic shades of black, white or brown hues and no other colors even though they exist in those months. (It sure is a boring pattern season.)

Five months as a break, starting from December to April is 'Multichromatic' season when we get to see all colours…

The season includes winter, autumn, spring, rains then finally summers paving way back to mono season again…
Some call the multi season "Whistles, Lantern,

Florochromatic, and Rainbow" season lovingly! We have a splash of colors and patterns everywhere!

The principle behind 'mono season' is to live a simple life. Focus over your work, not clothes and colors.

To implement it, galaxy houses have floor to ceiling 'plain' transparent glasses so that galaxy light can control the colors. The plain glass reflects only shades of three color hues: black, brown and whites. Rest of the colors are suppressed by the glass even if they exist.

But granny, she is a rule breaker and wishes to live with colors all twelve months! She uses obscure glass to obstruct the natural galaxy light and even 'imports' light from planet Earth. But importing is an expensive affair. It's far easier to retain all colors by using opaque glass. It filters natural galaxy light of three colors into seven and allows visibility of all colors inside her home. Quite a trickster.

Just town library 'Pinea' is privileged to use all colors year round. It's for educational purposes.

She tells the light dept. 'I am so old now. I was brought here at age two. Let me enjoy my life now.'

They always let her get away with a bit of fine. She is always with the best of makeup and colorful clothes, polka dots being her favorite. Quite a fashion fiesta. She also has a special hairband and bracelet that keeps her colorful in all places by breaking the mono light into multi light.

Zunu fell asleep again as he floated into the past. He was woken up by a loud 'THUD'. Zunu's thick candlewick like eye lashes opened up startled.

It was only the tall black rectangular tower importing some stuff from some planet and the nickel nails clamouring to it's walls giving it power. Zunu shook his head out of his sleep and put on a full sleeve sweatshirt and his canvas shoes. It was time to talk to dad.

He ran downstairs to the utility room and on the way tossed his smelly mat into the gun metal grey washing machine. He set it to a cold wash, after adding a few drops of liberal unchlorinated bleach and gentle cleanser.

'Done!' Zunu smiled.

He walked through the hallway corridor. Just then the oversized round clock at the left entrance wall, (that held the most distressed finish yet to be seen) went 'bong'. It was half past eleven now and Zunu had over dozed.

Aunt Maly 2x had gifted him the ugly antique clock on his fifth birthday and said to him,

"The big clock shall always be a reminder to do things on time. Work is a necessity for man. That's the reason man invented the morning timer. We cannot turn the clock back nor can we fix the harm caused. However, we have the ability to decide the future and to guarantee that what happened never happens again. It has a twenty four hours sand timer connected to it, to gauge your passage of time. Time has no beauty. This clock is no beauty, you have to make it worth it."

Zunu was exceptionally close to his two cousins, aunt Maly's son and daughter till they moved away to town side. Since then it'd been difficult to stay much in touch.

Zunu stared at the two glass bulbs connected by a narrow

neck. It showed a controlled trickle of sand from the upper bulb to the lower. It would flip upside down in twenty four hours naturally. Half a day had passed by already and the sand timer was nearly half empty, he had to find Antorio quickly. He should be at Pinea, Zunu speculated.

Zunu had sneaked into the town library of 'Pinea' where Antorio worked, many a times as a kid -however children were not allowed alone.

There was a hidden tricky route through Antorio's office to library 'Pinea' that Zunu had chanced upon. The library always absolutely fascinated Zunu.

As a kid Zunu would get to read a lot of books from town library Pinea, but the rule was - you could pick up books only twice a week from the library. It was to avert over indulgence and children below eight were not allowed in the library. Howsoever Zunu would break the rule via the secret route through Antorio's office.

Antorio's office was at ground level inside their home, close to the main entrance. The office was set just opposite the antique clock. Since it had an alternate shortcut through it to Pinea, Antorio would use it many a times if he was getting late for work to 'Pinea'.

Zunu peeped through the office door which appeared slightly ajar. He could see a long thin shadowy slant of light over the floor. As he opened the door, the narrow slant dissipated to a brightly lit up room now brimming with books, documents and wooden shelves. But the room was vacant. Antorio wasn't around.

The library was a good twenty five minute drive from their home **Obere Tuftra Plot No. 12** and just ten minutes via the shortcut route.

Antorio 1x Scrubs had the huge responsibility of being the 'culture ambassador' of Galaxy 1x. He had dropped the post of being town Mayor just for the love of books and knowledge. He preferred managing the library instead. He was into a lot of charity work and dedicated his income towards social welfare causes too. Every Christmas they donated away huge stacks of books, toys and old clothes in goodwill.

Christmas?(sounds strange). But Christmas was celebrated not as any mythological connection to god. It was just as a cultural energising spirited festival.

CHAPTER THREE

The Library

Zunu sneaked into the smaller adjoining room inside the office itself. It was a dimly lit room with some light filtering through the half open slats in the blinds. He saw the bookshelf standing in a corner. It was a light weight eight cube sleek bookshelf filled with books, mementos, a trug, file folders, and a shoe box. Zunu pressed a push button, it slid the cubical aside. Behind it was a five feet narrow old rustic wooden door with a lock. There was a shoe box lying at the bottom of the shelf.

The shoe box was jumbled with many keyset holders. Zunu fidgeted through the cardboard shoe box to find the right key. There it was!... a cute llama molded brass key charm with gold accents. A strand of wooden beads and colorful gems was attaching the charm to the key. ...Only these colors couldn't be seen due to 'mono' season, however Zunu adored the key chain!

Zunu grabbed the small antique bronze key, pushed it into the tiny key hole and opened the door. It led down a lonely sandy path, that curved up towards the 'Pinea' town library. Zunu walked down the isolated sand strewn path and reached the library in merely ten minutes. It held a back door entrance.

The eleven storeyed steel frame building had eye-catching exteriors. The interiors were equally enticing. Zunu entered the library, the skylight building was brimming with blissful light. The research library 'Pinea' made for a truly noteworthy sight amidst the city's bustling Hovern Lane.

As you looked up from the centre, there were glass windows fitted in the dome roof. They opened and shut in sync with the dome that pivoted every few minutes - clockwise and then anticlockwise refreshing the library air.

The small windows gave the impression of square gemstones studded all over the circular dome, from a distance.

Just outside the library, new passersby gawked at the structure and old passersby undermined and ignored the 'Zeeee zeee' breezy pleasant light humming sound emanating with every pivot, nonetheless disturbed by it.

This was the only place which was not devoid of colours even in the 'monochromatic season' as per the law of land. They could see all hues to facilitate learning and read invaluable books.

Ah! The legendary smell of the books… Zunu's perpetually running slightly freckled nose suddenly found itself color and electricity running through it, stimulated and awake. All the blockages were cleared turning him from purple to pink. He took a deep breath to preserve the essence of sweet, musky smell. The notes of vanilla flowers and almonds wafted into every corner, straight up book lovers' noses and lingered on... Nothing could be more addictive! He had always been in love with it.

'Dad'… he tip toed in without a sound.

'Are you there dad?' Zunu whispered, '– dad?'

There was no response. Zunu looked around the library, it appeared empty and silent. But on one side of the library hall there were long tables and benches and the library was actually packed with very quiet students sitting in corners like bibliophiles, oblivious to their surroundings.

They were now looking at him with agitated disturbed look. Someone said 'Shh —' and in few seconds they were all back digging their noses into the books ignoring Zunu.

Zunu could see specs falling out of frowned faces, and eyes fixed straight into the books. Their pursed lips and hands were tinkering with pen and notes, often running fingers into their heads as they jotted down precious notes with pens in their heads. "A used to sight."

The assistant librarian in black blazers, receding hairline and wavy crooked nose looked like quite a trained and qualified person. He was sharp as a scalpel.

'Sir, which section would be suitable for an eighth grade study,' the short thin guy inquired.

'You could move to the upper floor where you will find eighth grade and career related books in section 14– shelf 2,' came a prompt polite reply.

'Kindly don't spoil books by scribbling in them or tearing off the pages,' followed another swift command.

The assistant was offering counsel to understudies on the selection of books too.

Zunu found him busy all the time as he looked around for Antorio and he in turn gave him an acknowledging small gaze or two with his black tar eyes. Of course, he knew him.

The hall door cautiously read "GUARDIAN MUST ACCOMPANY CHILDREN BELOW EIGHT"

Clearly, not all of these books were ordinary. It was the treasure home of Zunu's ancestors kept safe for future generations.

Students were reading newspapers, journals and magazines; some taking down notes. Nobody was allowed to talk or disturb others. The calm and quiet atmosphere of the library helped the students work attentively. Bookworms were sitting and unwinding in cozy reading nooks, day dreaming and opening plan for a bit of inspiration, knowledge and fun, and searching for the ideal spot to get composing sizzling documents.

'Place for geniuses.' Zunu told himself raising his eyebrows in appreciation, and hands sliding deep into his pockets.

The long corridors lead past lovely wooden floor to ceiling shelves. The high flat ceiling of the corridor lanes had combination of different light intensities that created the feeling of depth and stars, with the matte black paint in backdrop being nearly invisible. The black paint added to the mystique of the sky roof, as the stars appeared just out of reach! greeting book worms warmly –plunging them into a new exciting universe.

Zunu trudged around, not knowing that his canvas shoe lace was loosening up slowly, merrily and naughtily. Suddenly in a flash he fell short of support, and just about balanced himself in the air, hands flying out like windmills as he almost squeezed and then crashed into the black board scribbled in white chalk.

A loud "CRASH"—

followed with THud! —and displeased eyes surveyed him.

A touch of white chalk finished over the tip of his nose, head and clothes. Zunu wiped the chalk off with his sleeves, cringed and rubbed his nose; his tongue was smothering out chalk powder. Kids around him giggled softly. A little owlish eyed spectacled girl offered him a pink lacey hanky pointing towards the tip of his nose, that still had the bearings of a white round smudge. The badly hurt nose was now turning red and swollen.

He was in dedicated section for children with plenty of family friendly materials, narrating sessions and even a devoted childcare space for parents with little tots.

Zunu adjusted the board back in position, onto its stand — that now read broken lines and bore white stamps of his finger prints :

A> Evry studen must ap ly for a card and get it. The librar is ues books against the card.

B No student can keep a book fo mor than fourteen day Defa lters ar fined.

C> Every clas has one library period onc a week. Studen mus visit the library only in th period and study.

A gentle hand tapped him lightly from behind...

Some people actually get better looking with age. Antorio 1x Scrubs in his thirties had an air of dignity, often of calm. He wore simple rectangular horn rimmed glasses, a square face with wide cheekbones and jaw. Mushroom brown thick hair with sterling grey eyes, his obsession with fitness and cool library programming could be sensed in his curious eyes.

'Dad! I need help. You will be very upset to hear what happened,' exclaimed Zunu.

'I don't know how to say it... You you-u will be angry-y.' he paused... and looked down.

'I had beamed the 'Guide book' to a friend over planet Earth and the book got lost.'

'That's the reason we don't allow kids alone in the library,' Antorio said in his knowledgeable and disciplined deep voice.

Zunu stared at his dad with a small face full of guilt.

Antorio took a seat at his desk… his forefinger now over his lips in thoughts.

'The book is our heritage and must be retrieved. It was a bad slipup, we have to address it unquestionably. Somethings are not meant to be beamed Zunu, galaxy 1x could be in trouble if anyone chooses to misuse it. It's not an ordinary book,' his fingers were steepled together. His eyebrows as straight as a bar, worried.

'I am so sorry dad! Let's just do what we can. We could go find it,' Zunu's square warm face went pale and shriveled like it had just been hammered into a can.

'Your grandfather never came back once he travelled outside of Galaxy 1x. He was fond of travelling. The guide book clearly states that we will be one of the people over other planets and shall have no supreme power. If we wish to be back, we have to find our way.'

'That's scary. Galaxy 1x is our home and memories. Maybe we shouldn't leave it for a book,' said Zunu.

'Galaxy 1x is the pride of our ancestors. Our education and value system say, we must always do the right thing. All actions have consequences. We will need to look for it. We have to bring it back somehow,' he paused.

– 'All mistakes need to be corrected, Zunu. That's the right way to live. If we have the determination, we shall be back home with the book. We have no right to lose things which our ancestors left behind not just for us, but for the coming civilizations. There is always a purpose.'

Zunu appeared sad. Antorio patted Zunu's head. 'It's ok, son.' He smiled understandingly with reassuring eyes. It flooded Zunu with an overwhelming confidence.

Antorio pulled out a paper from the note pad. He started to draw.

'Tell me, 'What is this?'

'It looks like a tree trunk with branches and leaves,' Zunu said thoughtfully.

Antorio flipped the paper upside down.

'Now what do you see?'

'The tree top has disappeared. I see only roots and a trunk,' Zunu gazed deeply with a puzzled look. He stared at the ragged edges of paper.

Antorio smiled, 'We like to believe that all things in life are exactly how they appear. Yet there's always more than one way to look at something and that is particularly true when it comes to situations.'

'Take the tree picture as example. At first, it pretty much seems fairly straightforward until you take a different look. Meaning you simply change your vision. Once you see the alternate ways to look at life situations, you will be able to unsee the solutions that are hiding within.'

Zunu hugged his dad warmly, 'I'm so proud to have you as

my father. I understand. We don't run away from problems.'

'Are people from earth our cousins? We look like them. Don't we?' Zunu asked with curiosity.

Antorio had no answer.

'Dad, what is god?'

'Earth planet believes god created them all. We don't think so in galaxy 1x. They worship him in strange forms,' Antorio replied with a bland unassuming expression.

'My friend said, god alone knows where the book is.'

'Ha ha! sure we can hope their god helps us cause we don't have one,' Antorio shrugged.

'Why can we see earth and they can't see us? Do we live above them? We live in heaven?' Zunu asked innocently.

'No. Our home is no heaven. Who told you that?'

'My friend said that up is heaven! and everyone from earth wants to go there.'

'I should meet your friend,' Antorio said with an unreadable expression.

'Dad, you said "there is always a purpose" ?'

'At times we don't have the foggiest idea what to do, simply take the minute in and leave it at that Zunu. Don't think too much. Be empty for it, let it stay an unknown purpose. Not always we know our purpose. Go with your belief to do the right deeds and the purpose will be fulfilled unknowingly, towards your destiny,' said Antorio.

The little owlish spectacled girl was peeping from behind a book shelf. She made a gesture towards Zunu with a waving hand and called out to him.

'Excuse me dad, I shall be back.' Zunu turned around at her.

He walked towards her. She led him to an empty reading room at the first floor towards rear of the building. They walked up the stairs and into twisted corridors. A huge arched door opened at a corner. As they stepped in, it's three sixty degree dome made it feel like you'd ventured into a universe of books. It felt like some old time room from an ancient castle with majestic wooden insides and shelves lined with everything from classics work of arts to modern texts with over eighty lakh books tucked away throughout its shelves, running to the top in a spiral fashion. They were home to an immense scope of various writings.

'My pink lacy hanky. Do you still need it?'

'Oh. I'm so sorry. I walked away with it. Here...' Zunu pulled it out from his trouser pocket.

'Thanks,' she said.

She held his hand and took him to a corner. She then blew a pink bubble gum. It became big, bigger, thick, thicker like some elasticated rubber and then with her mouth stuck to it, it started pulling her up. Zunu gaped at her as she rose fixed to the balloon like glue! He tried to pull her down by her frock. Suddenly she fell over her back and her two tiny palms spread over the floor . The balloon still went on becoming bigger. It rose higher and higher. It occupied the entire roof dome. Zunu and the girl stood squashed in a corner. It then changed to a thick solid. The girl fetched a long stick from a book shelf (

used for poking and dropping the higher up unreachable books in the shelf)

The girl slapped the balloon mildly with the long stick. Whirl… whirl whirl…. it started to rotate. Milky way, thousands of sun, hundreds of planets, asteroids, comets were shining and shimmering in a dusty cloudy spread. The fuzzy background too was floating and moving at a fast pace. The universe was being seen it.

'That's planet earth!' the spectacled girl pointed out.

'I'm from planet atlas. Geee!!' she blushed.

'Magic not allowed here,' said Zunu.

'I never break rules. We are immigrants with residential permit. And allowed some liberties to maintain our culture.'

'I heard your conversation with your dad. I thought you would like to see Earth. Anyways most of you galaxites are always talking about it,' she said softly.

'Yeps. I agree. Galaxites know a lot about it.'

'That white line is Astra Bastra. It's a hollow that you will cross to reach milky way. Earth is inside it. Geee!' she blushed once more.

She pointed back to the globe and tapped again.

Tap Tap Tap

The globe shrunk quite a bit this time to show up only Earth. And Zunu was amazed by the pristine, magnificent oasis of nature, right in the centre of the concrete globe . That was Earth. A land dotted with clear streams, water bodies, birds, animals, trees…. lights twinkling everywhere as the sun was down for some parts of the planet and the moon was out.

'I'm Gogola Gems and I was named after a search engine,' said the tiny girl.

'I'm Zunu Scrubs.'

'I know that. I told you I heard your conversation with your dad.'

'It's bad manners to eavesdrop from behind a book shelf.'

'I only overheard as I had tailed you to take back my handkerchief,' said Gogola fiercely defensive with her two front teeth sticking out.

'I'm sorry. I didn't mean to embarrass y....' before Zunu could finish his words the globe plopped to the ground. The structure, a huge concrete stone now was rolling out towards them.

'Run.' Zunu held Gogola by hand and they dashed for the corridor, out of the reading room. The long passage headed straight into finer laned corridors and huge monster sized arched doors. As the walls ran to the top endlessly, the ball was heading straight into them before they could set a foot anywhere out of the main corridor. Zunu saw a table desk in a side corner and both ducked beneath it. The ball ran and hit straight into the wall ahead. The wall fell off and heavy chunks of bricks dropped down, raining mercilessly onto the floor. A lot of paint dust and plaster residue and cement cloud filled the air. Zunu coughed. The flower pot over the table toppled down and shattered. The glass splinters lay over the floor, a small piece had flown into a close by passage and the fresh daisies (imported from earth) lay upside down.

'So! this is what you wanted to show me? Miss Gogola?'

'I'm so sorry. I had forgotten that the globe burst after usage due to the energies inside it.'

'That was a ticking bomb you set off on me!' said Zunu.

'I forgot that it should be set out only in open places like lawn, where it cools easily.' She adjusted her spectacles over her owlish face.

Then she continued, 'Eight planets revolve around the sun. One of them is Earth. This complete solar system is within a spiral galaxy, the milky way. It too revolves around itself.'

'Are you a nut case, is this the time to talk about Earth?'

'But you just taunted me… if this is what I wanted to show you. So I just extended further about the eight planets and the milky way. I wanted to show the real time revolution of the galaxy too, but the ball took off.'

'Really. Planet atlas is very knowledgeable. Thank you so much,' said Zunu sarcastically. He wanted to say silly girl, do keep shut. But kept himself from saying it seeing her three feet size. He had no bucket for her tears.

'Yes. We hold the knowledge of the universe.' She started to count, 'We know every lane that is square, circular, crooked and straight, every river twisted or straight, every ocean, every stream big and small and underground, every cosmic way and…'

'How much nut butter do you consume each day?' asked Zunu. 'Your head is a sharp nut.'

'I've only butter bread in the morning, and mushroom tea. Not fond of nuts.'

'Stop stop stop. Else I'll go nutty.'

'You mean non compos mentis?'

'Yes. If that's what 'you atlas' understand. I'LL BE MAD SOON. Please interpret it in your wordly comfort language and certify it.'

'Oh. You are displeased.' Gogola said with her mouth turned down, head conked over one side.

'We are under a table and bricks tumbling off the wall. For a change wise lady, you might want to take a look at your dress.' Zunu pointed to her dress.

'Your red dress 'show buttons' are creamy white now. It will need a good wash.' Gogola looked at her frock with dreary eyes. 'It was new. It was gifted over my birthday.'

Noise filled footsteps hurried down the old corridor. It was the library assistant, and a group of youngsters. A tall lady was peeping through the crowd calling out for Gogola.

It was her mom. She was under eight and accompanied by her giant mother, eleven feet tall. Gogola was a born dwarf though her mother was a giant.

Mother had a funny hair do. Instead of hair it was a hanging succulent plant bopping in the crowd. From a distance the top was a faint green strings of pearly succulent.

As she came closer she removed her hair do... it was all a hat. She had crimpy wire like bronze hair like her owlish daughter. She screamed nervously and rushed towards her daughter.

'What in the world is going on here? My daughter is unsafe

in this place,' she shrieked.

She gave her hand to Gogola, and pulled her out leaving Zunu behind.

'My daughter was attacked in this library,' she yelled loud, 'Are some decent people hearing it?' Turning all around, she gave an icy stare.

The crowd was gathering now. kids around stared and whispered in bunches. One of the kids gave a hand to Zunu and helped him out. A young boy picked up one by one, the white daises splashed all over the floor. He re-organised the pretty flowers that looked rumpled and frowzy.

'FIND OUT -- who did this! You need to expel them right away, Mr. librarian,' she lifted Gogola in her arms.

'Yes? Who did this? Show your face cowards. Can't face Gogol's mama?' she said with a dash of anger.

She hid Gogola's face in her thick neck protectively. She gave annoyed looks to all children. Two whispering kids dared raise an index finger at Gogola, only to withdraw back the pointer seeing the mom's monster purple raisin face. Gogola ducked further in the shoulder cave, upon seeing the fingers. A quarter of her top head poked up slowly, from behind the shoulder, and then her two eyes. The two boys squeezed their eyes tightly at her, their jaws jutted out. She slid in back quickly and her elbow flew out as she adjusted her frock button. The two boys jumped back as they saw the sharp elbow. She peeped out again, this time tiny from a side. She said, 'Hblu W' and stuck out her tongue at the two boys and spit out empty air.

The mother savagely spun around. 'Just who is teasing my girl?' … 'You?' she pointed a finger bringing down her beastly frowning face. The boy's collars stood up and the scared books flew out of hand. He trembled and gestured 'Nopes.' She spun around like a tornado and towered over the two boys now, 'you-u?' The boys inched two step back with a terrified pale face.

'There are no bombs here and such episodes are rare, we had just one similar case. I need to speak with you alone, ma'am,' said the librarian.

The librarian looked on with a blank expression. He adjourned them aside for a talk inside a room around the corridor, closing the door behind them. Minutes passed by. Finally, the three emerged.

'I think we'll have to raise the bar, 'Children below ten to be not allowed at all,' the librarian gave a hard stare at Gogola. The giant mother quickly hurried away dragging Gogola with her. Gogola's pitsy patsy feet turned around to look at Zunu and the owlish eyes behind the thick frames gave a diffident stare and left.

The public dispersed from the torn corridor slowly with mild discussions. The librarian inspected the damages. He ordered for quick repairs. Zunu walked down the corridor and picked up a splinter that had escaped to the adjoining corridor. He dropped it in his pocket and returned back to the main library area to find his dad.

CHAPTER FOUR

Pack Up

Antorio and Zunu walked back home, discussing all the conceivable arrangements. It was late evening.

Antorio entered the kitchen. He opened the fridge to get some chicken, red beans gravy, rice, marinated drumsticks and glazed carrots for dinner and set up the microwave. He quickly drew out some ice cubes as well from the freezer. He picked up a small hand towel from the peg and wrapped the cubes in it.

'Zunu, just apply this to your nose. It's a bit swollen. It should recover by tomorrow. Ice will help minimize the swelling around your nose, and reduce the spasms too.' Zunu grabbed the ice and the towel and started dabbing.

Shades of whites, greys, and browns combined with contemporary and simplistic straight wooden furniture lay a calm and tranquil atmosphere to the dining area. Zunu sat at the table and applied the cold cubes to his nose. It was too cold for his non stop running nose and the round cubes slipped and slid out of his fingers. As Zunu bent low to pick them up he noticed a hand written note at the casement window. It was pinned to the curtain with a ten inch tomato head pin.

It said:

Mr. Antorio.

Kindly sign the Alien Rights petition papers to be submitted to government officials over the weekend. They are lying over your sofa. The galaxy 7x community needs 'Whistles Season' all year round. This is the 49th attempt to get it done. My courage has yet not failed me.

Community leader

Mrs. Twiny Jansen

'Phew, can't she be normal ever,' wondered Zunu staring hard at the huge head pin with cheeks puffed out and eyes crossed. He picked up the petition papers lying over the sofa and carried them over to the table.

In three minutes, the food was warm, Antorio took it out from the oven wearing his microwave safe silicone hand gloves without any hesitation and placed it over the table. He was accustomed to handling the kitchen. Antorio doled out some cooked chicken for Zunu's cat in the feeding bowl.

'Dad, petition papers that granny needs you to sign.'

Zunu poked his fork and knife into the yummy carrots still patting his nose with the cold hand towel.

Antorio put on his steel rimmed glasses with thick lenses, without which he couldn't see a word. He had one look at the papers, dug out his pen and signed it. It was the twentieth time he was doing so.

'He he! You don't even read it anymore,' Zunu pushed some carrots into his mouth.

'Guess, I know the content by heart now,' Antorio laughed away as he picked up a napkin and placed it over his lap.

'Dad, how many hours does it take to reach planet Earth?' Zunu asked munching the carrots.

'Almost four hours,' Antorio replied with blinking eyes as he helped himself to some food and filled a glass of water from a jug.

'What will we carry with us?' Zunu inquired as he helped himself to some red beans. 'Dad, you need some?'

'Sure, that's just enough.' Antorio dug his spoon into the gravy.

'I have made a list,' Antorio scratched his head. His deep set eyes appeared lost as he bit his lips, looked heavenwards and started counting, 'Toiletries, snacks, hand sanitizer and wipes, medicines, pen and pencil, notebook and magazine, map, dvds, warm and casual clothes, eye mask and earplugs, and tech tools.'

'…That's a big list, will we be back?' Zunu muttered with a stressed look, and forehead creased.

'Stay positive… why not!' Antorio said narrowing his grey eyes. Planet Earth will be a new experience. You have a friend who lives there. You should look forward to meeting him.'

'Ya, that one thing I do look forward too,' Zunu said with twinkling eyes and the edges of mouth transforming up into a positive smile.

Today could be his last day in galaxy 1x... He glanced around at the grey table runner. He gently moved his fingers over the old metallic vase that added a pleasant note to the room. He checked his pocket for the splintered glass that he had picked up from the corridor. He dropped it inside the flower pot.

He swiped through his hair and stared at the small six glass lamps hanging vertically from top. He gazed in nostalgia at the oval acanthus leaf plaster ceiling roses right above the dining table. The big rectangular white dining table with the V legs… He had his every meal over this table and it might be just his last meal. His eyes were misty now.

Zunu's brown cat Tibby, exotic shorthair was lazing around on the super silk soft plush rug, all comfortable and warm. Mmmm… Indeed, the dinner was delicious and she could still taste the cooked chicken on her short straight paws! Her eyes sparkled as she peered into her empty food bowl with large round eyes, and flat nose giving it a few last licks.

Zunu picked her up as she flip flopped over the rug and carried her in his arms to his room.

Overly sensitive Mrs. Twiny cherished Tibby's gentle and calm personality and both got along very famously, with Tibby all teary eyed sad faced, even refusing to get off her lap when asked to come back home.

Well she'd already made up her mind about the cat being doubly awesome, even before Zunu knew it to be awesome! She even gave her a new nickname 'Libby' coined very affectionately –Needless to caterwaul without his consent but Zunu was ok with it, granny succumbed to absolutely no rules, he had had been aware. Her home was second home to Tibby now.

Zunu gently placed Tibby over the floor as she meowed,

smelled and licked his face, pawed him gently.

She walked away with her tail swinging slowly to her sweet fun basket - little kitten cat house.

'Good night Tibby. Could be long before we see each other again,' Zunu said gathering his courage and tightening his fist nervously. Tibby turned around stared into his pale face blankly, not understanding and walked off oblivious.

Zunu opened cubbies underneath the mattress that held books, boxes and baskets for additional storage.

There it was! His favorite fishing game "Pinchco", turning the bar wheel to reel the fish in, maybe he should play it for the last time. With all it's colors, types, shapes, and sizes, he had learnt for the first time about nature and art at age four.

Antorio had told him, 'It will better your hand and eye coordination.' As a kid Zunu was poor with it. He opened the box and his memories. It had in it an oval shaped pond with moss, rock and fossil images printed in it. Zunu brought water in a white mug from the washroom, and dropped all the floating fishes inside the water pond. Then he used a fishing rod to catch the fishes in the water.

There were four trout fishes: Golden rainbow, Brook, Brown and Rainbow trout.

One Fishing rod

One Fishing net

Sea creatures: Octopus, Squid, Pink frogmouth, Jelly fish.

Stones: Caddis fly, Moth caterpillars, Grasshoppers, Bees, Maggots.

At the end of the fishing rod was a fish snare, and the

mouth of all sea creatures had a small metal. As long as the magnetic hook was near the fish mouth, the fish would be straight up. His favorite bait was caddis fly and his most loved catch was the Pink frogmouth. Zunu smiled to himself as he played it again and nibbled on his bottom lip.

He reached out for his tall book case that displayed picture books with their covers facing outwards, dad always placed them outwards when he was little so that he could recognize the book at a glance. He picked up the book – 'Faraway Land of hopes', moved his hand over the cover nostalgically and put it back.

The clouds were shifting towards darkness and the light growing dimmer. Light breeze moved the frilly white curtains in window casting long shadows. Zunu lay over his bed, with his hands under his head and soon fell asleep as the cool breeze mildly patted his silky hair and lifted it.

That night something tried to squeeze in through the letter box. It tried hard and harder still, a small white corner was hanging through. But then there was some block. The letter box wouldn't open in. It slipped back for a pretty few seconds.

Something flew in the dark finally, but through the cat flap of the screen door that lead to the patio. It was some important documents in a sealed envelope. Passports and Identities that carried the home address as Vietnam. Antorio had had foreseen it.

Next morning Zunu and Antorio rang Mrs. Twiny Jansen's chameleon shaped doorbell, the lighted "Please Ring Me" brass doorbell button played rejuvenation chimes and helped enhance the welcoming home. There was a large door knocker too, a mystical green man to keep a careful gaze at door while greeting visitors with unique style. They knocked the door as no one answered the door bell even twice...

"—Mrs. Twiny

....Mrs. Twiny?"

'Yes, *who is it?*' a high pitched musical voice answered with eagerness...

'It's your neighbor, Twiny. Antorio and Zunu.'

The peephole seemed occupied for a second, there was a clang metal sound of the latch and the door opened rather quickly. Mrs. Twiny in her lovely red shading hearts and roses, vintage rounded collar, sleeveless knee length dress with crisp red vibrant lipstick, specs falling off her nose emerged with an ever warming smile.

As they stepped into her home the first thing to catch the eye was the colorful interiors. Colors were not allowed in the 'mono' season, but granny was forever breaking the rules. The use of special 'multichromatic' all color imported light reflected every color beautifully. Maybe that's the reason Tibby loved her home! ~ All colors every season. Wow!

She almost grabbed Tibby immediately from Zunu,

'Ohh! My sweet heart is here as well.'

Ignoring them she dashed off with Tibby into the kitchen and first offered her some ocean fish in a flat ceramic platter trimmed with a silver lining and stars.

'–My rolly polly must be so hungry   — My kuchi puchi.'

Tibby loved being in her lap and all the attention showered over her, she purred lightly.

Mrs. Twiny adjusted her specs, 'Nice to see you Mr. Antorio. How can I be of any help?'

'I am sorry about the ton of sand landing over your roof. Zunu wishes to apologize,' Antorio said regretfully.

'I am sorry, Mrs. Twiny,' Zunu looked up at her.

'Ohh! You are just a kid, that's ok. I lose my temper quickly,' her face broke into a smile as she tilted her head towards the sofa;

'Please be seated. Would you like some tea?'

They took a seat.

'No tea please,' Antorio gestured with his hand and then questioned her with a smile, 'Will you be willing to give Tibby your home for a few days please. We are off on a long journey. It could be long too.'

'You don't have to ask. Libby is my kid. You should know that,' she patted Tibby's head as she continued her conversation.

'So where are the father and son headed?'

'Planet Earth. We have some urgent work,' Antorio replied leaning back over the couch.

Mrs. Twiny excused herself with a grin.

The room was fresh and pretty, with botanical blossoms wallpaper bringing a splendid peach and pink hue to walls with a watercolor floral design that seemed lovely as well inviting. The lady was indeed stylish and very floral!

There was a drinking fountain in a corner. A few weeks ago, she had gifted an overly pampered Tibby one of those fancy cat drinking fountains because cats enjoy drinking from the tap. The fountain head had a funny soft 'fat rubber rat' sitting on top of it. Whole day Tibby would jump at it trying to make a kill. Tibby liked it so much that she started spending all her day playing in, splashing out and drinking the water. She was drinking so much that she was making herself throw up water all over the house and soon fell sick. Thankfully it only took her a couple of days to manage herself but it was a quite a few days.

Zunu could smell the fresh cookies being baked in the oven as he looked around the room. Mrs. Twiny arrived with a large tray of cookies, three cups and a petunia pink teapot.

'Before you leave, father and son must taste my butter cookies.'

'Sure,' Antorio replied and took a small piece in his mouth,

'The cookies are delicious and crunchy. Thank you, Mrs. Twiny.'

'Zunu, you like it?' asked Mrs. Twiny looking for appreciation.

'Ya... fantastic...' Zunu replied nodding his head. She handed him a package of baked cookies, 'You could use this for your trip. I have cooked extra.'

'Thank you! That's lovely,' Zunu grinned with wide eyes and accepted the brown packet.

'How is school going Zunu - lots of studies ?'

'Going very well. I am in fifth grade now.'

Just then there was a knock at the door. Mrs. Twiny had a delivery guy at her place. A funny looking spiky haired guy dressed in blue from head to toe was at the door.

'Ma'am where do I place this sack?'

The sack which looked like a heavy potatoes and onion sack had really no potatoes in it. Mrs. Twiny opened the sack and screeched in delight.

'At last! I have been waiting and waiting forever,' she scoured her hands together gleefully. She started to count the packages with her thick finger tip one by one. She tapped and knocked them with her knuckles to cross check none were empty. She shook the packages to see they had enough matter inside. Next, she got a small green weighing machine with a large scale flat pan fitted at top. She checked if the grams mentioned over the packages were accurate. The delivery guy looked on impatiently and shuffled his gaze around uncomfortably.

'Ma'am, the packages are sealed and not tampered with. I can assure you,' he rearranged his eyes around awkwardly.

'A double check never hurts and safe guards the buyer interest,' Mrs. Twiny grumbled, 'it keeps you guys on your toes too.'

'We don't steal ma'am.'

'Last delivery did have some stuff missing. When was it that I accused you of stealing. You only misplace, right?' Mrs. Twiny protested. The man made a face.

'Do you remember that? The pink umbrella that you had to re-deliver? What if I had not noticed it?' Mrs. Twiny barked.

Nine Triple Dippi Peanuts, Fifteen Milk Chaco Raisins, Quarter Dipped Chocolate, Hundred and one Malty Balls, Golden candies, deodap oozy, and silver chunky, yes! all were delivered! The man stood by restlessly while granny peeped into each silver paper wrapped box one by one.

'Ma'am we have a lot of deliveries from the black tower still pending. Can I just have your signature and leave now?'

'Sure,' she signed 'Received.'

'Chocoholic!' She raised her eyebrows while giving her signature. Do you love chocolate too?'

'Yes ma'am.'

'Care to binge onto the heavenly delight?' she offered him a malty choco ball from the box.

'Sorry ma'am. I am on a nut diet.'

'Oops.' She dropped it into her mouth and shut the door.

'The delivery man told me he only ate whole nuts, but I still gave him a malty choco ball and he loved it,' said Mrs. Twiny. Granny was a story teller too and Antorio had had heard a distinct 'No' to her offer. Granny pulled the jute sack close to her window and there it sat quiet. Antorio and Zunu looked at each other.

'Chocolates will give you a reason to bond with just about anybody.'

She added three dollops of spoonful sugar to her teacup and stirred it gently with a silver spoon as she spoke.

'You... You shouldn't have so much sugar. It's will ruin your health. Tell her dad.'

'Zunu is very right. He has concern for you,' Antorio

commented.

'Ohh! I am so old now. Let me just enjoy my life. A tad bit of sweetness won't destroy me.'

'But – No ways that's little,' Zunu added.

'You are a healthy sized boy. You'll be your dad's size in no time, don't worry about me,' she said holding the teacup with her thick fingers as Zunu looked on graciously and stopped advising further.

'…and Antorio, where is Maly Tar? I don't see her anymore?'

She slurped on her tea with the saucer in other hand.

'She shifted with the kids to level two, she finds the community better suitable for tech schooling as the kids are growing up.'

Antorio and Zunu sampled their tea.

'It was good to have Mrs. Maly around. I don't get to meet her these days except for in shopping malls. It's just once in a while that I bump into her – very fine lady –she is,' said Mrs. Twiny smacking her lips and splashing more tea in her cup….

'She had a lovely backyard garden. Her kids often turned up with freshly grown vegetables to my place, the best brinjals and pumpkins I've had –'15 feet size' ! — grown with very fine earthworm manure. I was thinking of getting lessons from her. I have never tasted anything better.'

She dabbed her mouth lightly with a hanky, and her curvy thick lips smutched over it.

'Maly is a professional chef, —a crazy gardening enthusiast and expertise right from childhood,' added Antorio taking his last sip.

'Would you like a cup refill...?'... eh?'

She refilled half the cup before Antorio could stop her.

'I need a small favor too. I scalded my hand while cooking egg omlettes yesterday,' she showed the brown bandage ripping across her forearm.

'Will Plastica please fire my plants for the next seven days?'

'Of course. Zunu, just please call out for Plastica,' said Antorio.

Zunu walked up to the sash window, pushed his head out and shouted out for Plastica who was busy washing the car. Plastica rushed in.

'I would like to show you the latest collection in my bloom shed if you could give me a few minutes and Plastica too can understand the chores I need of him,' said Mrs. Twiny.

She disappeared inside the repository and picked up a huge key from the byzantium purple cupboard that could lock up five Plastica's with ease. Not that the threat was never held over poor Plastica.

They crossed the lawn which was strewn with sand towards the bloom shed. Mrs. Twiny unlocked the cringy door of the wooden shed with the flat glass roof canopy.

White breathable cotton cloth sheet was covering the stuff underneath in four vertical rows as they looked around. Something entwined around Zunu's foot and bit him. Zunu thought it was a sand lizard. He pulled off the white cloak startled. It was a tiny drago tail plant. It shook its bifurcated tail which had a pointed tooth set that opened and shut with a red slimy tongue. It was long like a ribbon.

Mrs. Twiny immediately covered it back.

'Don't disturb the babies. They are still growing in their pots.'

'Plastica, I need you to spray the fire hose from that corner over each plant. Fire keeps the babies warm just like woolly's do and helps strengthen them.'

Plastica nodded obediently, 'Only fire and no water or sand.'

'Absolutely only fire and just ONE short quick spray, and—not a drop of water,' stressed Mrs. Twiny.

Zunu plucked the cloak off another one gently and slowly from the top of the center. There was a huge snap sound. Something broke 'clink' and fell down.

'Zunu! Don't draw up the covers,' said Mrs. Twiny. 'The Cross Square plant is very amateur and fragile till it's ripe.'

Mrs. Twiny quietly collected the broken soft tile pieces from the floor. She picked up a trowel and started to bury the broken chunks again into the pot, folding the malleable tile in layer after layer like it were some foldable hanky.

'Soon I will have new tiles for my kitchen wall,' Mrs. Twiny commented excitedly, 'Plastica - you need to fire this one thrice. Remember that! Meaning THREE short sturdy sprays. It should immediately be a stiff square and be pluckable right then.'

'Did'ya understand?'

'Yes.'

'Repeat then what I just said.'

'THREE short sturdy sprays.'

'Where did you get this stuff from?' asked Antorio.

'My sister sent it by post through the black tower delivery services. Got the courier through after a lot of tight scrutiny by authorities. Some imports are prohibited. But you know me! I convinced them it was no harm.'

'I love the smell of freshly heated ripe tiles. They ooze a lot of clay in their growing up months though. I have to clean up and scrub the floor really well.'

'Ever seen such velvety square leaves? Aren't they awesome?' Mrs. Twiny said feeling them delicately.

Zunu and Antorio bent double down.

'Such perfect immaculate squares. It's a big wow,' Zunu remarked. Plastica looked on with swimming wide eyes, dumbstruck. He too had seen nothing like this before.

'How is "chopsy" so quiet. CHOPSY is well behaved only in front of Antorio. Huh?' Mrs. Twiny gave a sharp cutting look to Plastica through the corner of her spidery long lashes. Plastic turned away choosing not to entertain.

Mrs. Twiny looked around the shed, tidied it up. Sand was always such a nuisance. She hung up the weeder, hoe and scissors in a corner. She re - arranged the shed, neatened it and put it in order. **Unused pots and pans of iron, and of copper and of black tin, hung from low fitted pegs.**

The four walked back across the sandy lawn to granny's plot no 13.

Antorio shook hands with Mrs. Twiny, 'I'm afraid we are getting late. We must take a leave now. We still have a lot of work to look over.'

'Let me know if I could be of any use. Good bye Mr. Antorio and Zunu you too,' Mrs. Twiny replied with a concerned look clasping her thick hands together.

'Have a safe trip.'

'We shall meet soon.' Antorio smiled.

'Bye Tibby,' Zunu held her in his arms, patted her and handed her over to Mrs. Twiny.

'And before I leave, these are the petition papers you'd left by. I have signed them,' Antorio removed them from his back pocket and handed the bundle to her.

'I am so thankful,' Mrs. Twiny accepted them gladly.

Back home they started packing their bags. Antorio opened his safe vault and wrapped a few gold nuggets carefully in a small box that they would need in exchange for planet Earth currency. He dropped the passport and documents in his bag pack.

He locked up all the doors and then bent low to check the three cabinet unit of the traditional grey sideboard. It lay there for ages inflecting a curving skirt, bold scrollwork cabinet fronts, and a weathered charm to it. His wife had bought it from an auction for a small price.

Antorio opened its drawer and picked up the beaded wooden frame lying upside down. He stared into it with moist eyes, corners of the eyebrows drawn in... Zunu turned around and saw him sad.

Eyelashes that drifted softly like dandelion blow balls,

soulful, glistening with unsaid stories that Zunu wished to still Unravel... that was his mother Zeva and Antorio together in their better days.

Thin lips, straight ash blond, shoulder length hair swept back neatly. Zunu had seen her just in some older albums. Separated from Antorio for years now, Antorio never talked of her. Zunu had no idea what happened and never questioned so as not to hurt his dad.

Antorio sat in a corner clutching the frame. He was falling down down, deep into a dark tunnel— pictures of his wife Zeva flickering briefly in front of him like shadows as he fell:

flash!

It was evening. The winter weather had turned unexpectedly mild and the streets of marketplace were crowded when he first bumped into her. It was love at first sight.

flash!

The day they first met for a date. Her smile lit from within as she walked up to him in the coffee shop.

flash!

His birthday. Zeva beaming with chocolate spread over her face in a ginger split wrap dress.

Her face smiled and rippled through the walls in waves all around and her voice calling out to him echoed in his ears...

No more flashes. All quiet and dimness.

A small squally wind scattered the old photographs from the drawer and was pounding at the window which swayed to and fro with creaking sounds. Antorio grabbed all the photos back and shut the windows tightly.

Antorio placed the frame back in it's place upside down again, and locked all the three drawers that were used to keep small yet necessary items like cutlery, napkins, table mats. After that he locked the three cabinets below the drawers that stored crockery and other dining essentials.

Zunu and Antorio sat together and wrapped up a nice gift for Danh, a 20" Laptop.

'Dad, Danh will love this. He has no net at home,' Zunu said delightfully, rubbing his hands together as he pulled the crackling gift paper tautly up over the far ends of the box. He creased the paper along the box edges with his thumb and forefinger. He double knotted the green ribbon, and tied it into a simple bow and ran scissors over the neatly tied lace. Then he clipped it gracefully.

'We will teach him to use it. He should see no problem after that,' Antorio replied.

Zunu ran up the stairs, back to his room. He pulled out his wooden chair and sat over his study table.

He scribbled a quick small note for Danh. Then he removed his torch from the drawer and adjusted its bandwidth to a 'candy' beam. The beam instantly flew the parchment as soft cotton pink fluffy ball though the space into Danh's room. The minute Danh touched the light candy fluff, it translated into a pink candy floss paper that read...

Dear Danh,

We shall be in Vietnam very soon.

Against all odds, it was decided by dad that this was the best thing to do.

See you soon.

Love Zunu.

Next morning was an important day and a sleepless night ahead. The backpack and a small trolley suitcase was ready.

CHAPTER FIVE

Midnight Crashes

At 12.30 am that night something swooshed into Zunu's window. It was followed by another swoosh. And then a clang of water pipes.

Zunu woke up, threw his blanket aside and struggled to see in darkness surrounding his bed. He rubbed his eyes to find his two daring cousins in front of him. Fourteen year old Baggy Tar and twelve year old Lavender Tar.

Baggy was a tall handsome teen, umber eyes behind thin intellectual glasses. Lavender had the sweet looks of her mom. Both had cedar brown hair just like aunt Maly. Lavender had dyed her head a tinge of cedar brown from her natural black after shifting to second level galaxy 2x. Second level was more liberal in culture and colors were permitted all year round. Just like planet earth.

Level one light had no impact over them as they didn't belong there anymore. They could see all colors.

'Hey! You two at this hour?'

'Your dad told my mom you were leaving for planet Earth.'

'We couldn't have just let you go without seeing you once, our sweet cousin,' said Lavender wrapping her flying skates in her hand. They looked gorgeous as she folded them very small and held them like some toffee in her closed palm.

Seeing Zunu's expression Baggy explained, 'We are now studying in a scientific studies school. Invents and discoveries are prime to us.'

Lavender nodded.

The clanking of the hollow pipes continued and the trio peeped down the window. A short silhouette figure in pink was trying his way up desperately.

That was Drinkiwell. A twelve year old friend who was in sixth grade with Lavender. Before he could land in Zunu's window his flying skates had collapsed out of fuel and hung him over the electricity pole upside down and then crashed him into the sand lawn leaving behind heaps of red sparks and carbon fumes. He could hardly breathe. He coughed and stepped out of the smoke cloud.

As he clobbered to find his way up the water pipe, Zunu quietly lowered a ladder for him to climb up.

Mr. Antorio didn't appreciate midnight visitors. The three of them had dropped in without informing their homes. Late night strolls were not a regular sight in the quiet lanes of peaceful Pinea locality. And certainly, the big ladder in Zunu's room was meant for cleaning up the top shelves and hauling out books. It was totally not meant for twelve O'clock past bizarre invites and activities.

'Thank god granny is not awake. She would create a huge tantrum. She knows mom well and would call her up right away,' said Lavender. Lavender gave a hand to Drinkiwell who caught the bottom rail of the window and quickly slid in. He held an antique box in his hand.

Drinkiwell looked like a cross between Kobolds and human, but was a figolf.

Heart of a human, but cleverness and ambitions of a kobold. His head was a hut shape funny triangle. Red hair fell on both sides through the middle parting and he had a very long nose and a thin voice. He was just two feet tall, very pointed ears and his shoes had large holes.

'Drinkiwell Jot studies at our school. He has migrated from planet Alexa where it became tough to handle the ill intent of the ghostly powers to finish off the rest of fraternity,' said Baggy.

Zunu waved at him and Drinkiwell smiled back gawkily.

'We got him along to show you something before you leave,' said Lavender with big mocha eyes.

There was a small shadow that moved just outside Zunu's closed door. They knelt over their fours and peeped through the slit beneath the door.

'Shh,' said Zunu, 'It's Plastica.'

'The clanging of the pipe must have woken him up,' said Baggy.

The shadow moved away. There was sound of footsteps descending the stairs. It faded off. They breathed a sigh of relief.

'I think we should move to the lawn,' said Lavender.

The trio climbed down the ladder one by one. Not an expert at it, Drinkiwell's foot slipped and he hung by his hands looking for a foot hold. He was about to fall when Baggy held his foot with one hand. After placing it back in the rung, they all got down cautiously one by one.

The lawn was silent as the sand in it. A metallic mail box stood right next to them. The four huddled together on the sandy lawn and lounged around the antique box. It was a rosewood writing box with fluid inlay in pewter depicting motifs. The box stood on turned rosewood feet and had turned rosewood drop ring handles.

Drinkiwell opened the small box. The lid opened to a sloping writing surface with compartments for ink and pens. There was a lift out tray and place for storing paper beneath. Further detachable velvet pads had been fitted in and there was fluffy soft cotton inside the pads.

'This is what you wanted to show me, a writing box?' said Zunu.

'Hold up a second,' said Lavender.

Drinkiwell sorted the cotton aside in one of the pads and there was a silk cloth draping something tiny. It looked like a crescent shaped milky pearl swaddled in silk. As he undraped it, it started to bawl!

Drinkiwell immediately closed the box.

'It's unhappy cause we removed the cotton around it,' said Drinkiwell.

'What the heck is that?' questioned Zunu. All crouched around it slouched over their flat palms.

Drinkiwell took out some cotton from his trouser pocket and laid it in his open palm and then opened the box again.

The crescent pearl yelled and noised again. It wept out loud unrestrained.

Drinkiwell then lifted it smoothly and placed it in the cotton. It quit crying immediately. He looked at Lavender and smiled, who nodded at him positively raising her eyebrows.

Drinkiwell blew wind over it softly and pushed it gently towards the sky with more and more blows. It grew bigger and bigger and took its spot in the sky right above Zunu's home Obere Tuftra.

'That looks like a moon,' Zunu said softly.

They slumped down into the sand and watched it rise.

'How beautiful it looks amidst clouds now. It's dipped my home in mild silver light,' said Zunu.

'When it's packed in the box with cotton it feels it is home. It assumes the cotton to be clouds. If you remove the cotton around it screams mad,' said Baggy.

'It won't cry anymore. It now at home howdy!' said Drinkiwell gazing upwards.

'We don't have a permanent moon in galaxy 1x. This will last just till morning. After that it will move away. I am afraid,' said Lavender.

'How did you capture the moon in a box?' asked Zunu.

'It's something to do with my planet,' said Drinkiwell, 'Grewins don't step on planet Alexa due to dark, very dark entities. A million years back they cried in the woods and left the planet Alexa. Where ever their tears dropped and mixed with the first dew drop of the morning a bow moon seed was born. It was just the last sign of hope for some of us against the dark evils. Just a very few, so few fortunate people could find them. My family ancestors were one of them howdy!'

'What is Grewins?' asked Zunu.

'They are white swans with five hundred crescent moon shaped wings. It's widely believed they are the carriers of moon carriage. The spectacle is seen once in five hundred years only and no one truly has witnessed it howdy.'

'Dark Alexa doesn't permit you to keep moon seed. It hates

light. We migrated to galaxy 1x and kept it hidden in a box. Sometimes we leave the moon seed to the sky. Whenever it leaves the box, it drops a part of the crescent seed in the same box. It sleeps tight around cotton as it believes cotton to be clouds in the sky. If you remove the cotton you are waking it up howdy.'

'Bro, the moon will bring you luck. It will direct you,' said Baggy thumping loudly Zunu's back.

'It will console you when your heart is sad. Whenever your heart wavers it will give you courage. With every heart beat it will remind you who you are. Whenever you loose powers it will empower you back. The moon will look after you. Cause this moon is a blend of Grewins precious tears,' added Drinkiwell in his thin voice.

'We are aware you will have no powers over planet Earth. Ever feel lonely, look towards the sky. And you will be back home soon with moon luck on your side,' said Lavender.

'Is there only one moon?' Zunu asked with curiosity.

'There are several moon seeds which are a part of the moon itself and look exactly the same. These seeds influence the parent moon. We have been studying universal energies and their impact,' answered Lavender.

'Why Galaxy 1x doesn't have any real moon?' Zunu questioned.

'Hi munchkin! Hi bottom fries! Finally!' Baggy said looking at Zunu and the rest two, 'It's just a moon seed, for heavens sake. Don't hit your heads too much. For all I know it could be a plant seed that flies off to the skies and fits in there. All mythology fails there.'

'But it leaves behind a real moon seed in the box howdy,' replied an agitated Drinkiwell.

'Call it the power of multiplication or simply choose as you wish to believe,' shrugged Baggy.

'It will disap-pear tomorrow morning definitely?' Zunu stuttered.

'Yes, great shakes. You arrived the point! But it will still watch over you phew hopefully — not conclusively,' said Baggy. 'You guys get far too carried away. We are in a world of science and planets. Damn.'

'Some midnight snacks anybody. It's 1.30 am,' grinned Baggy adjusting his spectacles and opening his mouth hungrily.

'Let's get back to the room,' gestured Lavender.

They climbed up the ladder one by one, once again and hopped off the sill and squared the ladder back into the room.

Back in the room they swept their hands over a handful of roasted peanuts and popcorn packets. They tossed the peanuts in the air and caught it with their mouths open. Soon there were peanuts flying across the room as they tried potshots in each other's mouths. The timber wood floor was littered with popcorn puffs and half crushed peanuts. Iced milk and empty lemon tea cartons too lay around scattered. Baggy had loaded them out from the kitchen fridge.

Drinkiwell just moved around casually fiddling pen, pencils, caressing the green walls and staring into photo frame with an iced milk moustache and a paper cup filled with milk in his hand. He jumped over Zunu's double poster bed and did somersaults too. He spilled some milk over Zunu's bed but refused to let go of the cup.

'Time to leave now,' said Baggy. The three agreed.

Baggy checked out Drinkiwell's skateboard quad roller. The rollers were grinded out.

'Drinkiwell still has some fuel left, but the rollers are burnt out. Power slider is working, if only we could give it a fierce push.'

So, then what do we do?' said Lavender.

We go back home skating down the streets and that will take Drinkiwell hours with such rough rollers or we could go my way,' said Baggy with his hands over the hips.

'And what's that howdy?' said Drinkiwell his bat like ears standing up.

'Escape through chimney. We climb the ladder first to the mouth of the chimney. Then we use the hot fire as propeller to the skateboard and dash out in no time. Otherwise go skating for hours. Make a choice.'

'You must be whackers!' said Lavender.

'You'll be toasted. Sorry three skeletons to be precise,' said Zunu.

'We'll be scrambled like eggs!' said Drinkiwell.

'We'll be ashbroth soup!' We'll be dead turkey! Noo. Me scared of it,' shouted Drinkiwell.

'You're joking. Tell us that was a joke,' said Lavender.

'I'm not joking.'

'oh howdy! I wish to live longer,' screamed Drinkiwell and disappeared under the bed sheet. The golden gift paper he wore was shining from underneath the sheet through a small hole. (It had thin silver lines all over it. The triangular crunchy paper was stapled and held to his fragile shoulders as the only outfit. He always carried a tiny stapler in his small pocket, for change of outfits. Of course, he loved lights, shimmer and the sparkle. All kobolds do, and all figolfs do too, if I didn't tell you. Only I don't know if the dress was stolen. They could be offensive burglars. Tendency runs deep in the culture.)

'At the most a few scratches and some soot, Now guys this way or that. Decide,' said Baggy impatiently.

'Ok. I'm on, till we are not human con queso,' said Lavender.

'Howdy, what is that?' Drinkiwell shot back in a squeaky voice nervously.

'Chili con Queso is a dipping sauce of melted cheese and chopped chili peppers. It's in our kitchen shelf imported from Texas, planet earth. And human con….'

'Enough of garbowhacklylumy talks. Need some action now,' said Baggy.

'Wait a minute. Let me complete. Drinkiwell, human con Queso could be, rather would b' a dipping sauce of melted body and chopped chili peppers and soft bones that's if we walk into an open chimney, unless and least we live with our wits and heads.'

'That doesn't sound terrific to me one bit,' said Zunu.

'Are you quitter or warriors in shining armour?' said Baggy.

'Drinkiwell the coward. Miss Lavender the scared rabbito. Please wear your boards nice and tight around the neck.

Drinkiwell your gold dress won't gel well with the black board, now would it,' said Baggy.

'The chimney flue flu,' Drinkiwell said popping his red hut head out of the bed sheet with tiny confidence. The brave man inside him was stirred and worried about the fate of the golden dress if at all Baggy decided to award the board. Kobolds can never refuse endowments from friends.(It's impolite and curses fall during the day if you turn down gifts at night, especially after evening, say anytime after sunset to begin.) Lavender turned around and looked at Drinkiwell and then Baggy in sorts of agreement.

'Pretty exciting,' said Zunu.

'Good. Follow me fellas. Up the chimney ladder with your fuelfiller bottles. Fit it in behind the skates. Catch the fire and get a quick lift. As soon you get an uplift, get the first gear correctly and push into second.'

They twinkle-toed down the stairs to the kitchen place. The three climbed into the cold brick lined fireplace, and went up the long ladder to the top of chimney. Drinkiwell broke into a song:

knock knock knock

Up the ladder, one step then two step

We go, we blow!

Look who is here

Drinki, laven and bagss

The glowing warriors

The boldest we

The best we
the fearless three

The trio will fly
Hunkington streets we come we come
Bhum bhum buum
Lum tum lum!
Fun fun fun.

No chilli con queso
No human con queso
Only fun con queso!
Wheeee!

They reached the top. Baggy gave a light knock to the dark sooty chimney wall and gestured Zunu to light up the chimney. Zunu lit up the fire pit. He dropped a few waxed pine cones into it. They were lying over the mantelpiece in a small wicker basket. The tall smoky flames swayed, flicking and curling this way and that, crackling as they burnt the dry wood.

Zunu heard a swoosh…

Yet another swoosh and then an unusually bigger plooosh. Then all was quiet. Zunu went back to his room and slid peacefully under his warm blanket with eyes open to the ceiling.

At 3.00 am, plot no 12 woke up with long lasting activities. Zunu had not slept a wink. Plastica somehow kept giving suspicious looks to Zunu. Drowsy Mrs. Twiny too was awake and gave a small and curious peek through her washroom window for a second.

Plastica helped load the jet and muttered with drowsy eyes, 'I see something like moon close to our chimney and an upside down winged bat.'

'Plastica hasn't slept well at night,' Antorio dismissed it off abruptly while Zunu stifled an upturned grin.

Lesser known and unknown Drinkiwell lay hung by the smokestack upside down, all very upset, while the moon gleamed in the sky. He had pushed in the second gear too early and his skates had jumped right up into the sky and then suddenly fallen flat just over the chimney edge. As the moon moved right behind the chimney his dim flailing arms could be seen clearer.

It was sometime late before it struck Baggy that Drinkiwell was amiss and he finally plucked the terrified two feet from the chimney top. His syrup green mint eyes practically melted into an overflowing water tap when he saw his savior Baggy. Drinkiwell Jot was still in one piece and howled a lot that whole day. The tap flow wouldn't stop. His red pocket handkerchief, a cut out shred piece from a coffee shop table cloth was so wet.

'Bad Baggy lies about gears.'

'Baggy almost murdered me —' to almost anyone who would willingly give a fitful ear.

'Lavender's sibling make me cry, so wicked.'

'And who saved you finally? Tell them that too,' blurted Lavender all annoyed with the rumors in school Wifthshift, the school of science, that's where they studied.

The Hunkington town and the street was buzzing and lapping the odd and lowly treatment meted out to Drinkiwell, especially the kobold crisscross figolf community who loved to believe every possible told untold story without any briefs or explanations, forget clarifications, each one already had a twisted story of his own. An exaggeration that fell off into newer exaggerations, tumbled into fresher distortions and newer widths and gained dimensions, in all directions. Along with a lot of wits added in surplus like salt and pepper.

The common salt that humans use, in all wonder is not so uncommon after all. But sometimes! It just makes things saltier, spicier even without a dash of chilly and by all accounts magnificently sordid too. A great fallout in great friendships thus, as in the future who shall see.

'Wore pink and dazzled in golden when we left. My cousin maintained a cordial silence over it.' Lavender let out the small burglary. And the school Wifthshift windows roared with it. The doors thundered with it. The roof broke with it. The sound of it echoed everywhere. The figolfs were seen gossiping in corners and galaxites 2x tattling in another.(Gift wrapping papers were pretty expensive. If you were unaware.) It costed 5-2/3 Sanddunes for a single paper glitteri sheet and additional Sanddunes if it had design on it.

The moon and sunprints always did cost more cause people had always a fascination for things that were amiss since times immemorial, even over galaxy 1x... (That would be roughly six dollars for a country like United States) who can afford it, a surprisingly high cost for common though. They were imported of course as galaxy 1x hardly manufactured anything.

Next two weeks the school in the mountains stayed busy. Baggy and Lavender often thought of Zunu.

Back home an annoyed Plastica had broomed away the crushed peanuts and the empty lemon tea cartons, grumbling every now and then. He had snooped around almost everywhere, especially the fridge and underneath the bed too - but the roof top. So there— he remained in the dark.

CHAPTER SIX

Journey to the Blue Planet

Flying into the air, the past and the future separated and the world started shrinking. Zunu started taking photographs, as memoir. Antorio was in the pilot seat and it was meant to be nearly a four hour flight. They had started from galaxy 1x at 3.30 am.

They had carried with them a three tier collapsible stand with plates, a cake and some fruit trays, a munch bag in case Zunu felt hungry. It was windy and cold. A lot of empty space around and a land of nowhere. Nothing seemed to be moving around except the Jet wings that sped through the long, deep dense darkness and some silvery bluish horizontal flashes of light. Antorio was flying for an hour now. Zunu had a good time playing puzzles while Antorio gave him an occasional nod. They crossed a white line called Astra Bastra, Gogola flashed in Zunu's mind.

After three hours the jet entered the earth atmosphere. They could now see the ocean, land, and ice-covered surfaces which looked like pieces of a jig jaw puzzle waiting to be fitted in together. The ocean and rivers looked like twisted warped white snakes cuddled together. The top of the snow covered peaks were ready to eat glittering ice cream cones. They started on breakfast with yummy ripe sliced melons - cantaloupe and Galia, some toast and a nice cup of hot green tea, as they enjoyed watching the new unfamiliar miniature terrain below in sheer amazement. —A toy land it looked like. There was some hot water in the flask and they managed to use it for all purposes. It proved a great take away for tea, coffee and soups that they occasionally sipped on.

Wind smothering off the north post made it very cold and water beads were now precipitating onto the jet window. Zunu was cold and his nose was running. He drew out a faded woollen blanket from his travel bag pack and wrapped it around tightly squeezing his stiff head into it. He pulled his warm socks higher up. The thermometer now drifted around the freezing mark. The atmospheric water vapour froze into tiny little ice crystals, and hail started hitting and banging the windows furiously. Flurries of stones roiled in the air under the hold of erratic roaring breezes. Icicles dangled at the windows as Zunu peered through and mopped away his watery dripping nose with a tissue paper.

Furious black mist spat lightning mercilessly onto the jet, as it sliced through the sky. Zunu lowered his head down and wrapped his hands around his ears as sharp claps of thunder pierced his eardrums. A numbing coldness gripped their hearts.

Suddenly a gust of wind seized the jet, and the jet rattled its wings up and down as it hit through the dark clouds and annoyed birds looked on gawkily.

Just then a mad Bar headed goose chased the jet, stuck its beak in the window and kept hitting it hard to break it. Zunu smoothed his nose up against the damp soggy glass, raised his eyebrows to him and kept prodding its entertaining assaults. The bird was adamant and unshakeable.

Zunu quickly plucked out his camera from the bag. He then tapped the goose reflection with his finger point and it wheeled in reverse; confused, all ruffled with conked out wings. Zunu caught the amusing bird in his camera. He smiled to himself.

Again, there was a clean patch, with a dramatic decrease in curiosity. Heavy rain poured down in cold sheets. Zunu kept himself occupied with in between meals, some cheesy crunchy frito pie topped with chili, cheese and onions, and would give periodic bites to Antorio too.

Not a bad trip. Time flies by when you're having fun. He ate a lot and fell asleep. Antorio woke him up to tell him they were now three miles away, nearly five kilometers from his friend's village 'Na Rang'.

They were now in country Vietnam. Antorio had been flying non stop and the jet engine did need a refill. He decided to land in the fields. Earth was pretty near, and there was an incredible spread of land underneath them with mountains and timberlands… at that point fields and trees… and then a small town. Down and further down plunged the jet. Ever closer came the Earth underneath. Sea and land gushed up to meet them, getting larger every second that passed by…The sharp jet wings pierced the strong cold winds for a swift landing, Zunu found himself skidding onto the grass carpet as soft husky paddy fields silently crushed under the jet wheels. Suddenly the thundering engine halted with a loud screech.

'We have landed safely,' said Antorio emerging from the cockpit.

Zunu was left speechless. Antorio was yet calm.

'So, this is PLANET EARTH!!!! Never seen something like this, my first trip outside of home,' Zunu screamed in wonder with eyes wide open.

It was 7.00 am morning. Antorio asked a passerby if he could get a jet refill from anywhere nearby. The stranger said he would contact Hanoi city headquarters, and inform it that a jet was stranded for a refill in the fields. Antorio was thankful for his courteous support. He further added that Na Rang was around three miles walking distance.

'Chúc một ngày tốt lành -Have a good day!' The stranger walked off.

Antorio replied back, 'Bạn cũng vậy'

'How did you understand his language?' Zunu asked surprised.

'As you grow older you will learn all languages like I did,' Antorio replied with a wink.

It had yet to sink in that they were over a different galaxy. Funnily no one questioned their identity. They looked so like one of them. Antorio was tired, Zunu could tell from his face.

'Zunu, are you happy? You will be meeting your friend.'

'Yes dad. I'm soaking the reality.'

The sun shone splendidly and the water in the nearby pond sparkled. Besides the mountains and close to the backwoods there was a cascade with white water sprinkling down to the stream. They filled some fresh water in a bottle from the stream. Strands of fog had soon started clearing the dew loaded grass and the webs and they could see better. New breezy cool gave them mild chills; fresh air began whistling - eventing the start of September.

It was 8.00 am now. They sat around on broken rocks and took a quick stroll sometimes. Far off they could hear faint voices of children playing and see local communities just starting their day. Planet Earth had warmly embraced them as its own, as though they were a large part if it. They were so much at home.

The tremendous paddy field stood like an illustrious royal

residence and the thick dried enormous branches of trees swayed as people passed by. Zunu saw amidst the grass a vast, towering scarecrow and circled around it. There was a scary look originating from it's dark sown on frightened eyes and battered old garments hung from its straw made body in shreds. Zunu didn't understand why the dead body was over sticks and gaped at it. He poked it with his middle finger. He shook the fragile leg to and fro. He smelled its clothes. So sad! to be reduced to dry straw after death, thought Zunu. 'I think human beings and plants interchange roles after demise. One turns to wood and other maybe to human.'

Charming butterflies skipped and flooded them, up and down — all around.

Whenever Zunu appeared very anxious or extremely worried about something, it could instantly be read by Antorio. At the back of his mind was still the lost 'Guide book' and a sense of guilt.

'Good luck, surely you will find it and …you rock Zunu,' his mind said to pacify him. But reality check said this was just poor humor. '— No, this wasn't going to be easy or soon. Soothing words won't help either at this point. You are in trouble.' He started twiddling his thumbs and tapping his feet, his shoe soles were muddy.

Zunu found it difficult to sit in one place. Antorio gave the permission to look around but he should stay close by.

'You're not the only one suffering from anxiety, that happens to me too at times. Not always though and when I do feel anxious, it usually subsides with a few deep breaths,'

Antorio said stretching his own feet a bit to relax out.

Zunu sought the opportunity and ran off. Antorio sat patiently, his sharp disciplined and silent personality absorbing the new world. He had till now only read about planet Earth.

Antorio realised that there had been some rainfall the night before. The air was crisp and clean, and the grass still moist. A robin flew quickly over the open field, streaming along with the delicate breeze, brushing his head and then back to its cautiously placed home on that of a tree. He didn't see it at all. His gaze was fixed across the fence. There was a stout wooden fence pole held at closures by a spiked barbed wire. Just across the fence there were some chicken species roaming in the grass field, looking for food.

Tau Vang a funny yellow Chinese chicken was looking for a place to stretch out. It was not one bit appreciated by Ga Noi the Vietnamese chicken who controlled that area— It recognized it as an invasion, Chinese invasion; overseas foxiness possibly towards territorial expansion. It headed to lock horns with an upright neck and aggressive temperament, very angry just like some bull. Tempers flew midair! Ka vroom bhoom! Vek vek vek! Bright shiny feathers tore in the air! There was a spectacular cockfight, as possibly even birds understand which country they belong to. The Chinese squeezed away silently. Ameraucana and the Jungle fowl,(a red Indian chicken) apparently thrilled with the Chinese washout then formed a quick gang with Ga Noi. Antorio simply looked on the interesting threesome as they scouted for food together merrily.

A few moments later Antorio saw a tiny bird playing in the mud. It announced its presence with a loud penetrating cry and musical burst of "kweep" notes. Its wings fluttered uncontrollably and it had very beautiful copper colored wings. The three friendly chickens thought the little bird was onto a new food source and hurried over bawling and yelling, alarming the bird away. But soon tired of the game, they strayed off to other parts of the field leaving the sloppy terrain open for the copper bird. The tiny bird came back scurrying about after the little bugs.

Antorio removed a bread piece from his bag pack, crumbled it into tiny pieces and offered the bird mashed crumbs. It looked at him with sharp eyes and flew off, and perched over the fence. It then watched him intently till he decided to step back and leave the ground open for its re-entry. It flew down again, and started inspecting the ground once more. The bread offer was quietly rejected.

Antorio studied the interesting bird which was now gathering building material and carting it up to the nearby fence pole. It soaked the leaves and the grass in mud and then rushed off to its budding nest. Antorio clicked its pictures. The bird was actually a pair, but he never got pictures of both at the same time. It returned right back and continued picking up leaves. It blended them with mud before flying away with sloppy mouthful. It fascinated him.

The nest was a thick walled mud cup almost complete now with a frontal opening. Looked like many days work… The pair sat over it proudly and warded of other birds from their territory. Guest were unwelcome. Antorio opened his colored pencil box and started outlining the small winged creature. Whenever he got too close to it for detailing, it would take off and gaze at him from far. He was clearly an intruder and the winged bird was displeased.

'I can best describe it for you as a brown bird with tiny tail and brown bird with a mud home,' he scrolled a note in his diary. I am trying to understand planet Earth and its root. I have read about the Darwin's theory of territorial dominance and survival of the fittest. I just experienced it today in the very first species I laid my eyes over. We don't see such fights on galaxy1x as everyone has lots and lots space.

Galaxy 1x is very peaceful, though we have our share of problems. Guest are always a pleasant and a welcome sight. I do see competitive spirits over planet Earth, beginning with the small bird. No… actually it was first the chickens. I had only read about it earlier.

We galaxites do look like humans but have a different inherent system. I wish I could track down galaxy 1x complete history, and why we resemble humans? Antorio nibbled his pen and frowned lightly in speculation.

There seems to be enough of free space available over planet earth and it does appear far more enormous than galaxy 1x, diameter being 12,742 km while galaxy 1x is only 3,000 km. Earth is round from heights while galaxy 1x could be best described as a three layered rectangular biscuit, each layer has people living in it and can travel from one layer to another via vertical good speed wooden cable cars that stop at main station 'Planoi' situated at every level, every sixty minutes. My sister Maly 2x has shifted to the second level and quite likes it.

Such a big planet! Is then aggression an inherent tendency towards want of inner domination or defensive impulse triggered by self protection… I wonder. Theory of evolution states that dominant genes will survive in the long run. Are all species considering aggression excessively important for survival of genes?

That's not the way galaxy 1x operates. Antorio twirled his pen, paused and then started to write again with his lips now hard pressed, eyes deep focused.

Regarding dominance, I have read about the old times, stone age caveman era. Men hauled women by their hair with daggers in their hands and viewed themselves 'victor' of the lady. There were thunderous loud applauds and a trophy too for the winner. He could marry the woman.

I assume dominating approach made 'man' evolve more stronger, broader and more masculine. Continually subduing women made women less forceful, fragile and accommodating. It had an impact on their physical development as well… Call it lack of dominance, genetically.

21st century as I understand from books and pictures, is about women strength, fashion and empowerment and now you might just find strong well built ladies utilizing broom sticks (their dagger) over spouses, yet to be seen by me in person he he! That's just my humor, but could manifest into a reality if books are correct.

On a lighter note: Will women grow stronger and taller than men eventually? Every species is looking for dominance in the long run. I wonder!

Brisk note:

Planet E finds aggression normal. I find aggression unnatural.

Territorial aggression doesn't exist over Galaxy 1x as we know no fear or insecurity.

Planet Earth is very bright and confounded, yet I seem to like it as it seems familiar somehow. I also met a stranger full of 'inherent' respect and courtesy. I thank his kind genes and wish to study humans further and why we look so similar.

Love Antorio.

..

Zunu's walk through the rice field was pleasant and breathtaking. Further down the creek the water gathered to shape a little nature lake, consistently enthusiastic and brimming with activity. Zunu removed his shoes. He walked barefoot on the soft tiny pebbled lakeside, and sat for a while sifting through the fine gravel with his thin fingers. He collected a few spotted slate and feldspar pebbles to take home to remind him of his journey.

He found numerous stones. A stone that resembled a round

ball, some wonderful light pink sandstones, a white one with a broken heart shape. Many had unusual hues. The colors ranged from translucent white to black and included shades of yellow, rust and green, with rusty stripes (the red due to iron staining).

There was a time when he collected pebbles in his pockets till one day the pocket had a hole. This time he cautiously placed them inside a plastic carry bag. It was tempting to hear them 'clink' when he laid them gently inside the bag. He'd good fun shaking the bag, and hearing the 'cling cling.'

He carefully marked the location over each bag and took some pictures. The photos were excellent to recollect where a rock originated from. Each stone in the accumulation spoke to a period and a spot as he studied them carefully. He felt he had hit upon a superb collection of colorful stones. 'Grab the best stone and feel the essence of the planet earth in your palm!' his heart screamed out cheerfully.

He sat by the lake and started throwing stones in it. A tall Buddhist monk in saffron attire passes by. Zunu waved out to him.

'Hello there, how are you?'

The Buddhist smiled and waved back at him.

'I'm new to this place. I have collected a lot of beautiful stones. I like to collect pebbles, clean them and watch them under a magnifier lens,' said Zunu, fairly looking for some response.

'That's a decent leisure activity,' the gentle Buddhist answered back. 'These are great tokens gifted by mother nature.'

'Look! I can even see through one of the white stones,' Zunu said and looked at the Buddhist for friendly approval while he locked the stone with his fingers and reflected gentle light playfully into his face. The Buddhist smiled affectionately.

'Gracious! you have uncommon powers to see through the stone,' the Buddhist commented. Zunu burst into rolls of laughter. He found the man amusing.

'What kind of a water lake is this? When I toss a stone in it, it creates circles. First there were smaller circles, then they grew into bigger circles and bigger still and then slowly disappeared.'

'That out there is the center of universe,' said the Buddhist raising his hand and pointing his fore finger towards the lake. 'It releases vitality in different forms. One energy is me. One energy is you. Smaller circles are lesser energy and bigger ones have achieved more energy. They can change their forms and disappear silently.'

'I don't see my stone any longer, where did it go? The circles gobbled up my stone?'

'The stone is inside water now.'

'In any case, that isn't fair! For what reason wouldn't I be able to see it. I need it back,' said Zunu looking to pull the man's leg.

The Buddhist recognized his whims with a 'hmm.'

'Is the stone god? I hear we can't see god? He gives a brief presence and disappears.'

'Truly son, God is everywhere. Everything you throw in water has god in it,' remarked the Buddhist.

Zunu threw a dry leaf. 'Look! It's above water and I see it.

Meaning it's not god?'

Buddhist smiled at his quest to seek answers. 'It's protected by god.'

'Earth is so complex and people's beliefs confuse me. They say something and following two minutes they overlook what they said. So finally leaf has no god in it, cause despite everything we still see it,' Zunu exclaimed. 'It's just protected by god.'

Buddhist laughed gently with wrinkles around his hazel gold flecked flaming eyes.

'You know my dad says, we all have a purpose. Purpose determines the destiny. So, I guess our destination is Galaxy 1x as per the purpose. Our home is like the leaf that learned to float and rose above the water. That's why we have hardly water and only sand. We stay above the water protected by god and can see you from above.'

'I have not seen god but I have seen many other planets through the cable car as it goes up and down,' said Zunu. 'I just press my nose flat to the cable car glass and my eyes too. You stroll through the carriage to an area surrounded by glass walls. That piece of carriage is a thick glass box. It changes to a telescope as your eyes press over on it.'

'A glass that is adaptive, it must make each small size gigantic,' said the Buddhist with big eyes.

'You can see Jupiter with umbrellas. People carry purple striped twirling umbrellas all the time be it night or the day.'

'Then you have planet ICO. Ico is a huge block. A huge cubical chunk that looks so cold. It keeps dripping into the space small beads of water. Jupiter gets very disturbed and mad at it. They have to carry umbrellas to deal with the leak most times. Jupites are always looking up and reviling with umbrellas in hand. Short Gnomies with sharp screwy noses carry ice lumps over their backs to Ico factory all twenty three and a half hours. It delivers ice cream to my planet.'

'You also have a small boy who sits at the edge of his two hundred centimeter round asteriod over a chair. He loves to see the sunset. He too had visited planet Earth and so many other planets.'

'He draws beautiful pictures of ten desert palm trees each day and drops them over Earth. His only friend is blue bell plant.'

'Have you met him? Maybe you could be friends with him and he won't be so lonely?' the Buddhist commented.

'No. I cannot meet him. His asteriod is too small for me to put a foot on. It will crumble in tiny pieces and nothing will remain,' Zunu said fearfully.

'I now wish to travel to all these places too, you must take me,' said the Buddhist longingly.

'It not always possible to go all places great man. Destiny takes us. There are rules,' Zunu shrugged in a helpless way.

The bright sun was casting a glare now. The light blue sky was brilliant against the warm lake. The sun shafts were warming the side of Zunu's face. The Buddhist looked around and grabbed a banded tulip shell from the wet soil and told the boy to put the shell to his ear.

'Umm… am I meant to hear something? I don't hear anything,' said Zunu.

'I have done that many times to understand the mystical energies, and heard the sound of the gentle sea splash. The shells found in the sand still carry the ocean, because it's a part of it. That's the terrific gift of origin. The ocean too continuously draws back to the sand to pull it back in the waters.'

'Are you trying to tell me my home was built out of water and not sand? —But we have sand all around mostly.'

'If there hadn't been a transition, man would not exist; A broad valley wouldn't open up leading to a high level flat plain. The flat level wouldn't rise to be a tiny slope, and a hill wouldn't one day be a precarious mountain. It's true that everything has it's destiny, one day that destiny will be realized unknowingly.'

'So, each thing has to transform itself into something newer, and does that acquire a new fate?' asked Zunu.

'Transition will always assert. You are a bright boy. We shall meet again.'

'Where will you meet me?' said Zunu excitedly.

Buddhist just waved his hand as a gesture of departure and disappeared down the curvy village road. Down and down he went till he was reduced to a point in front of the faraway hills. Zunu marched right behind him playfully and then turned around to go back to dad. He looked back till he lost sight of the modest saffron figure to the dusty cloud filled horizon of the South-west.

CHAPTER SEVEN

Cafe 'Pho Co'

Antorio and Zunu had been waiting for a refill, with no signs of arrival for sometime. They decided to walk down as it was just three miles. Even though it was just after nine o'clock, the rice fields were already twinkling and sizzling under the hot morning sun rays.

On the path that wound up through the paddies, they encountered farmers on motorbikes commuting to work, women and child who timidly walked past them. They yielded the way so that ladies carrying large planks of wood, and packs of grass clippings on their heads could pass by easily. Smiling rice farmers were attending their crops and remote villas dispersed the hill slopes.

'Dad, just imagine working under the bubbling sun daily on the same plot of land. Would it be comfortable to be free from the cares of modern day and work in the fields? So much physical labor would outdo us, wouldn't it? This really looks so tiring…poor farmers,' Zunu commented, his brows knitted, making a strong point and marveling their efforts.

Just then a farmer shouted out eagerly to them, waving frantically, his hand up and down, 'Sir, you could stop by my restaurant for a cup of tea. It's managed by my wife. Be sure to order our legendary bánhmì for breakfast.'

'What is bánhmì?' Antorio shouted back, waving out to him politely giving him a response that possibly he longed for.

'The bánhmì means breakfast sandwich,' the farmer answered eagerly, 'If it's not too much trouble please take the road on the left. Keep walking up the small street (about two minutes) until it snakes to the right, you'll see a narrow path on the right side which isolates itself from the street by a concrete wall. That is bistro "Pho Co." '

'Alright, done!' Antorio raised his hand, giving him a thumbs up.

They were not as such hungry, but decided to stop by for a cup of coffee. They wanted the poor man to earn some money.

After giving a positive nod to the farmer, they followed his directions and headed towards cafe 'Pho Co', watching the farmer alongside as he took a sickle in his hand and cut through green stalks with a smack, and then another… Iridescent pearls of water flew through the air with each slice like showers.

There were in development numerous little eateries and coffee shops along the path, all unremarkably mediocre normal looking, some small, some big - however, by no means over developed. They were just out and out plain, simple and sweet for regular easygoing meetups and drained out working people. Some played lovely exquisite background music just at the right decibel, could hear them as one walked by.

They stumbled across this cute little shop with a small board labelled 'Pho Co'. They were greeted energetically by frog eyed Mrs. Tran who peeped out of a tiny window to state a brisk inviting welcoming hello. The farmer's wife ran the family business all alone, her eyes squeezed shut often and jaws trembled while talking to them. She kept wiping her sweat soaked head with her hand, her loose hair strand ran into her mouth.

She was rushing from one customer to another, handling everything together, with no helping hand, frantically jotting down the orders placed over a neat paper and trying to keep a cool at the working surge hour, her pen everlastingly tucked all time behind her upper ear.

Zunu and Antorio put in the request for two *ca phe sua* (milk coffee) as they occupied the simple plain oak wooden table with round small chairs. With the set up being in the inner market circle, it made kind of a quiet surroundings in spite of the hustle, hubbub and swarm…. and on the off chance, if you loved your coffee more than the clamor around – you might just want the spot and quite like the place.

Mrs. Tran came out rushing with a metal tray carrying two small coffee cups with equally tiny handles, and poured the warm coffee through the steely narrow coffee pourer into the cups… the coffee had a strong, bitter nutty sweet flavor - a smooth milky concoction made with dark roasted coffee and sweetened condensed milk. Though too sweet, indeed it was 'REAL COFFEE' for them after a tiresome trip as they took their first sip! It smelled so great!

Just then an airplane flew above leaving a white trail of smoky mist. Its lights twinkled white in the daylight as the pair looked up. It's thundering engine noise muffled and distracted people from the cafe coffee mood. Nobody noticed Mrs. Tran had pulled in a chair too amidst all her customers. She sat close to Zunu.

'Where do you come from?'

Antorio answered, 'Dropped from the skies, today.'

Mrs. Tran laughed as her froggy big eyes gave an amusing look. She said lifting her fore finger, 'Naughty sense of humor.'

'As a kid I stayed at a place called Bolivia by the pacific ocean. It was so vast, so sparkling white, I lost my soul to the ocean of mystique. Standing in the endless frothy splashing waves, you could feel your modest tiny size and gaze hours at the cerulean horizon that appeared so far away. Whenever it rained the slight layer of water transformed the salty flats into an amazing impression of the sky.'

'The area still sustains something that isn't alive any more. A railroad burial ground. I miss it, 'she rested her knuckles over her flat cheek. 'Trains carried salt and miners to and from the flats. My father carried me in his arms every morning and I used to watch them chugging everyday,' she got up from her chair, did an imitation of the wheels with her hand and laughed away heartily.

'Once I even sat at the wheel. But after salt robberies by native people in the area, the train was abandoned. My father lost his only job and we decided to move to Vietnam - Asia. What a contrast. But both are close to my heart.'

'Vietnam is a very friendly place, and we are still discovering it. Every place has it's charm— but surely home is where your heart is,' Antorio replied and Zunu nodded heartily.

'Sometimes destiny takes you away from home and you must find your heart elsewhere,' Mrs. Tran replied.

'Quite right you are lady!' A customer seated at the next table interrupted in. Mrs. Tran smiled turning around, waving at him and throwing kisses at his three kids.

'You're not just simply missing your home. You're feeling the loss of what's ordinary, what is standard routine, the bigger feeling of social space, in light of the fact that those are the things that help us survive,' George stated, ' – and myself an American,' bringing down his hat.

'A lot of my companions got hitched, have young kids and I'm not part of that since I'm not physically there, so you just sense that you're missing out,' Mrs. Tran included.

'I miss my things as well, 'George's seven year old blurted out softly, his head buried in pizza, '– the comfort of eating macaroni and cheddar with a fork in front of our twenty one inch television with my squirrel Baki; And to know it's your kind of macaroni and melting cheddar – and the TV set too, also it's only one Baki that nibbles nuts so neatly.' A blonde lady sitting next to him patted his brown hair and slobbered, 'O my baby.'

Antorio turned his chair around to their table, 'It's normal and natural to feel homesick sometimes. It's only your mind and feeling letting you know, you're out of your space,' Antorio said shaking his hand with the seven year old.

'We are on Asia tour for three months now,' said George's blonde wife; a bright hibiscus flower was pinned in her hair. She bit into a plain potato sandwich and spoke, 'To leave the nest and all the battling with siblings, to deal with new task that the trip is feathered with has been very daunting for my kids. Three of the kids are left in my sister's care take. We have a total pack of six.'

'We long to go back home at times, we do love our home so much more,' she added munching upon her sandwich. 'Although we still have some stuff out here that brightens us when we're not feeling to our best, my kid still misses Baki quite a lot. If there was nothing on the planet that we were attached to, then I guess we wouldn't learn to value them when we're away,' she shrugged and rubbed her kid's hair gently.

'If you try to do something else with your life you will sense you are missing something too. We can always schedule time tables into our day, whatever little we enjoy, just to do away with the woes. We can look forward to some socializing, maybe a nice hot shower!' said Antorio. 'Sometimes enormous changes like school too can be whelming. If you look at a seven year old boy at a day camp, you would see the same symptoms as that of your kid. The same would be true for an eighteen year old heading to an engineering school. Research has proven it.'

'We can always start to fill in the holes with new faces that get comfortable to be around with; share their favorite places to hang out, be it late night snacks or foods that they love. It should begin to resolve a bit,' added George.

'Right! When you initially get into a pool, it doesn't feel any better. It feels cold,' said Antorio, 'you question quickly should I get out of pool, or for what reason did I get in, it's so cold. However, at that point, upliftment sets in as you drift freely in water! You hang in there and it starts to feel much much better! But nobody changed that water, or even warmed it up. We simply balanced it out. So, with change, even enormous changes, we should be happy to feel that underlying uneasiness, ride it out or more so,' said Antorio.

'If you experience discomfort and balance it out, like slowing down slightly before a big bullish bump in the road, you surely won't get a lumpyhumfadumpa over your head and it won't send you flying out in the air when you hit it!' George's other eleven year old spoke in, 'dad simply slows down the car.'

Everyone laughed.

'Words of wisdom by my customers! I already feel so good. Thank you, gentlemen,' said Mrs. Tran, 'not that I was too sad. Happens sometimes, moods isn't easy to fly past,' she grinned.

'You are welcome,' the eleven year old drawled plucking his nose.

Just then another customer called out for Mrs. Tran and muttered something to her. The lady needed some tissue papers.

Mrs. Tran surged back into the kitchen area, her red A line long dress stuck on her tightly as she fast paced her footsteps. She came out quickly again, this time with a jar that had a gleamy blue top and tissue papers that she handed out swiftly to the lady. The medium sized glass jar smelled of coffee beans at a distance too. Mrs. Tran walked up to them, opened the fat-mouthed jar lid, but it had instead cherries in it. 'Surprised?' she said.

She placed the jar over the coffee table decorated with a lime yellow chequered cotton cloth. She then held the sweet looking red cherry in her palms that looked somewhat like grape sized tomato. Next, she squashed it.

'See this? The pit —They commonly contain two stones with their flat sides together. That's your coffee bean. I love to show it raw to all my customers. Not many know where it comes from and they are joyful to see it. We've much coffee plantations up the hills.' She stretched her right palm forward to show them the fresh bean.

'A bean or a split kidney?' wondered Zunu. (what it looked like was – a hard stone pale kidney and not truly a coffee bean.) 'But it does carry a raw, short lived flower fragrance of espresso coffee,' thought Zunu.

Next Zunu got up and bent low to peep into the jar, his freckled nose literally dunking into it. The side table American joined in. His blonde wife too craned her neck in like a giraffe, and so did his three kids. All were now trying to peep in one by one. Seeing so many elbows, so many noses and so many eyes into one small jar, Mrs. Tran hurriedly acted.

'Do not get so close! You will breathe germs into it. The purity quotient gets spoiled.' She waved her hand as though asking drain flies to disperse. Then a worried Mrs. Tran, carefully pushed the jar aside. She dropped the metal lid onto it and fastened it tightly. Zunu jumped back. The American man, his kids and the blonde were back at their table now. The light faint music continued playing from the old radio in kitchen.

A light breeze started blowing and ruffled Antorio's shirt and tickled the ringlets of hair on his neck. The air was filled with the haunting smell of gulmohar blossoms from the trees outside. Suddenly a water droplet fell into the empty cup. Spat! Then another tiny drop. Splat! Zunu looked at it and looked up. 'Hey dad.'

Lightning spiked through the darkened sky, the clouds looked menacing in their glory. Antorio opened the red striped porch umbrella. Soon a bunch of umbrellas were hiding the sky and children were running around screaming in the light shower. They formed a train and Mrs. Tran joined them in the front as driver. Some adults joined in behind. The long train moved with whistles that Mrs. Tran blew and they sang songs;

chug chug choo choo
A three quarter empty train…
Saturday noon, Windows down
To Cantho - over the hill
To Da nang - through the cave
Then Haiphong
Then Hanoi –then up, then down

A four quarter empty train…
Windows up
From Ho Chin Minh to Singapore
chug chug chuk chuk….
Through Bishan East - over the sea
From Marymount to Upper Thomson
To Alexandra Hill, then Alexandra North
To Bukit Ho Swee, Bukit Merah
From Depot Road to cafe Pho Co
and then STOP!

Kids dispersed. They had a lot of fun.
'Thank you all very much for your time to wait for tasting our coffee,' said Mrs. Tran now with half lidded droopy eyes.

She did have a tiring day and her hands were aching rest that she hardly saw.

'Thank you too. Could you please give me some of Vietnam currency in exchange for this gold nugget, if it's no problem? We are new to the place and are unaware of the right shops for us to initiate the exchange,' Antorio inquired with a straight gaze hoping the generous lady obligates, she appeared responsible.

The 'speedy' Mrs. Tran dashed inside, her long hair and creased dress hugging her thin dainty frame in the breeze. She took snappy paces like a deer and returned back with 'Dong' currency. Antorio was charged merely 11,000 VND per cup, but gave an additional 6000 VND as they deserved to earn better. The lady politely gave Zunu a small water buffalo statue as a gift, and a thank you note scribbled roughly on the spot.

Thank you Zunu and his Pa

See you again! :)

It was a great pleasure to converse with the proprietor Mrs. Tran, she had been quite accommodating with a great deal of data provided free to them, that dealt with the most ideal approach to set up the coffee beans; how to… when to…. to that which are grown by her father in law at a remote town village high up in the hills. Their forefathers had learnt to ace it from French who introduced coffee plantation to Vietnam. Antorio and Zunu exchanged good byes and took a leave.

The side street proudly displayed a sign with all the contributor's names who had had donated to pave the narrow road. They walked past tiny shops and family compounds each with their own distinctive temples. It was fascinating to see people worship god, their belief and conviction systems were different from galaxy 1x where they have no god, yet both Zunu and Antorio could feel a deep unknown connection with the people, though they were complete strangers and it was a new planet.

Turning onto an irregular foot path trail now, it took them across the river which translated into a dirt pathway. As they walked the wet mud sloshed and splashed onto their trousers. As the shops became less frequent and less continuous, the rice fields could be seen emerging on both sides once again, challenging them to take strides in the mud drenched soil.

Sounds sputtered and gurgled from the enduring steady abundant flow of water from the irrigation trenches. It reminded them to drink some of their own water before they continued on their way. Antorio opened his backpack and hauled out a bisleri bottle. He ripped apart the blue ring crown with a swift motion and unwound the bottle cap to drink some water and offered it to Zunu.

'I've eaten rice so often in my life, but until early today, I'd always taken for granted all the hard work that goes into cultivating it,' said Zunu with eyes reflecting admiration.

'Meeting the local farmers changed my outlook too,'

Antorio replied sympathetically.

'It's something that I cherish so much about travels, my level of gratitude and appreciation just grows each day impacting me largely along with a sense of wonder. It's a feeling of miracle and contentment. Traveling trains us and educates us about the beautiful world, culture and people surrounding us. I do want you to experience it too Zunu and I am glad you are doing it.'

Antorio silently looked for his pen and started scribbling…
Brisk note:
Planet E is a persevering planet. Locals eagerly showcase the most striking side of Vietnam and their kindness is worth the diversion.
Zunu loves the water buffalo. It's the conventional symbol of Vietnam.

CHAPTER EIGHT

Na Rang Village

Na Rang was an hour's walk. The local communities were closely knit and they found themselves easily guided, as everyone knew where Nguyens' stay. The locals frowned upon them with reservation, gave them fancy looks of mistrust; the ladies murmured, and children tailed them out of curiosity. They rarely had outsiders visiting their village. A cyclist passed by merrily ringing his bell and pointed his finger to the Nguyen home.

From a distance they could see a roof of thatched palm leaves with a small courtyard. Coming closer it was a traditional earthen home, the walls were actually woven bamboos smeared in mud and had an earthen deck. Someone was already waiting for them at the entrance.

An old conical strawy hat flew over her eyes, she placed her hand over her mouth and chuckled just like Danh. Her eyes closed and shoulders shook as she covered her mouth each time a giggle erupted. Mrs. Nguyen Hang was Danh's mother, a thin body like a matchstick.

Mr. Nguyen Bay looked like a simple man in white trousers and long flowing grey shirt. Eyebrows like hedges, black deep set eyes with laugh lines underneath that reflected worry. Medium statured and thin, around in mid thirties.

'Welcome to Nguyen home sir, we are very pleased to see you. Danh is very cheerful too that you could make this trip,' Mr. Nguyen said warmly lowering his head.

'Thank you so much,' Antorio replied. 'We are equally pleased to be a part of your community and such lovable people. It's a dream.'

Ever talkative and much excited Danh appeared to be shy and hid behind his mother. He was well informed that Zunu would be visiting him. He was nibbling his nervous fingers, his round beaded Chinese black eyes popped out as he saw them. He puffed away the few fringes falling over his chubby face, and broad forehead and stared at them long.

'Hello uncle,' Danh suddenly rushed to Antorio, held his hand and Zunu's tightly dragging them into the house.

'I have so much to tell you about the book and moo!' he said swinging their hands.

'Danh, first let your friends take some rest. Later you can show them around the house and play as much you like. This is not the way,' said Mr. Nguyen.

'Oh No, Mr. Nguyen. Let him talk. We are not one bit tired and look forward to spending the day with Danh,' Antorio was quick to comment and defend Danh.

'Of course, Mr. Antorio. However, it's post noon and you must be hungry,' remarked Mr. Nguyen.

He led them to the tiny kitchen where they sat over the mats on the floor chatting away, while Mrs. Nguyen prepared the food on a roaring charcoal stove in the kitchen.

Danh had a problem in sitting as he had gained weight due to over eating. Mrs. Nguyen always pampered him and a bit of indulgence did finally go down to great extremes. Danh's back dropped down a few inches as he sat down in wriggling trousers causing the front to be pulled in. The tight buttons pinched his waist and his gut was spilling all over the front. At times it was so terrible, he routinely had to unbutton his pants, even partly unzip them in order to sit down and eat comfortably.

The kitchen, was set at the center of the house and served

as a common place where the family gathered at the end of the day with or without reason. It was almost like a conference hall.

'I'm so outraged with moo,' said Danh throwing his hands up in the air. What is it we didn't do for it? We made it national animal!'

'He he!' Zunu laughed almost rolling out on the floor.

'Zunu, it's nothing to laugh about at all. We have many serious problems,' Danh short cute window in front teeth showed up as he dismissed Zunu's comment with a slight grin and then shifted uncomfortably on the kitchen floor as he adjusted the pinched trousers, that dug like a knife into his buttock.

Pinched pants was just very normal for Danh, thank you very much, till the time others kids were not around making fun of him. He hated if mocked.

'Antorio uncle,' Danh exclaimed, 'The high density of 'moo' animals in the area leads to direct defecation and urination in the watercourse, as well as reduced river bank stability due to much soil erosion and poor conditions for vegetation growth. — We all kids know it, we are enough intelligent! — We see it everyday. The water smells so bad because of 'moo' activities. But we still clear off the faeces quietly and never scream.'

'Quieten down, save your irritation Danh,' Zunu cautioned him.

'No! Moo always tramples the banks of the watercourse as it drinks water and also cause loss of plants and grass which is so important to us. Yet we tolerate it and compromise.'

'But it gives you milk, and milk makes kids very strong.

Zunu too drinks one glass of milk everyday,' Antorio smiled.

'That's what I'm trying to say, dad. Moo is not bad!' Zunu added up grinning.

'It ate up all the trees near water. We had to put up fences and rocks, ask my dad please. Why did it take off with the book and then kick it into river? It just couldn't eat it, so then kick it? I have always treated it well, but look at the amount of trouble,' Danh remarked gravely.

'We will be able to find the book. It had a plastic cover and won't sink in the river. Don't worry,' Antorio consoled Danh. 'Don't be angry.'

Mr. Nguyen gave a confirmative nod, 'Danh is impulsive and gets worried easily, but otherwise he is a very good boy. He loves all animals without a doubt. I have promised to take him to wildlife sanctuary someday.'

'The lunch is ready,' Mrs. Nguyen interrupted. She spoke very little, but smiled with a periodic gaze at them occasionally. She got up and fixed her long dress trapped in her toes, snipped the thread caught in the toe nail with her fingers and sauntered towards the other room. Her frame was so petite that she moved like a shadow.

From far, they could faintly seize the glimpse of a stone tablet with carvings over it. She placed offerings of the cooked food and some marigold flowers at the altar.

'Ah! Don't be surprised... When alive, one must have a house, when dead one must have a tomb. It's a saying. Connections to the past are important to us,' Mr. Nguyen explained as everyone continued to hear intently.

'The food offerings are generally placed on the altar only for symbolic purposes, and remain there briefly before being eaten by the family. We provide for the sustenance of ancestors as a mark of respect towards elderly.' Mrs. Nguyen immediately joined them back.

There was Canh – a clear broth noodle soup with vegetables, boiled fish, salted eggplant, and pickled white cabbage, a clay pot of steamed long grain white rice to go along with it. Mrs. Nguyen sat right next to the rice pot to serve rice as they needed, her fingers as quick as bird claws.

The food was simple and delicious. They finished the meal course with món ngọt, a sweet dish which was a fruit pudding made with just a few teaspoons of sweetened milk.

'Our cuisine traditionally combines five fundamental taste elements: spicy representing metal, sour (wood), bitter (fire), salty (water) and sweet (earth) and we finish off with a sweet dish. Danh loves banana pie. Our menu has it every second day,' Mr. Nguyen said stroking Danh's head lovingly.

'So content peaceful and happy in their lives,' Antorio thought to himself.

'It's time for some rest now. Let's move to the other room. After an hour Danh can play outside with Zunu,' said Mr. Nguyen.

They all lay on a simple mat on the cold floor. Mr. Nguyen quietly played conventional music on a flute carved from bamboo. Antorio almost fell asleep quickly.

In sometime Danh and Zunu slipped out of the room

without making any noise. Danh showed Zunu around.

The house was divided into six small rooms of varying size. 'This primary room is the central focal in which the ancestor shelf holds the spot of respect,' said Danh bowing down to his ancestors with both hands folded, muttering something while Zunu looked on in a funny way. Corner of mouth half tweaked, not really understanding it –

The alter was draped in a red and gold cloth. It stood for the concrete representation of the ancestors (since his or her name could never be spoken by the family after death.) There was a display of incense, candlesticks, scrolls, burners and tapestries around the shrine containing the ancestral tablets. Danh lit up an incense and told his ancestors in a bated breath to shower all their blessings and keep looking after him.

'The names of our past ancestor is inscribed upon the stone tablet through the four generations to whom our devotion is encouraged and expected. Ancestral spirits are regarded as constantly present to observe happenings in the family,' he said seriously, giving an idea to Zunu how deeply confounded these beliefs were. It was like the ancestors were still living alive in the home!

The family slept on slender mats spread on the floor, there was no sign of television or internet. The family compound was attached just outside containing shelters for the buffalo, ranch tools, grain storage, ducks, the inescapable pig sty and the chicken pen.

The interior of the compound was enclosed in a nice wall of greenery. There stood an old brick cement tank used for storing rain water in one corner, (an important low cost option for storing water gained through harvesting.) It was splattered with sand, gravel and mortar after fresh repairs to its old structure. It was far cheaper than ferro cement tanks and easier to build by the communities. There was a pond as well just outskirts of the wall where the children and adults showered and washed both clothing and dishes.

A well cultivated small rear garden with vegetables and fruit trees could be reached through a low wooden gate with a rounded top arc. It had a chrome yellow picket fence border (dirty dark yellow) with sharp wedges pointing to the top, wide at the bottom running all along the fence. The wooden boards raised, held and split the compound from the back yard garden, just a few yards away from the tank.

'We've to re-paint the fence, only Bambi seems to adore it,' said Danh bending low and stepping through the wooden gate.

'Where is she?' asked Zunu.

'Not around. Must be sleeping or grazing out in the fields.'

The rear side had a huge screening wall of growing climber plants and riot of fruit trees – Jack fruit, flame trees, mango trees, areca palms, guava trees, bamboo clumps, banana trees, orange etc. shielding the occupants from curious locals and other people who passed by.

Morning glory, moon flower, sweet pea and exceptionally large flowers in pure pastel pink– a color rarely seen in climbing roses, were climbing the weak fences and boundary walls into the neighboring yard. And that's exactly where the neighboring goat Bambi loved spending her time! It liked the old fashioned roses in full form. —The strong, sweet scent as they opened all the way to the ground on sturdy *10-12'* canes! Blooms were on both old and new wood, so they did have lots of flowers throughout the summers and then the falls.

Danh jumped up to pluck an orange from the ten foot long big tree. The tree had a smooth brown bark, and it could be climbed. Just nobody wished to. His finger tips just about missed the plump orange and he fell back over his bottoms almost ripping his tight shorts. His fat stomach bulge was now showing. His yellow turtleneck t-shirt had given way from the bottom revealing his double tyred waist skin. Danh got up slowly using his left hand support, squirming. It was difficult to get up with all that weight his mom had had asked him to loose.

He jumped up higher again! This time attempting a pluck at the sweet ripe orange hanging from the lowest tree branch covered with lots of sprouting green leaves, but it just didn't wish to be in the reach of his fingers. Another finesse jump and the orange did finally give away along with a tiny branch sticking out some twigs and young leaves. There were highly fragrant waxy white flowers in small clusters in its leaf axils and appeared very lovely. Danh smelled them… he was pleased! He chucked the orange into the air, and as it came back caught it proudly.

He looked at Zunu, 'Vo-hoo!!! Task accomplished.'

He split the orange into two and gave one half to Zunu. As his old habit was, he then crushed and squeezed the orange rind peel. The tang went straight up Zunu's nose causing him to sneeze hard! and HARDER!

'AChOO—'

At this point he squeezed it into his face as well grinning away silly, enjoying the drama jumping up and down literally, waggling his eyebrows at him.

If this was not enough, his loud hearty laugh generated tremors all around poor Zunu.

'Eeuks!– Just what are you up to, I have tears in my eyes.'

'This is crazy!' said Zunu horrified, his chequered blue shirt now soaked with his sneezes as he took a few steps back, his eyes glazed and almost blinded.

'It's good for your eyes. It will bring tears and cleanse your eyes,' grinned Danh. His chubby cheeks broke into a cute dimple inherited from his mother as he shook his bums and bulging stomach in a dancing mode, making him look cute and funny. He sure was having a good time teasing his new friend and the little sweet bully in him had just shown itself up for starts.

It took Zunu ten minutes to be normal again as he rubbed his nose, and continued sniffling - the sneezes just wouldn't stop. The air was loaded with tang, and there he went again…

'Acchoo — !!' his eyes were flooded with tears, as he propped his head into his hands.

'Do you know why my dad planted orange tree?' Danh chatted on playing oblivious to Zunu's sneezes. He was used to playing squash rind game with kids and knew it would be just all ok in ten minutes, it was like he never had played any mischief. He stayed very calm and cool and continued peeling the big fresh oranges he plucked now and then; with cool jumps; anything that fell in his notorious reach —

'I had a dream that I was eating oranges from my backyard. Following day dad had a huge profit. Our rice stock sold at a very good price. So, we decided to honor the event with an actual orange tree plantation. It's been three years, it's always brought us luck,' grinned Danh.

'We believe such a dream is a very good sign, usually indicating fresh beginnings.'

'How can a dream be suggestive to anything? I could sit and dream entire day, if dreams came true,' Zunu was pensive.

'Well, you can choose to not to believe it. But it happened with us. There is no reason for us not to believe it. My dream was genuine.'

'In fact, I tell you something more – if you dreamt you were eating oranges which tasted sour, such dreams usually aren't a good sign.'

'Uhh- hh, that sounds superstitious,' said Zunu.

'Em… Danh pushed an orange segment to his mouth, …… If you dreamt you were buying oranges, such a dream might indicate someone asking you for advice in the near future or indicate unexpected gain of money, — you know like getting a legacy from someone you never expected to or winning some lottery,' his face puckered, eyes squinted as the sweet sour orange tingled his tongue.

Zunu sneezed again.

'If the dream is about green orange, it reminds you to watch your health as you may fall sick.'

'Oh Ok. Before sleeping I will tell myself not to dream of unripe fruits. That sounds quite insane to me,' Zunu replied.

'The dream about stepping on the orange and slipping suggests the death of a close one,' added Danh.

'I just stepped on a peel, Danh! You saw it and just made that one up.'

'But it wasn't your dream, right? So, then no harm to you. Except for you may just get a broken leg if you slipped again,' Danh chuckled.

'Achooo…' Zunu went off again and wiped his mouth. Flecks of spit splattered the air and Danh jumped aside.

'Just before I was born, my mother dreamt of orange. I was born a boy.' Danh rolled another piece inside his mouth.

'Could be a coincidence,' said Zunu turning his mouth down dismissing it off.

'I mean– **sorry** it was not about my gender or the gender of the child. The dream about eating oranges confirmed she will have a "smart" baby boy,' Danh said proudly.

'So, you are the smartest kid over the face of Earth.'

'Exactly. Now you came down to understanding my point,' Danh laughed and trees shook. He ate his last portion.

The barking of numerous dogs and the presence of many small children, made the arrival of a stranger in "town" a well known fact within an exceedingly brief time. They could sense some chaos outside.

'Maybe we could buy you shorts with a bit of stretch to them,' said Zunu staring hard at Danh's shorts.

Danh gave him a 'not amused' look from the corner of his

eye.

'Hey, I'm not making fun of you.'

'We could get loose trousers for you, a belt might just help keep the back from dropping down, that's a much better position to be in as it can be adjusted anytime. – Not much you can do about pinching of the gut aside from losing weight, if you wish to still continue with your tights.'

Danh hated the talk and royally ignored Zunu suggestion. Of course, he could lose weight, he wasn't born fat. Why can't people suggest better solutions, Danh faked a plaster smile. ...deep inside he knew that Zunu meant well for him.

Zunu and Danh walked out of the Nguyen gate to take a stroll around the village.

'You know while coming down to your home, I met god. You should meet him too. Just like the stone thrown in water, he too disappeared down the horizon in dust. He was surely god, you see, he knew everything and disappeared too,' said Zunu.

'Really? We must go find him in the fields. He must not be very far right?' Danh gasped with mouth hanging open, eyebrows like crescent moons now, pupils large and fist clenched with excitement.

The dogs were still barking in the backyard non stop, new visitors were welcomed in great style if they dared crossed their territory. The supremacy rule.

Zunu and Danh headed for the fields. Behind was a trail of small kids following them and giggling away, whenever Zunu would turn around they would disperse in small corners.

"*Look! Look…* some new boy in our villeegee–" whispers could be heard. Tiny footsteps were crushing the leaves right behind them.

"Looks like Danh friend —"

"O Yeah —!"

"anh ấy trông thật dễ thương –"

"Danh has grown fat no ?? – more than last time."

"See his bums —!" peals of laughter could be heard.

"Tummy looking like half cut potato he he —!" someone chuckled.

Disgusted and annoyed Danh now turned around to give a hot pepper look and stood with his hands over his hips, glaring eyes, nostrils flaring like rockets ready to shoot off on anyone in sight.

"That's enug-hhh —!" with grinding teeth, he stormed his foot over the ground enough to generate a mild quake.

Small hidden eyes were now peeping out from behind the trees, still amused. Danh did hate being poked by the kids' gang that too younger to him.

There was silence for ten minutes as kids decided to back off.

Next instant the nasty fiery eyed, stray dogs gang decided to chase them and an aggressive medium sized pariah dog with rust short coat, thin scraggy limbs now started to sniff around Zunu and jump at his knees, wildly.

"BOW Bhow BhOW-WW —"

It roared madly at Zunu, as though Zunu was about to be

his first delightful meal for the day.

Zunu freaked out and just lightly yanked him, so he knows to stop. Now the adamant dog with his pointed muzzle started pulling at his pants all the more fiercely. Zunu panicked and started to run. The wedge shaped head went right after him aiming at his t-shirt, gleefully looking to tear it off! Danh too chased Zunu, his shorts midline getting tucked in his buttocks making it so difficult to run.

Danh screamed, 'Don't run, he will attack you all the more. Just stay calm and stand in one place. It will leave you alone.'

Zunu pulled his hands upwards, took a deep breath and stopped with a tense face. The dog jumped up and down barking at him, pulling his pants, now barking less furiously and smelling him. The small kids following them offered the dog biscuits, calling out to him. (So, they were still following!) The dog immediately quietened down and moved away from Zunu. He appeared familiar with the kids and starts wagging his tail playfully.

'Thank you, friends,' Zunu said swallowing hard and still trembling.

'What's your name?' Kids seemed pleased with the acknowledgement and inquired bashfully.

'Ahem... Zunu 1x,' he replied.

'1x.. ?'

'umm... I mean just one Zunu.'

'Awl rghttt- ' the small kids ran away giggling.

'When did we say you are one into two?' some kid turned around and hollered naughtily.

Danh exclaimed panting out loud with his hand over his chest, 'Thank god, you are safe and not bitten up,' his hands shifted to his waist, as he looked to breathe still short of breath.

They started looking around for the Buddhist in the fields, twenty minutes had passed by. They turned towards Rilly forest woods. Rillywoods was round and round from inside, one layer set inside another layer like some riddle. No start, no end, only thick crooked trees running into skies allowing mild splash of sunlight, and in some spots not even that. As they walked in, it tapered upwards like some hill, an anthill, then suddenly downwards again and then behold! Gracious, upwards once again. So tiring for precious me feet... It was funnily wavy and spooky a bit, to guess. Just how deep it ran was a feat accomplished by none (yet). After a while they would be all back to same spot, dazed nevertheless. Getting lost was easy though if you were not native to the place. They caught a glimpse of the back of a man, hidden in trees at some distance, folded crossed legs, orange clad robe meditating in silence.

'That's him,' said Zunu.

'He has all the answers.'

His eyes were closed, he looked so peaceful, with an aura of radiance around him.

He opened his eyes and smiled at the kids, 'So we meet again.'

'Great man, I want you to meet my friend. He is Danh and I am Zunu.'

'Hello great man, I am Danh. We have lost a book. When will we find it, please guide us?'

'When the time is right, you will find it or it will just come flying to you,' the Buddhist said with an amusing expression suppressing his smile.

'Can books fly?' Danh inquired.

'If you wished very hard, why not?' the Buddhist smiled again.

'You are joking, aren't you?' Zunu remarked.

'Oh! So, you are fooling us,' Danh said with a grumpy look biting his nail.

'How can I trick such intelligent boys. I am not as well read as you are,' the Buddhist replied back with eyes that blazed like the sun.

They heard some chants of odd mantras and recitation just behind. Some very young monks in saffron robe were seated on the ground right behind.

Was it some kind of a study class? Danh wondered. When did these monks come? They didn't hear them. What were they reciting in their breath? Zunu and Danh folded their legs into a cross and sat adjacent to them.

It was indeed a strange class. The Buddhist offered them all jaggery and sesame seeds. He asked them to gulp it down. Danh ate it pronto, he loved sweets. To his embarrassment no one in the study class had eaten it. They had all placed it over a banana leaf on the ground. Not even Zunu had eaten it.

Embarrassed... Danh face turned red, he pretended his mouth was chewing nothing, it was empty!

The Buddhist then started to explain greed and desire and gave a paper, bamboo stick and inkpot to everyone to start writing the four basics. Everyone started jotting down trying to understand the deeper meaning. The Buddhist briefed:

"Number 1: Greed brings sorrow."

"Greed is a pursuit which races the individual in a ceaseless effort to satisfy a need while never genuinely accomplishing genuine satisfaction. Some individuals just don't comprehend the importance of satisfaction. All humans have wants. When the desire goes over board, beyond the acceptable definitions, then it establishes 'greed.' The minute greed enters, happiness says good bye automatically and flies out of the window. It needs no wings."

"Number 2: How Does Greed find roots?"

"Greed grows from ignorance of one's self. It distorts the psyche, corrupts your intelligence and crushes the voice of conscience, and we find ourselves in a dark alley. It is shut to any kind of reasoning and thinking and evades guidance from all sides. As we lose the right track, spiritual insights get blown out too. The judgment starts to confuse and the mind starts to sink in the mess of illusions."

"Number 3: Too much of Anything is Bad"

"We should live a life of moderation otherwise it can be unhealthy. Even if a thing is good, if you overindulge in something, it will get to the point that it is no longer good for you. Even drinking too much of water can be dangerous. Insatiability is about failing to be happy with what one has, continually needing and anticipating more. It is a ravenous craving and a significant type of gluttony. Hence, overdoing anything will bring tragedy and cut off the ordinary span of life. The nature pursues the standard for equalization, proportion and extents. Fulfillment lies in appreciating all what we have and not being fascinated by what we want."

"Number 4: As You Sow, So Shall You Reap"

"Sowing and reaping are a part and parcel of the law of nature. According to the Law of Karma (as you sow, so you procure). You require a seed to grow a tree. But if you don't water it, give it sunlight and manure, it will never develop."

"It is not enough that you sow a huge quantity of seeds, and spread over a huge farm. The quality of seeds, fertility of seeds, right manner of sowing, water, right maintenance, including protection from weeds, these also matter. This applies not merely to reaping a harvest but to all aspects of life as well. Work hard with honesty, filling in right values, you will be paid effectively later."

'That is all for today,' Buddhist said.

Danh's face turned small.

'We are not greedy or are we Zunu?' said Danh pressing index finger to cheek.

'No, we are not. Don't take it personally. He is a great man. We should visit him again. I already feel like I know him long.'

'I ate the jaggery because he asked us too, not out of greed. I also drink my tea when mom calls out for us to have it. I only followed the instructions,' Danh face flushed and corners of the mouth turned down.

'That's the thing. This not about eating jaggery, or drinking tea. It's about following what is told to us indiscreetly by any trusted source. We have to give up on impulsiveness, reflect upon our actions. This is not the time for food. So, we don't eat untimely even if it's offered to us. We live life in a disciplined and controlled way. Otherwise it sows the seed of greed. There are multiple messages in the great man talks,' Zunu said with twinkling eyes and brows closed together.

'Now before you ask me how I know it, I have no answer Danh. It's just inbuilt. I feel I know the man,' Zunu lowered his chin over his knuckles in a 'I read you Danh'.

Danh kept gazing at Zunu like an alien. 'Thanks for explaining. I'm glad nobody is thinking I am greedy.'

Zunu rolled his eyes. Danh was impossible.

'Zunu, how did the young monks know they shouldn't eat it?'

'Dunno— Their hearts knew it, just how I knew it,' said Zunu.

'There is no 'why' for everything – just knew it,' Zunu shrugged as they walked away.

'You knew it. Why didn't I know it?' said Danh.

'Good question. I have no answer to it. Maybe the "great man" has. You should ask him!' Zunu slapped his head hard.

CHAPTER NINE

Coconut Guy

Meanwhile Antorio was all set to go across the river bank and hunt for the book after a quick nap.

At the river bank the mud was still fresh with a lot of animal foot imprints. Looked like most visitors were animals. The weeds were trampled and crushed. The bank had been alive with nestling ducks taking advantage of the shade provided by the tall reeds. It quite looked like a sewer and dumping ground.

Frogs were jumping in and out of water. The river current was slow, the book couldn't be very far off.

It was 3.00 pm. Before dawn he could reach the other side and speak with the locals. He waved out to a ferryman and asked him to drop him to the other side.

'Sir, that will be VND 4,000 to MeoVac town market, half an hour distance.' Antorio agreed quickly.

He was the only passenger. Rowboat was handled swiftly by the efficient boatman, it could carry up to six people. He propelled the large flat oars smoothly, cutting sharp slices through the water. His boat and oars were in perfect harmony of motion and balance with the soundless tranquil waters.

'We fishermen love such quiet rivers, because the calm water makes it easier to find hungry schools of fish. We stay a whole day without worrying about being carried downstream by current,' the boatman commented as his oars slapped the cold greenish waters behind.

'That's good to know,' Antorio said politely. The boat bopped, jived and bounced further, friendly to the current.

The boat cut through the water slowly and steadily. Antorio found himself at the other end in no time. He paid the service charge and walked away.

Antorio met up with two farmers – one was pumping

punctured bicycle tyres, and another who had just finished scaling coconut palm trees.

The middle aged coconut farmer lamented, 'I don't have a job, so I pick coconuts which I then sell to 'Green Karst' restaurant up the hill. I picked thirteen this morning and hope to sell them for VND 211482.

The *aroma* of coconut suntan oil rubbed all over the body, a whiff of tobacco smoke and leather was in the air each time he sashayed past. Antorio gaped at his hands and thought with hand as big as a boxing glove, he must have picked all thirteen coconuts in one go.

The man still dabbling in coconuts showed Antorio a golden paddy of rice that was likely to be harvested next day. He also removed a few kernels for him to sample. Bahir Ali was indeed a sharp man. Dark complexion, around forty five in age with an eighteen year old son, five daughters, and a wife. His son's name was Halim Ali, it means 'gentle.'

Halim often travelled to Middle East to trade in spices and leather as it served a better market for them. Bahir Ali was getting older, so it was his son who would now travel frequently for all trade jobs.

Bahir Ali stuck to his old routine work of selling coconuts and tending the fields. They were living in immense poverty. They could put some food over the table through spice sales in Saudi Arabia. Antorio felt sorry for him and asked him if he could help him in anyways. Bahir Ali was a man with pride and refused.

'We have survived till now and will survive with god's will,'

Bahir said with great faith.

'Planet E belief in god does seems so strong. Praying and worshipping makes them positive towards life. I applaud the inner strength.' Antorio thought to himself.

'I do need some help. I have lost a book. It was as important to me as god is to you. It was swept off the river bank from just across to your side. Can you please help me conduct a search? Has any of you seen it?' said Antorio.

'We haven't seen it, but we can help search it. MeoVac is a small place,' remarked Bahir Ali.

He offered him to sit over his cycle and they pedaled through the countryside rice paddy fields, enjoying the nature and fresh air along the way. While passing through the village, there were a few painting and craft shops, small restaurants and a handful of accommodation options. Finally, they ended in a small locality, where Bahir Ali stayed.

Antorio had never been treated more warmly than getting to know the people living in Meo Vac. These families opened up their homes to them, put up with his buggering and incessant questioning, all while refusing to let him lift a finger, and bombarding him with delicious home cooked dishes that he had never ever seen before.

He did have some strange, call it funny and jubbly not to be forgotten 'seating' experiences. One time he found himself seated over a choir four legged wooden bunk. It shilly shallied, screeched, wobbled like the leaning tower of pizza and then pummeled to the ground with a loud crash, while he held tightly onto his tea. In any case someone did have the tea, the huge black ants that came crawling in for the sugar in it. They sought his trousers too till Antorio shook them off. In all generosity, he was offered another glass of tea.

Another time he had a generous offer to sit on a potter's wheel. – While he refused, he was pushed politely to be seated, as guest just don't keep standing. So what if his pants had a patch of mud that looked like the full moon (it could be washed away with a charming conversation and some water later on). Old ladies grinned and offered him a pail of bucket. Antorio refused as he didn't wish to get wet. The ladies thought he was being just shy –'Our little chocolate headed boy.' A garden hose head sprayer was plugged in from behind and Antorio stood drenched, startled, speechless. The witty ladies had to clear up the messy guest before he left and before he gave their generosity a foul name. So a dry towel was offered too.

In another home was so lucky to be offered a chair (phew) but it was just too narrow for him.

In yet another home he was seated on top of an upside down big fat blue drum and he thought it was for storing *oils!*

Then came a stool with a nail flying out from one corner, it was somehow alright till it caught the best of his pants.

MeoVac village had all sorts of arrangements for seating guest. One and all flashed biggest warmest smiles. Soon Antorio walked around with a lovely mud patch, oiled bottoms, torn buttocks and looked like one of them.

He was taken to place of worships and made to say 'hello' to their gods too. Gods stood as stones with pretty garlands around them, in all houses. He was asked to place red Zinnia, Nelumbo, yellow Daisy, Cape Jasmine, and Marigold at god's feet and burn sweet sandalwood incense to achieve his goal quicker.

Only Antorio couldn't spot their feet? He tried very hard with glasses and without glasses too.

He was further gestured to immediately bow down as well to the holy feet. So he did bow to the invisible feet that only humans could see and placed the flowers too happily at the unseen feet.

'How are you?' was a definite question everywhere by every person.

'I'm good' became Antorio's ritual answer! Some of them even snapped pictures with him. Unfortunately, none had seen his book. Six hours had passed by. They were tired. Antorio decided he might just need to stay back for a day. He booked a stay for the night at a hill resort. Antorio had a nice hot shower and a good scrub that night.

Antorio scribbled a brisk note that night:

Planet E people always put up a question 'How are you?' every time they meet you. Twice a day means two greetings. This is not the everyday norm in Galaxy 1x. Thrice a week is good enough.

Generally, I'd say "I'm good" because they're not really asking a question. What they mean by 'how are you' is simply 'I acknowledge your presence'. I'm good means, 'I acknowledge your presence back'. So, you're actually not lying even in ill health. If someone is genuinely asking about your condition, then 'I'm good' could be a funny unexplained lie or compulsive courtesy. Antorio scratched his head. Really they're not asking how you are. It's just a colloquial way of rolling a conversation...

I must add they have great seating arrangement plans for visitors with a range of styles.

Typical rural family's assets include: A work area, desk, seating chair, table, cupboard, a couple of books, two cycles, siphon sprayer, slippers, shoes, two beds, stoneware urn, big metal pot, diggers, rakes, other ranch agricultural tools, bamboo seat, sideboard, a tea set, an electric fan, a roof fan, cane baskets, serving plate, pots, cooking pan, dish, bowls, two stools, chest with nearly 2,000 pound of rice. They also have 3 pigs, 2 piglets,10 chickens, 10 ducks, 40 banana trees and many other fruit trees.

A handy garden hose nozzle to water guest and water plants.

Maybe I could pickup a few tree species for plantation for our home too. I wonder if they will survive the 'monochromatic' season though. Cactus has survived well.

Antorio

CHAPTER TEN

Yellow or Orange

Next day Danh and Zunu ran to the Rilly forest woods to attend the morning class at 6.00 am. They went and sat right in the front. They heard the chants once again and turned around to see monks seated behind them.

'Zunu, why are they wearing yellow robes today?' said Danh.

Zunu turned around and said, 'No, they are all clad in saffron, just like yesterday.'

Danh turned back again…

'Why am I seeing yellow… What's wrong?'

'No idea,' said Zunu.

'Oh my god! have I developed color blindness? Now how will I pluck oranges! They will look like lemons!' Danh whispered.

Zunu picked up a dry orange colored leaf. 'Can you tell the color?'

'It's orange yellowish,' Danh said.

'It means you are not color blind,' Zunu replied. 'I don't know why you are seeing yellow though.'

'Wise man, why do I see yellow robes everywhere while it's actually saffron?' Danh said.

'You have chosen to see it,' the Buddhist replied.

'No, I didn't make this choice,' said Danh.

'Without knowing, you exercised this choice,' the Buddhist said.

'How is that possible wise man?'

'It's the mind, energy and aura playing games.' The Buddhist removed a red color pencil. He dipped it in water, and rubbed color red gently on a piece of paper. Then he dipped green color pencil and rubbed it over red color.

'Combining red and green together cancels both colors and gives you a brown. Brown is actually a mix of red plus yellow plus blue and yellow plus blue is green, so finally red and green is brown.'

'There is no way to make green into red though.'

'Similarly, there are varying layers to the mind. Our auras combine to give different energies and colors. We perceive what is reflected to us or what we choose to see,' the Buddhist said.

'There are a wide range of people in this world, those who say "I can see something" and those who say "I can't". And they're both right. Also, the events in our lives are outward projections of what's hidden in our subconscious mind.' added he.

'What does subconscious mean great man?' Danh questioned perplexed.

'Your conscious mind can be thought of as the gardener, your subconscious mind can be thought of as the nursery in which the seeds germinate.'

'So if I plant a seed, it will be subconscious and when it's big enough it will be conscious?' Danh queried.

'Ha ha... somewhat.'

'The power of the subconscious is around a million times greater than conscious mind. The conscious mind is like the part of the mirror that you can see over the surface and reflect. The main part of the mind is the subconscious and is underneath the surface of the mirror,' explained the Buddhist.

'The most important thing you need to know about the subconscious mind is that, it is active all day, regardless of what you are doing. However, you cannot hear this silent inner process with your conscious effort.'

'Your subconscious mind does impact your aura, energies, choices and inner self,' the Buddhist remarked.

'Thank you. I understand somewhat –' said Danh. 'I know you didn't understand, but you will someday,' the Buddhist remarked kindly.

Danh started to look around. He found a small oval spiny seed dispersed under a crooked tree. Danh picked up a broken twig, started scratching, raking and scraping up the soil. He dropped the seed into it and covered it back with mud neatly using both his palms. His hands were a pool of wet mud.

Zunu looked on confused. Next Danh ran and filled a jug of drinking water from the earthen pitcher under the tree. He watered the seed slowly.

'Zunu, I am trying to grow conscience,' Danh said proudly. Zunu caught his thick hair and whacked his forehead loud.

The Buddhist smiled joyfully and said… 'Let him learn.'

..

Colorful Kites… Noon

'It's a breezy day today. We must all fly kites in the fields and test the winds,' said the Buddhist.

Everybody shouted, 'Ought to be enjoyable!' They moved to the open fields' outskirts of the woods.

Zunu and Danh searched for sticks and fallen tree branches to make a simple newspaper kite. They hit a jackpot pretty soon. Zunu tied the sticks into a cross. Then strung the red thread around the ends of the stick. Danh cut a newspaper into a quadrilateral pattern to match the shape of the kite frame. He then folded the paper edges over the stick and glued them firmly.

'So simple. Done!' Danh screamed in delight jumping up and down, 'Zunu, your turn first.'

'Thanks, Danh, yet how about we begin with you. I just want to watch a bit, I prefer throwing the kite.'

Danh and Zunu both were good at flying kites. Danh gave Zunu a 'Thumbs up.'

They took position in the field. Danh had super fun trying to control the kite properly. Zunu enjoyed giving the Lift offs and holding the winder.

It was a bright day, with a steady soft breeze caressing their faces and brushing their trousers gently. It was extremely exciting to put the kite through the grilling paces. However, they had to wait for the right winds to pick it up.

Once the wind caught up Zunu stopped and let out more line quickly, spiraling the reel one way and then back the other, while being pulled across the grass trying to control the line. The kite was surprisingly strong with thrilling swaggers. It was cool to build up a feel for the kite and the wind.

If the flying line went slack, Zunu would bring in a little. If the kite begin pulling too hard, he would let some line out.

As the wind went around objects such as trees, buildings, and mountains, it got bumpy with slight turbulence. The gullible kite now seemed wild and desperate to escape, to fly on its own will, testing Danh's strength.

Suddenly an unexpected monster gush of a wave picked up the kite and along with it Danh too. He was alarmed, hair stood straight, and chest tightened… blood flowing fast to his cheeks… quite unnerved…

— Danh screamed, howled, yelled as he went up with force about two feet into the air. A second or two felt like minutes… Looking around he panicked to see all the pointy sharp corroded metal objects lying around looking to stab him. Luckily the wind just stopped slowly and settled him down without as much a thump.

"*Heelp!*" Danh yelled madly with popcorn terror struck eyes, but Zunu found him already on the ground in seconds… Once Zunu stopped laughing he was actually understanding Danh's state of mind and offered him his hand to get up.

'Should I like rope your feet to some heavy weights or something to make sure you don't get blown away like that? I mean if that's a risk.,I'm sure we should try to tether to something as a precaution,' Zunu grinned.

The Buddhist started laughing too, 'You could, but that's generally not a good idea because then when the tether suspends you mid lift, you'll have lost your catalyst for controlling the kite, which is your weight and balance. Once you lose that, most kites will take a brief plunge and you will have a strong force pulling you face first to the ground faster than you can fall naturally.'

'Ohhh.' Danh exclaimed with fright.

'Weighted harnesses sometimes work, or simply lying on the ground helps too. The problem was that Danh slouched his shoulders a bit too much, which made it a lot easier for the kite to pull his whole body up,' the Buddhist remarked.

'My worst nightmare would be finding myself hundred feet in the sky clutching that thing,' Danh said forehead puckered.

'Yeah, once you're up seven feet, just think 'I'll be down soon, no need to let go just right away!' Zunu giggled.

'Then suddenly as a gust gets you ten feet further off you still stay relaxed, 'It's just one small serious drop, I'll be back down soon… let me ride it out some more!'

'– Then when you're in the jet stream above the clouds amidst planes— SCREAM Ohh shit-tt! I knew I should've let go at ten feet. he! he!'

Buddhist explained, 'I mean you can let go of them fine, as long as there are no streets near by for them to fall on to. They won't travel very far and letting go of a runaway kite is honestly the best way you can bring it down securely if you don't know your maneuvers.'

'Should I take my chances and hold on hopefully, until the wind sets me down gently? Or should I take my other chances, let go and take the fall?' Danh quizzed.

'Depends on the intensity of wind,' Buddhist replied.

There was again a huge rush and unforeseen current in the winds and Danh got blown right off his feet yet one more time.

He quickly slid across the moist grass nervously with shaking hands, and scrambled back on all four. He landed on his two feet trembling, and decided it was time for a break and some rest.

'Few things are as liberating as watching colorful kites dance gracefully in a splendid blue sky,' Zunu said looking up at the sky with immense pleasure.

Danh sat slumped with his legs sprawled out and elbow propped on his knee, 'You know when things didn't go right, I would spend most of my time unraveling the two disorganized flying lines, running to and fro like a stupid person. Friends would be bored and disappointed to toss the kite back into the air after each crash.'

'It's just a game and wind is god,' Zunu remarked.

'What did you just say? I thought only I believed in god.'

'I picked it up from you, that's the best way to explain you —right ?' Zunu chuckled.

They could see there were many people far across the field flying kites and they were attempting to take over kites. As they cut loose the opponent kite, the shouts of diều bị cắt (kite is cut) roared through the air.

Mostly all were boys, it was an overwhelming kite flying game where the goal was to maneuver their own kites to cut the other person's kite string during flight, followed by kite running where participants raced through the streets to grab the free floating kites.

They reclaimed the kites, after they had been cut loose by running after them. That was a popular custom amongst kite flyers. Line contact was utilized trying to cut each other's kite lines, either by letting the cutting line loose at high speed or by pulling the line in a quick and repeated manner. There was lots of excitement, kick, buzz, shouts, struggles, competition and screams.

'It was always easy and good fun to make kites from newspaper, sticks and string but most were a let down as they got stuck up in trees quite easily,' said Danh.

'We had kite flying lessons in school as part of hobby classes. On many episodes when my kite crashed into the ground, I would quickly repair it and it would be back in the air pretty quickly,' added Zunu.

The purple red light was casting silhouettes now as the sun started reducing to a pinpoint. Cool wind blew into their faces.

'You know we have kites that are flown without tails too. Instead small flutes are attached that allow the wind to murmur melodic tunes. Many Kites here have different designs like winged animals, dragons, insects, and mythical serpents,' said Danh. 'But it always is much more fun to build your own.'

Danh went on and on… and on. Zunu heard him out patiently… sometimes a hmm, sometimes a nod.

Zunu handed a round white translucent pebble from his collection to the Buddhist and said, 'from me to you.' The Buddhist extended his welcoming palm.

It was evening, both Zunu and Danh headed home. Zunu was still stressed over the book at the back of his mind.

'We must reach home before dark. It's not good to be out late. Mom gets worried,' said Danh.

'It's not so late. It's just late evening. Everybody is out.'

'I know. But it's a lonely path through Rilly woods. Ghost could kidnap us,' Danh moved with quick steps like a duckling.

'What– Are you serious?'

'Yes. My mom says they shove you down potato sacks and

kids disappear forever, never to be found,' Danh gulped nervously.

'Three kids from our village vanished thirty years back from the lake side at dusk.'

'Maybe they slipped into the water? Could they swim?'

'Don't know that part. But I am not allowed to go in lonely areas. Even adults don't move out at witches hour.'

'Now, whatever is that?' asked Zunu.

Danh whispered low to him, 'The witches hour is a deadly hour after midnight when witches fly. That's when every tyke and all grown ups are sleeping tight. Witches brew elixirs in hot steamy big pots and they seek more powers. Black magic is most effective at the hour. All the dark dim elements come out from the caves and from behind the bushes,' said Danh as he peered into a fatty fubsy thick clump of shrub. 'Powers of witches and magician are believed to be very strong at the hour.'

He circled the dark wild bush twice suspiciously craning his short neck into it and remarked, 'and you know they have the world, flying everywhere. They even walk around with daggers to capture us.'

'What are you looking at?' said Zunu.

'Hell's bells. Special signs,' Danh said sniffing at a wild thorny fruit.

'You mean witches ring bells in hell, are they very noisy witches?'

'Noo... Nobody rings bells. It's a plant name. Seeing this wild hell's bells plant? It's called Datura. It's a very poisonous flower used for making potions.'

'I wish to see the process, we should camp in a tent at midnight,' said Zunu.

'I don't want to be hung down by some tree or be changed to a canary bird. Please spare me.'

'They have these shiny copper cauldrons. The witches stir the stuff in the cauldron. They stuff in striped snakes, datura plant stems, fat roots and tiny flower, big frog eyes, tender human heads, cow hair, pig skin, monkey tail, a yellowish-brown woodland moth, and soft slugs. The cauldron boils up in frothing flashes of green and yellow and purple and red, and white and silver and sends out a fleshy inhuman scent. They empty it out into a pot and set it to cool and drink it,' said Danh.

Danh and Zunu took quicker strides now as they continued walking further down. They turned around the bend.

'You skipped out potatoes in the bubbly potion with smoking fumes. Now please say, I don't wish to be boiled like potatoes in a brewing pot.'

'Walk fast. Talk less,' Danh retorted.

'Look who's advising, blabberburps!' laughed Zunu.

Suddenly there was a streak of bangarang and unhinged footsteps flying through the woods. Hearing the tiny shrieks, the pair jumped behind a thick bush. They caught the faint dim outline of kids' gang in the haziness and behind them the scraggy limbed pariah dog… all running for life. Fleeing at a fast pace. They had still been following Danh and hearing about the witches tore off in fright. Danh and Zunu looked at each other and walked out from behind the bush. Zunu had a small scratch as he had run into a prickly thistle. The sun was shining into the right side of the creamy silk moon, hidden behind the misty clouds.

They walked towards the north, then turned left as the path curved up into a shabby shaky scaffold. They climbed into the slim creaky wooden bridge as it shook and swayed. The lake below was greenish murky with a couple of air pockets as the crocodiles popped their scary greedy eyes through the darkness. The pair caught the sideway ropes and moved ahead slowly. Danh halted right in the middle. 'You know this is the place where the three kids disappeared.'

'Ohh really?' Zunu exclaimed.

'After the disappearance there were some odd stories of the three kids being seen sitting in tree limbs after dark. Some saw them even playing marbles together around the lake.'

'Sounds pretty creepy to me,' said Zunu.

'It's just too sad. Their parents threw their toys, their clothes and all the belongings, also the marbles in the water with the hope it reaches them. Everything was packed in heavy silver trunks with chains around them with thick padlocks.'

'You know, people avoid crossing this bridge,' Danh looked at Zunu. Both stood straight, still and silent staring into the lake. The waxing gibbous moon was out now from behind the smoky clouds. It gleamed white and melted into the water like cheddar as little fishes bounced up and down.

They crossed the bridge quietly, this time without dread and walked further down as the trees cast lazy and apathetic shadows through the border of the forest and the fields and back into the old boulevards.

CHAPTER ELEVEN

The Belief

It was 6.00 am when the rooster first crowed, every five minutes or so the cock split the silence. Antonio had a pillow covering his ears, finally around the time he actually woke up, it went quiet. The morning was sweet and fresh, someone banged at the door. The attendant knocked again, Antorio got up yawning with a couple of long stretches. It was his morning bed tea. Antorio said, 'Thank you.'

He was ready to face the day now, to pour his day in his diary, adjust, modify, compose and pack it back in yet again. The hotel room was clean, quite small but the bed was comfortable and the staff was friendly, a perfect place for a one or two night. Antorio rose and peeped through the small window. There was a pale glow of light towards the east. Bus office and bus stop were around the corner.

Antorio showered, dressed quickly and went downstairs. There were many people moving around. At breakfast there was a good selection to choose from; tea, coffee, boiled eggs, waffles, toast with jams, fresh fruit and even some hot Vietnamese dishes.

Antorio had already informed Bahir Ali that he would come down that day to his snakes' farm and then decide the future action. Bahir had conveyed that his son was not in town, otherwise he could have had him picked up. Antorio had countered back, that it was not too far for him and he could easily travel by bus. As he walked away from the hotel the sun was breaching the horizon towards the east. The sky was light blue above the deep orange streaked horizon. He walked the long walkway bordered by rows of Petunia and white

Bougainvillea, took a right and then headed down south. A blue sign board at a corner pointed the 'Cycle Route'.

Antorio stood at the bus stop, in half an hour he was dropped by an old and shabby yellow bus at the snakes' farm. Bahir Ali was into leather business.

'Good to see you, sir,' Bahir Ali welcomed him with a hand shake. 'This is my snake farm in collaboration with some five local people. They have also contributed to it, as we share common business interest.'

[The outside board read 'Vac Snakes farm']

Owners:

Bahir Ali	Trang Quynh Tran
Huu Duy Vu	Nam Le
Hiep Nguyen	Do Thuy

Antorio smiled. Bahir Ali started to show him around casually. Amongst the first few shops was refreshments by 'Nam Le', and then there was a store by 'Do Thuy' with leather goods that offered bags, belts and wallets made out of snake.

Antorio's disappointment ran in right after that. There were several snakes kept in incredibly small concrete and metal enclosures that were found all over the farm. All of them were kept in the same about one square meter enclosure, with hardly any space to move at all.

The biggest snakes were kept in a separate building, and treated as objects rather than living being. Their confines were totally vacant aside from bowls with water. Some cages had wooden floors, some had only wire work. The snakes could neither hide nor move.

The rooms smelled unpleasant and warm, with snake poop and uncleanliness. Some snakes were sleeping but others were poking cages looking for an exit from the three feet area. The poor wild creatures lived in enclosures so little for them, and would be turned into shoes, bags, belts and purses without compassion. It disturbed Antorio greatly.

Even if Antorio didn't agree with it, this was a way of life for people so that they could put food over the table for their families. He watched everything quite upset but didn't convey his disapproval.

'Bahir, I wish to be left alone for a while.'

'Ok, no issues. Are you upset with me sir?'

'No Bahir.'

Bahir pulled out a chair for him and cleaned it over with a cloth. He threw the cloth piece over his shoulder and walked away. Antorio sat over the chair outside 'Nam Le' refreshments sipping coconut water. He gazed at the passersby quietly. After an hour he decides there was only one way to get Bahir Ali out of this.

After much thought he went up to Bahir who was waiting for him at a corner and asked him to summon all his business partners.

'I would like you all to buy a land and setup rubber plantation. Rubber market is a fairly new industry with currently not much competition. If you work in collaboration and discipline, in time you will yield rich dividends,' Antorio told them collectively.

'Are you joking sir?' commented Bahir Ali. 'We don't have the money for that kind of business.'

'Three main things – I will fund all the resources, labor charges, material, land, fertilizer and soil required for it. I will buy you a land too. I will get you enrolled with some institute where you can be trained for this job before you start off.'

'That is very kind of you sir, but it will be a very big debt. How can we take such a big obligation?' Trang Quynh Tran seemed skeptical.

'What if you change your mind later?' said Nam Le.

'We will be in trouble. We are very poor,' Do Thuy agreed with Nam Le.

'I will give it in writing that you don't have to pay me back anything in case of losses or failure. If only you generate double the profit, should you even think of returning back any money. How and where, I will inform you in future. For the moment, please don't take it as obligation. Bahir Ali is a friend now. A friend can help a friend.'

'My son will be thrilled to hear it. He has to travel so far for trading. It will be nice to have some stable job in our own country,' said Bahir Ali.

'I am glad you all have agreed to it. I look forward to it. But I also have a condition attached with it. I want you all to stop this leather business and release all the snakes back in the wilds. I understand absolutely it is a means of livelihood for you. To compensate you, I am giving you all some gold nuggets. Please change it to your currency and you may keep the money to run your homes.'

'This will be our first step towards the new business setup. The money is sufficient enough to take care of your home expenditures for the next eight months. You won't go hungry.'

All six of them gave a big hug to Antorio and told him he was 'god' to them. They would do as he said.

Bahir Ali had tears of joy in his eyes. 'Now I can easily settle my oldest daughter and get her married off,' he said with gratitude.

'Now folks! You can do me a favor too. Please someone help me locate my lost guidebook,' Antorio exclaimed with hands in the air.

'We must visit the tarot reader. She does give great guidance. Once my niece had lost her precious middle finger diamond stone ring and the tarot reader helped her find it in a jiffy,' Nam Le exploded with excitement.

'Do you really accept that randomly rearranged cards have supernatural capacity to disclose you anything about an individual ?' Antorio questioned them.

All began narrating their encounters and beliefs. And they believed in it quite strongly.

'Tarot is never never a speaking parrot, meaning replying yes or no to your questions like some parrot just when you wish. Sometimes it gives you a very direct answer and at times pretty vague and yet again at times no answer. You got to decipher the silence too, that too sitting under the full white moon. Helped me at least!' Nam Le said with an unmistakable squint that never kept his gaze steady. He was talking to Antorio but staring at Bahir.

'Every spiritual lesson we meet in our lives can be found in the seventy eight Tarot cards,' Bahir was quick to add.

'There are total seventy eight cards?' Antorio quizzed.

'Indeed!' Bahir reacted.

'And when we consult the Tarot, it's like holding up a mirror and getting the answers through yourself. If you disrespect it, it will insult you right the hell back. Meaning you kick yourself in your butt,' said Trang Quynh Tran enclosing his palms excitedly. His half broken silver tooth stood out as he spoke.

'We have been through hell,' said Do Thuy. 'My twenty year old daughter Anh was suffering depression through a break up. She was left crushed, when she first decided to give healing crystals a try. Her heart felt blocked, like it had cracked into a hundred thousand pieces. Her shoulders were hunching forward badly. We were so stressed.' Do Thuy eyes welled up as he recalled.

… 'And so Anh's friend, who was studying shamanism at the time, placed a series of stones along her chakras, that is a string of seven linear energy portals over her chest. Then she placed a pale pink piece of rose quartz known as "The love stone" upon Anh's heart. She said it opens and mitigates aching heart and removes negativity.'

'Then?' Antorio questioned intently, his jawline leaning over his clenched fist.

'We had great hope once again. She was able to move some

of the stuck energy that was there,' said Do Thuy. 'We remember the weight that was once on her heart being lifted and she felt lighter and happy. We saw her smiling and getting rid of the dark past. Anh has married since her first chakra cleanse, but rose quartz remains her most loved precious stone,' Do Thuy said relieved as his hands rubbed his misty eyes.

'For me, I rely upon spirituality and going within, to a belief in something bigger,' Antorio said with arms crossed over the chest. 'The crystals really becomes more for me about pulling out, drawing out what was already there.'

'The crystal is a wonderful magical reminder, to be open to new opportunities throughout life's journey!' added Bahir Ali bouncing his excited head.

'I always had quiet mystical influences around me, with a father that read palms, and an uncle that practiced Reiki healing,' said Hiep Nguyen. When I was around twelve, my grand dad bought me my first tarot deck and introduced me to our local crystal shop. I never pursued it. But I always had a curiosity for the esoteric. It wasn't until years later that I reconnected with that part of myself again.'

'If you believed in it, why didn't you pursue it?' asked Antorio with a deep gaze.

'I had settled down early, my wife's wish was I pursue farming over my father in law's land. She was the only child,' said Hiep Nguyen as his mouth gasped and heaved for relief from the day's scorching heat. 'Many people kind of misunderstand tarot. It's far more complex than I'll read your future.'

'You mean it doesn't tell past and future, but people simply choose to believe in it? Are people not being naive?' Antorio reflected.

Huu Duy interrupted, 'If we already have a fixed answer, a fixed past or say a fixed future then we are not allowing cards to guide us. What's the point in chasing your spouse around town, hiding behind the walls with binoculars to see if he is having an affair. Say he is. Later questioning the reader if he is betraying you makes no sense. We are looking for solutions not simply delving on past or future.' He rested his arm over Bahir Ali's shoulder, and removed his cap to fan himself.

'Also, if the reading is for you, you must make sure your question centers only on you. Just ask about your book. Don't involve any third person, from personal experience I advise it,' said Bahir Ali. He blew and plucked his shirt to and fro. It was drenched with running sweat. His athletic shoes were smelling too as he tapped the floor.

Nam Le tried to fix his squinty eyes over Antorio and clarified further, 'Say the tarot hints at you any day that your relationship is going to burst out, take the thought into consideration and reflect over it. If you reviewed it and then dismissed it as unfound fear, so then great for you!'

'Guys! Let's see the tarot reader!' Antorio said pushing up his glasses over the arc of his nose.

The mystical shop…

The party took several turns before finding the shop, tucked away just off a bustling convergence alongside an eatery, a shop called "Crystal blue". They were surprised as they didn't expect to find a magic shop to be more accurate a spiritual store in such a locale (precisely next to a bakery shop). They expected a haunted lane.

The moment they walked into the cozy shop, it smelled strongly of earthy incense. A handtied white sage wand coated with dragon blood resin lined the walls. The store had Crystals, Oracle Cards, Crystal Sets, Zodiac Crystal Sets, Pet Charms and so much more to help fulfill a happy soul.

Antorio had come here on a mission. It seemed like a place that would help him with his quest. It was truly a mystical shop, offering everything from precious holistic crystals to stunning, handcrafted jewellery. A tiny board read Lady Zamonta also hosts beautiful crafts and mindfulness workshops.

They paid the consultation fees and patiently awaited their turn. The area in the back of the store was large and open, partitioned off by rows of movable dividers and curtains. Green and weird orange cloth pictures hung along the walls.

Antorio sat on a sofa with large thick cushions, enormous round arm rests and a velvety fabric. A grey eyed woman in a crazy long streaming robe walked in and sat across in a comfortable chair, the curiously oversize round chair could easily fit two people. She was now leaning over a small table in the candlelit room and her disheveled curly hair touched the floor sweeping it.

She spun her long skeletal hands around a burning sage, like a spider, envisioning and determining the looming fate. Her mysterious eyes shed reflections of the burning Palo Santo, and the lighting candles in the room.

She didn't have a crystal ball, although they did sell it at the store. Rather, there were a few piles of cards that looked quite like the cards Antorio had envisioned. They had ancient, elaborate illustrations trickling with a feeling of enchantment.

'Tarot is the magical untold story of our life, the desire to explore the heart, and key to our soul,' the lady said in a mysterious tone. Her red rimmed watchful rabbit eyes gave Antorio a very strange look.

'The twenty two Major Arcana cards speak to life's karmic and spiritual lessons, and the fifty six Minor Arcana cards reflect the hardships that we experience on a daily basis. Disclose to me your concern and let the cards help you.'

'I need to locate my guidebook. It got swept by the river,' said Antorio. The woman gave him a baffling fixed gaze again.

'Now that you have grounded yourself, please select the cards we must use for your Tarot card reading,' the woman said.

Antorio saw her pencil thin bony hands and wondered if she ate tarot playing cards for meals. She was as flat as the cards and looked like one of them. She wore over her head a small baroque style gold royal tiara. It was card shaped and inlaid with artificial gemstones, red ruby and crystals.

She gave him a set and instructed him to shuffle. At that point he cut the deck, to one side explicitly as she instructed, and re-stacked them. She asked him to shuffle again and cut a few times. Next she directed him to pick exactly fifteen cards. She took the fifteen cards and spread them out in what seemed like a random pattern.

'Can I see the cards?' Antorio questioned with his eyebrows raised.

'Not yet. Now please take a moment to breathe and draw out ten cards one by one… with a good pause. After the reading, I will give a detailed explanation of each card. The position of the cards in the Celtic Cross Spread impacts the answers you seek.'

Antorio drew out the ten cards slowly without seeing them. The Celtic Cross spread was a complex spread where each card had an assigned position and a meaning for that position. Antorio begin with the Celtic Cross layout, and as they were talking, she moved the cards around. It looked like the point of the cards were whispering to one another. By the end of the reading, the spread looked totally different.

'It's really about the connections between the cards. Depending what cards are around a specific card, it will influence the meaning. They're all being influenced by each other, occasionally their energies are amplified by each other,' she explained. Antorio gaped on in silence drumming his feet impatiently and fingers crossed.

While she shuffled the cards, her eyes gave him a freakish inspect again. Antorio handed her three cards: Six of swords, High priestess and Tower.

'Six of swords is quite a somber looking card, I have often interpreted this as a trip by water or air. It's my "Journey" card and I cannot tell you how many times this has proven to be true for clients,' she said twirling the card with her fingers.

'Hmm, well ya… I already had a comfortable trip by water and air too.'

She picked up the second card and remarked, 'She sits in between light and dark at the gates of the incomparable mystery, the High Priestess wears a blue robe and holds the Torah in her hands. Known as the "guardian of the unconscious", she speaks to insight, serenity, learning and understanding. Since you have uncovered the High Priestess, it's time to trust your intuition and engage in "mystical" practices.'

'What mystical practices was she talking about,' Antorio wondered.

As if reading his mind, she answered, 'You would be wise to give a touch of consideration to the signs that come to you in dreams.'

'The Tower card– your third card, depicts a tall tower on top of a rough mountain. I can see lightening strike and flames bursting through the windows. People seem to be falling from the tower in desperation.'

She shrieked and suddenly exploded out of the chair, her body stiffened as she stood there with her eyes big and round like watermelons. She held the temple of her head for a few seconds, then shot her index finger sharply at Antorio. Antorio reclined back into the chair nervously. His shocked gaze fell over her distinctly padded bottoms and her tops that had thick cotton pads spilling out of her bosom, now toppled over the floor. Antorio shuffled awkwardly and uncomfortably in his chair, shifting his gaze to the orange cloth over the wall. But the lady was a warrior.

'Excuse me,' she said shoving back the lumps of cotton in place very normally with a frozen unfazed look.

'The Tower tarot suggests you may be about to embark on a testing obstacle or difficult time in your life. Although you may face a period of destruction, you're strong enough to survive, thrive, and emerge wiser and more powerful than ever before,' she looked up at the ceiling and drew a deep breath.

'Good to know the danger before hand,' Antorio grinned.

Then she held his hand and closed her eyes, 'The color blue shall be very fortunate for you.'

'Alright, I shall bear in mind,' Antorio replied gracefully.

She spun her head ten times, her bulging eyeballs rolling in an eerie spooky fashion and said, 'session over.'

Suddenly she shrilled and screeched like a mad cat, 'Leave now.'

'LEAVE NOW — LEAVE NOWW,' drawling in a far more hoarse manly voice now. Her eyes turned from grey to fiery red.

Antorio jumped out of the chair startled and hurtled out of the room. Hesitantly he peeped back through the silky drapes and said, 'Err – Thank you for your precious time.'

Her face was lying knocked out flat over the table as though someone had clobbered her.

The party dispersed out to conduct an inquiry once again in the town. Luck favored them with a little piece of information.

Trang Quynh Tran said his neighbor's daughter was playing at the riverside that day. She mentioned that she had seen someone pick up a muddy book.

'Please give us a week to track down the guy. He might revisit the spot. We cannot promise you anything, but MeoVac is a small place. We can try,' said Trang.

Antorio was a bit relieved. He could return back to Na Rang and wait a week. He headed back to the resort, and packed his bags. Next day he could venture out for the return boat ride to Na Rang.

CHAPTER TWELVE

The Disappearance

Danh saw the mess in his room, the worn out thick bundle of the unwashed messy clothes lying in one corner and the stupid stool he always tripped over in the dark. Soon there would be colors and traffic rolling in, the smell of other homes making coffee and toast. Zunu was still fast asleep. He woke him up.

Flaring sun rays swept in over the compound wall, the freshly cut grass smelled raw and pleasing.

There was not just chaos in his room but outside too, and he could sense that the chaos wasn't the right type. It wasn't the usual peace filled community.

Both him and Zunu peeped out of the window. Locality appeared grim, people were standing in groups holding grave discussions. Women looked frightened. Kids carried serious faces.

'Whatever happened?' they wondered. Stepping outside their home they saw men preparing a funeral.

'Has someone died?' Danh inquired.

'The monk who stayed inside the cave has not surfaced. Last he was seen going inside the cave by some and since then no one has seen him. Upon conducting a search only fresh bones and skull were found. Looks like the man was eaten up by animals,' said an elderly man.

The entire village was sad. The community strongly maintained that a person should die at home and be surrounded by his family. They had the belief it was a bad misfortune to die away from home. Many people were carried to the hospital if they were unwell. But if it became evident that they would die, they were rushed home with all possible haste so that their demise may be made there.

It was concluded that if the ancestors didn't get a burial at the hands of its own generation, their ghost haunted and soul could never be at peace. It was a bad omen.

'Which monk are they talking about?' Zunu and Danh looked at each other and speedily rushed off towards the Rillywoods.

Everything was as it ever was, there was a profound quietness and a pleasant breeze. A skylark was trilling and the crooked trees were whispering to the winds as though they wished to tell it a secret. The pale yellow dry leaves softly crackled under their feet as they ran. The forest thrummed with their foot steps and the unceasing yackety yak of frogs. The hard parched ground was clay like and very dry. They heard the swishing sound of the warm wind as it swept past, whispering to the vicinage. The shriveled trees emptied their lonesome softly to the wind which swallowed their rustle and muffled them. The morning sun shone dimly from behind, washing them in soft, amber light, the woods remained darker at a distance.

They looked for the man under the tree. They looked around at all places. Everything was standstill. The mat was lying dusty and abandoned. His students were missing too. The only thing live was large, handsome and spreading, the albizia tree above them that was easily recognized by its umbrella like canopy of evergreen, feathery foliage and puffs of pink blooms. A flower dropped next to the empty mat. Danh picked it up and stared hard at it.

He caressed the land beneath the tree while his still face intently looked towards the sky. The canopy was dotted all over with pink and white. His brows crossed and eyes bathed in anticipation. The trees, the leaves, the sky now all stood out enclosing their presence, with a slight radiance that proposed life, perhaps cognizance.

'Is this flower a sign of life?' asked Zunu.

'I dream it to be,' Danh replied.

The man had truly vanished. Were the villagers telling the truth? Both Zunu and Danh felt very sad. The last place left to be checked was the cave itself. They returned back to the village.

Meanwhile monks were invited to perform Buddhist rites and deliver sermons. Mourners and members of the Buddhist community presided over the service, whereby chants were led by the monks. Mourners too join the chants and sat silently.

At the end of the service, locals and mourners carried the casket to transportation vehicle, and followed the vehicle in a procession. Then the casket with the remains was placed into the grave with recitals.

Zunu and Danh watched it silently and unbelievably. They needed to find out what really happened in that cave.

..

'Zunu, I hope you know what you are doing.'

'My dad has taught me about caves and it's exploration. We can't just give up, we have to look for the great man. He maybe in some kind of trouble.'

'Many species of land dwelling animals use these caves for nesting or accidentally enter them and not being able to find their way out, they die,' said Danh. 'I'm not yet prepared for the worst.'

'Why are you thinking over on such lines? I'm shouldering the responsibility of getting us out of here. If we give up, we won't be able to forgive ourselves. He was a good man. He was good to us,' said Zunu. 'I need to see it with my eyes, what went wrong.'

It was evening as they walked. Small, loose stones littered the stream causing them to trip as they got closer to the rock face. Their feet were cold and socks watery. Zunu shone the beam of his torch ahead and a roughly oblong cave came into view, the entrance was so small they almost missed it. The cave was built under the earthy grey rocks into the cliff. The stone guarding the entrance was jagged and slippery, and arranged in such a way, that it would be difficult for any passersby to spot.

'Alright, here's the cave, what next?' said Danh.

The gigantic rocks around the cave, stood as though somebody had recently placed them there. Inside their small cracks; mosses, thyme, fern, oregano and different plants were alive with astounding tolerance and steadiness.

The entrance was so small, they had to squeeze in carefully. They first extended the left arm through, then firmly planted the left foot to the inside and then angled the body accordingly. It appeared to be the livelier part of the cave since many small animals such as night butterflies, flies, bats, and mosquitoes were going in and out at the time. From that point on, they could see a clear way to the inside of the cave.

'Danh, place this chewing gum in your mouth,' said Zunu.

'Why?' asked Danh.

'To keep your mouth shut,' Zunu said jokingly. 'On a serious note it will make you less nervous and unlikely to scream. If you make noises, it will wake up the cave.'

'Is the cave a ghost to wake up,' Danh was intrigued.

'Yes, if that's the only language you understand Danh. Take it as a ghost. We need to tip toe and not make a sound. Ok!'

'Yeps.' Danh replied. 'I like chewing gums and sometimes I swallow them too. Then I get a bad tummy ache. Mom has to give me hot soup to wash it all out. He he!'

'Danh, please keep the chewing gum in your mouth right away. I don't want you making sounds anymore.'

'Ok!'

' - But if I see a ghost please don't expect me not to scream,' said Danh.

'Eekkkkksss... What is it that you will take to stay quiet!'

'A small finger right over my mouth. My mom does that to me.'

'Enough! Sshhhh or you don't accompany me.'

The cave mouth was of impenetrable obscurity, as they stepped further. They watched their shadow dissolve into the surrounding darkness. It was damp and the only sound was the dripping water.

The cave was very broad and there were numerous stalagmites and stalactites stones inside it. Some were so big that they almost reached the floor from the ceiling. There was a small pool of water too with fishes living in it. It had an eerie moonscape look to it. They could see clumps of plants with deep pink flowers growing in very dark condition clinging to the vertical walls.

'So pretty,' Zunu murmured touching the flower, flower petal melted in his hand leaving a pink hue. As Zunu stepped ahead the flower had revived its pink petals.

Deeper inside the beam of Zunu's torch was enveloped and lost in the blackness. They had to move around by following the damp wall of the cave with hands. Unexpectedly, flaring lights started to life, illuminating the passage ahead and washing the whole natural hollow in a glimmering orange sparkle. Danh rushed his arm to his eyes in fright.

'What is that?' said Danh.

Moving closer they were left spellbound.

There was a swayambhu (natural) Shivling at the end of the cave.

'Looks like local people come to worship here,' said Zunu,

'Once in a life time experience.'

It did give them a lot of courage. Somehow, they felt they were not alone. So many people had been in and out of the cave already.

'This is Indian god,' Danh murmured to Zunu.

'Stone god, please save us from ghost, please - Jai ho,' Danh mumbled in his breath.

They walked past the passage into an extremely narrow opening to the right. It opened to a dark chamber, at the end of which stood massive arched pillars. The pillars had some sort of spiritual carvings. The ancient text and sculptures couldn't be understood by Zunu and Danh. The calcium carbonate stone wall was mirroring the light, making the lithomatic stylistic layout sparkle. It looked precious. Starting there on, the cave was confounded with many columns which made for huge divisors.

The roof in the next chamber was collapsed and the floor

was huge boulders that had fallen off it. When they looked around the blocks, underneath some old stalactites were cropping through.

'I understand now why the great man chose to meditate here,' said Zunu in a soft hush.

The pair sat down to rest for a while enveloped in the body of the dark walls, feeling the cold stones underneath their feet. In the darkness they felt their blood return to a comfortable warmth –their hearts and spirits were now firmer. They sat curled in a safe corner and stretched their arms out.

Zunu's unblinking eyes quietly absorbed the darkness as though he was in a dream. In those minutes without the interference and diversions of the world, in that immaculate harmony, Zunu told himself, 'I have to do this. Doesn't matter if a monster holes up out there, we will face it. I'm prepared,' he took a deep breath.

Cold water ran as a thin stream from the cave opening down the crevices, feeding smaller springs in nearby spots. The water shimmered even in darkness and had silent waves. Underfoot the loose stones shifted, and Danh suddenly stiffened. Danh's fleshy ankle twisted one way and then the other. It was all blue and cold. The noise from the tiny shifting rocks echoed off the dense stone walls. His heart galloping Danh let out a cry,

'Ahh–' Zunu quickly gagged it.

'Noise can wake up dangerous animals, shhh!' Zunu warned.

Just ahead there was the sound of water dripping slowly into water. Inside the utter darkness and the absolute quiet, animals living in the caves walked softly, crawling inside the endless galleries created by the cracks of the subsoil, seeking scant food and a mate to couple. Many black poisonous spiders were waiting for some insect to get caught in their web. Zunu and Danh cleared the meshes away. Their fingers tips had fragile pipes of white spidery threads hanging from them. Rodents ran around, sniffing and crossing their shoes.

The sound that met their straining ears and nystagmus eyes was their own echoing footsteps. Danh wrinkled his nose against the moldy smell permeating the air. At a curve, Danh reached out for the wall and lumbered his feet slowly to feel his way. He stumbled accidently into a forest of stalactites and stalagmites, and fell thud over the splintered solid floor.

'Not again, please Danh!' Zunu gave him a hand. That moment more rocks gave away, Ploosh! Danh found himself slipping vertically in the dark shallow water, his feet were frozen with fear and blue veins jammed. Zunu held on to him strongly as Danh found himself bubbling out air in water. Danh somehow broke the frothing barrier and quickly managed to grab a rock. Zunu helped him out. He stood there shivering with chill, coughing and spluttering out water as he struggled to regain his feet. He spit from his mouth noiselessly.

'You ok?'

'I guess so,' Danh fumbled meekly. Thereafter they moved on very carefully.

The last chamber was dim… but it was unusually lit up by a small wood fire in one corner that no one seemed to have put off. In the center was a small simmering earthen pot and in the far corner there was a braided tangled mat made up of dried grass. Zunu wished to scream out for the man, but he knew it was useless now. This was a dead end - There was just no one anywhere to be found. There was a small stream of water running out of the cave through small cracks— the only way out.

Right in front of them lay lower jawbone and a few other bones, mainly fragments. No creature could have escaped as there was no other opening. 'Maybe people were right?' they thought. It was his skeleton found intact by local people deep inside the cave.

It brought tears to their eyes and the acceptance came by that he was no more. They were so lost in thoughts and grief, that they didn't realize they were out of the cave in no time. Their shadows were shrinking to their feet.

Rebirth was his first thought as the drowning azure mellow golden sun hit the face. Zunu stared at it. His heart prayed, 'May his soul rest in peace.'

Danh was exceptionally quiet all the way home. A curtain of light shower beat down from the sky. A big fat rain drop hit his cheek and flew down his face to the neck. It was followed by one more raindrop then yet another. A gasp passed through his lips and he wrapped his hands firmly around his waist. The drops of rain hung on his lashes. Then ran down his face. The rains patted his cheeks streaming away the tears. The wind was now sighing and swaying the tree tops. The cicadas were buzzing and a frog croaked as it peeked out from behind a stone.

They walked upon ageless stones listening to the wind. The wind assaulted their skin leaving them with small cold pricks. The uneasiness closed away when the passage light of Nguyen home was seen. Houses were lit up like candle flames on the farm land. They were back home and Danh's mom was on the lookout for them whole day long. Danh got a firing. They were put to bed immediately after dinner.

'What is ahead and how far will we need to go? I wish to go back all the way, and do much miss my galaxy 1x.' Zunu leaned on the sill and gazed at the dark cotton clouds sifting the sky. Zunu raised his fingers to his lips, and gave a flying kiss to the sky, his home.

..

The horizon tossed shades of taffy pink to orange to canary yellow and changed the shade of waters to a brilliant lemon tint. The endless vast expanding river in front of Antorio filled his heart with unknown depths. The boat man rowed quietly. Antorio heard him sing and the cool wind was loaded with his charming notes.

'Một đàn chim xinh đẹp trên bae tori ánh sáng
Hãy cùng bay nào!
Nhớ đến nhà tôi!
Bạn đang ở đâu, đàn chim trắng?
Tôi thấy bạn ở mọi hướng, khi bạn bay tới chạy lui
Đến và đi!

Một đàn chim trắng trên bầu trời ánh sáng

Hãy đến gặp tôi trên thuyền của tôi, vì vậy chúng ta sẽ cùng nhau bơi về nhà.

Tôi nằm trên một cánh đồng hoa! Tôi đếm từng con chim vượt qua đầu!

Chim trắng bay tới chạy lui.

Chim trắng bay tới chạy lui!'

'What does it mean in English?' Antorio asked and the boatman explained…

A flock of pretty birds in the light sky

Come let's fly together!

Remember to come to my home!

Where are you off to, flock of white birds?

I see you in all directions, as you fly to and fro

To and fro!

A flock of white birds in the light sky
Come meet me in my boat, so we'll swim home together.
I lay in a field of flowers! I count each bird that
passes overhead!
White birds flying to and fro.
White birds flying to and fro!'

'Sir, where are you from?' asked the boatman.
'Up there!' Antorio pointed towards the sky.
The boatman laughed.

The Sun was subsiding into its bed, as Antorio walked past the riverside and the shimmering of the river… the majority of the neighborhood locals were out by the riverside doing chores and the kids were playing. Dispersed with poppies, the brilliant green waves of the cornfields got blurred as he arrived home.

Antorio quietly tip toed to check upon Danh and Zunu, both were asleep. He felt for his pen and scribbled slowly…

Brisk note:

Meo Vac people are very poor. I don't intend to reclaim the cash I offered for the business. It's only a little commitment towards a valuable future.
These people have tremendous self respect too. If I tell

them I won't take back the money, they wouldn't accept it.

Also, Planet E is superstitious. You get these obscure thoughts and leads from the cards, if you start believing in them, you will automatically extract some parts psychologically and try and identify them with your life situations. It's possible the readings are nothing honest at all. Everything relies over your outlook.

I think individuals mentally depend upon some heavenly power overseeing their moves, it makes them feel nicer that they are not going to be blamed. It assumes liability for your errors and potentially inadequacies on the off chance, you can accuse something outside of your control
Additionally, who wouldn't care to know what's in store.

But I don't trust that tarot cards have any genuine mystical realities to tell us. It can be a lot of fun though and give a simple reason to sort out life. But just how far do you enable yourself to extend the implications of the cards to apply to your life.

Antorio.

CHAPTER THIRTEEN

Grand Plan

Zunu and Danh discovered Mr. Antorio at home, having breakfast, and ran to give him a hug.

'Dad! You are back. We missed you. How was your trip?'

'Kind of successful. I had a talk with the locals of Meo Vac. They are very co operative and helping with the searches. We will need to wait a while.'

Antorio over seeing their dismal faces remarked, 'Why such grim faces? You ought to be cheerful to hear it!'

'Dad, we lost a friend. He won't ever come back. He died,' said Zunu.

'Whatever happened? Who was it?'

'We have no idea what happened. He just disappeared from the cave where he stayed. Locals found fresh bones and skull. It was very heart breaking. We had connected so well with him shortly.'

'Life and death are a part of life cycle for planet E. One has to accept it gracefully. I don't need my two young men to be so upset. Unfortunately, we cannot help it. Planet E believes it's

god's will,' said Antorio.

Danh made a small face and asked, 'God can send him back too?'

'We will have to ask your god,' Antorio reflected.

'But he never replies back.'

'Hmm, yet perhaps he hears us,' Antorio grabbed Danh in his lap and said, 'Now you will have your breakfast and not think too much.'

Zunu joined in, 'Decent pancakes and lovely tea, –Aunty it's delicious!'

'It's Bánh cuốn,' said a smiling Mrs. Nguyen. 'These are a kind of Vietnamese pancake, made by steaming fermented rice batter over a cloth to make thin, wavy sheets.'

'We have at least seven days before I head to MeoVac again for inquiry,' Antorio spooned some pancake from his dish. 'Meanwhile is there anything you kids might want to do?'

'We could set out for town and watch a movie,' said Zunu with flashing eyes.

'I want to see animal movie something like Serengeti national park,' Danh added wistfully.

'Dad, can't we make a trip to Serengeti park? That should be fun,' Zunu said excitedly.

Mr. Antorio thought for a while. 'Hmmmm…. Ok guys! done. Pack your bags! We are going to Serengeti.'

Both Zunu and Danh's face lit up with huge smiles. They started dancing, jumping up and down, clapping their hands.

'How will we go?' Zunu asked.

'Mr. Nguyen, which airport is closest to Serengeti?' Antorio inquired.

Mr. Nguyen got an old ragged map from inside his cupboard. He picked up a red pen and started marking the routes in red.

'At present the national park is served by a number of airstrips; Seronera being the busiest. Major airports in the park's proximity are Mwanza Airport (166 km to Ndabaka Gate), Arusha Airport (226km), Kilimanjaro International Airport (284 km).'

'Best option would be Arusha town which is the starting point for Tanzania's most mainstream northern safari circuit. Kilimanjaro International Airport is situated 46 km/29 miles east of Arusha. There are direct and one stop flights from overseas to both,' Mr. Nguyen informed scrawling through the map.

'Danh always wished to go to Serengeti. I had spoken to some tour agencies too, but it just didn't materialize then,' Mr. Nguyen said pouring himself some tea in a cup.

'When is the best time to visit Serengeti?' asked Antorio.

'Actually, all month are good depends on which animals

you prefer to see. – February, April, June, July, and August are favored though. It's amidst dry season that a lot of animals try to find some water, so they are moving from one spot to another. The local guide said that the very interesting period is February. Zebras and gnus are giving births and a lot of predators around too,' Mr. Nguyen answered spinning his pen.

Danh peeped over Zunu's shoulder into the map and said, 'Serengeti is so big. It's written 14,760 square kms. If we wish to see it all, at least need a week…'

Mr. Antorio too scanned the map and exclaimed, 'Large! Almost 15,000 sq km. If you count the Maasai Mara portion in Kenya, it is about 30,000 sq km.'

'Dad, we could drive around exploring for days!' Zunu looked at him with excitement. Danh loomed behind, craned and hovered over his shoulder with curiosity. Danh fetched a small round lens from the base shelf of the storage rack in his room. He tried to see the map through it.

Mr. Antorio said rubbing his hands tightly, 'We don't need to cover all area. We will just visit some attraction areas or best ones according to the season.'

'You could fix up a program with a professional tour company "Hiliedu wanderings" or any other that operates in the area. There are so many. You can get a permit, and stay in one of the public camps,' Mr. Nguyen commented.

'We must all carry a good camera, and make sure the camera has magnifying ability,' remarked Mr. Antorio.

'Surely you must have zoom lens, otherwise it will be no fun,' added Mr. Nguyen.

'Yes, and a selfie stick can be useful too,' said Danh. 'Just imagine me posing with all animals in background he he.'

'Sure, till they decide you are their next meal,' Zunu guffawed heartily as Danh freaked out.

'Can't you think anything better! Think good, talk good always – my mom says,' Danh scrunched hard and scratched his stomach.

'Sure.' Zunu crackled a lively boisterous laughter holding his stomach as he leapt playfully on two feet like a frog. Danh's cherubic face was very red, very beefy now, he was going red to purple.

Seeing his annoyed tomato face Zunu quietened down immediately. Zunu was never going to have Danh falling over him in any worst case scenario fight… and Danh wouldn't want to chase Zunu any day.

The last time they played a chess game, Zunu was made to feel the worst person on earth.

—How bad he was… he was cheating to win. One month of friendship seemed like years with usual dose of blackmails like… 'You-u are older to me don't forget that Zunu…..'

So older Zunu was left with no choice but to give in to the hugely pampered sentimental Danh.

Mr. Nguyen broke the silence, 'I would recommend three cameras; crop sensor ds with 300 mm or something more prominent with a zooming focal point, a second dlsr with a 55-250 zoom, and good cell phone for wide edge shots. This avoids changing lens in a dusty environment and all must use sand bags as camera rest in safari vehicles.'

CHAPTER FOURTEEN

September Special

It was eighth September. Antorio marked it on calendar. He booked a flight through an agent from Hanoi, Vietnam (HAN-Noi Bai Intl.) to Kilimanjaro, Tanzania (JRO-Kilimanjaro Intl.) at the price of USD 1,229 per person. Danh was supported by Mr. Nguyen who declined any help. He had been gathering money for Danh's trip for long.

Next Antorio called up 'Hiliedu Wanderings' guide tour services. Someone at the desk picked up the phone. A professional crispy voice from the desk spoke up swiftly.

'The cost for the Serengeti Safari Tier one (Premier Experience) rooming & safari activity rate in Tanzania is from USD 760 to USD 1270 per person per night sharing on an average.'

'The topping is around USD 1750 a night for an exceedingly elite, upmarket and private experience,' the man added up smoothly.

'And where do we head from the airport?' Antorio questioned.

'You will be picked up by the tour operators from the airport itself, you need not worry sir.'

The person at desk further informed proudly, 'The continent might be underdeveloped, but it's leading camps and safari lodges are amongst the most glamorous and costly resorts in the world,' he paused…

'Park charges for Ngorongoro Conservation Area will cost USD 50 per person each day. Expect the additional cost of USD 30 for each vehicle and USD 30 per tent. Sir, we do give back value in return,' he said in a strong confident yet polite tone of a polished salesman.

'We have a decent budget that works for us,' Antorio replied back and booked the safari. The call ended content at both ends.

Danh was travelling by flight for the first time. It was a difficult tear jerky good bye to his mom dad and he had to be reminded he would be back home soon.

They arrived at the airport early. As airlines do have a specific check in time they want you to arrive by, which is usually two hours before the flight. They just sat around watching people go by. It was quite an occupied terminal.

Danh was gazing all around unusually quiet and appeared intimidated by the crowd. He just followed shyly Antorio's instructions.

Finally, they boarded the plane.

Antorio whispered in Zunu's ear, 'Danh could have a problem in take off due to drop in air pressure. Give him a chewing gum.'

'Why this chewing gum? You want me to keep my mouth shut again?' said Danh.

'No Danh, it's to protect your ears.'

'Then it should be sticking to my ears right?'

'Oh god! Danh is impossible,' murmured Zunu.

'What did I do now? Why did you just complain to god?'

'Eeeeeee, Danh! You just cover your ears and chew the gum while takeoff, ok!'

'Dad please explain him.'

'Danh, the pressure in a plane during take off is low and can cause ear ache. Chewing helps it,' Mr. Antorio explained.

'Oh, I see! Chewing gum has multiple purposes, I understand now.'

Zunu gave a funny glance to his dad.

'Dad, why can't I ever explain him anything! Funnily even I call out for god now. Courtesy Danh companionship,' Mr. Antorio grinned with wrinkles in his cheeks.

The takeoff was just perfect and Danh had no issues. He was sitting at the window seat with nose glued to the glass, watching the land beneath. The crew gave them a hot towel, bunch of food, etc. It was awesome. There was a bit of unexpected turbulence, but nothing worse.

There was this lovable little girl sitting in front row just across them. She was about six and was as chatty and energetic as could be. Her mom was very patient with her, however they could see the mother was also additionally occupied. A couple of times she touched her own eyes with tissues. It came across as some irritation in the eye.

"I am going to the Grand Canyon !" The child would tell the flight attendant and any passenger who smiled at her.

Danh waved out to her and said, '— and we are going to Serengeti national park. Many animals.' He cleared a frosty patch and was peering out of the window again.

The girl replied back jumping up, ' — and I get to see many mountains.'

It was only later when she and her mom walked down the aisle to use the restroom that her name ID flash. She was one of those Make-a-Wish kids and going to Grand Canyon was her wish.

The plane accelerated down the runway…. 16 hours 35 minutes + 2 stops had gone by like wind… in no time they had landed.

It was wonderful as they finally touched base at Kilimanjaro air terminal. The CEO and team were incredible. They had a vehicle, driver, guide, lodging, parking, meals, in other words everything pre-arranged by them. The driver drove them to a hotel. They rested for a while in the early morning hours.

Then they sped out of the hotel in a white Land Cruiser and drove straight into the vast mountain ranges, the impressive peaks of Mt Kilimanjaro inspired awe and roused a spirit of adventure in their hearts. They were left spell bound.

A mile later they took another road which headed due east towards Arusha. The driver kept the car at a steady sixty, the power line poles flashed past them as the subtropical sun shone bright in the blue skies. From that point the car rumbled straight into Ngorongoro where they took a short break at a gas station.

The late afternoon sun had the barometer pretty high. They shared a few slices of water melon, some water and the car raged over the highway like a tornado moving north central towards Seronera. Farms, cattles and canals swept past. Seronera was a small settlement within the Serengeti National Park. Finally, the car halted at a lodge. The loose board at a corner read, 'GONTYP'

The guide had already pre-picked a comfortable lodge for them. He was familiar with all the formalities needed and no one had to do anything. They waited patiently as he did the running around for check in. After getting them settle in comfortably the guide and driver camped right outside the lodge. They were available all the time.

There was a knock at the door. The manager walked in and introduced a fat guy.

'Sir, this is your personal butler. He will attend to only this room. You can call out to him with the red bell that hangs in the corner whenever you need something.' The manager smiled and left.

'How hospitable. They offer personalized services!' said Zunu.

Antorio was overwhelmed by the lodging and their gesture. As they peeped off the wooden railed balcony the umbrella thorn trees stretched far and wide in the rolling flats silhouetted by the red setting sun. They slept well at night.

It was an old fashioned lodge. Zunu wanted to take a shower. He was led to a bathroom in a funny tree house just adjacent to the lodge. They ferried up hot buckets of water with a rope attached to the tree branch. The water was heated over a wood stove in a pure village style. Zunu climbed up the ladder and placed his foot over the dais made up of loose wood blocks.

He was into the shower when he felt muffled footsteps over the floor board. The muted strides got only closer. Zunu stopped and turned around. His heart quit beating and voice paralyzed –

Zunu screamed, 'heeeeeelp! TIGER –RR ! Tiger in window….'(A tiger was in the treehouse window peeping at him in the most fascinating way.) He found his voice dead and muted as he opened his mouth and it stayed just open. He froze right there with his hands back to the wall, heart beating furiously. His eyes terrified. A flush crept up his face and an abrupt coldness hit his stomach. He just couldn't get himself to move.

Somehow, he took one step at a time against the wall. Still staring at the window, he snatched the towel. He stepped out nervously with the bathing towel in one hand, and water trickling all over the floor; soapy eyed, foam getting his feet slippery and dripping down in small splats. He almost slipped due to wet feet and suddenly found Danh just outside. He was rolling all over the floor with a tiger mask that he'd just purchased, thumping the floor with his clenched hands and laughing away.

'I could've got a heart attack!' Zunu made a fist at him.

'But you didn't.'

'Where did you get this mask from?'

'The lodge desk is pitching many such mask to tourist.'

'Cool! Make sure you keep that away from me.'

'Why Zuny? You don't want one?' Danh flipped out on the floor in another hysteria.

'NO. Thanks,' Zunu replied annoyed. Danh threw a mask over his back as he turned around. He had bought one for him too.

'Dat is for you.' Zunu turned around and picked it up.

Danh then did an impression of a bawling Zunu, 'help me, hlp me!'

He lay over the floor panel throwing up hands and feet like an over turned helpless turtle and kept teasing Zunu. That irritated Zunu further. Soon they were not talking.

..

Zunu sat in the simple Cane Chair nest hanging from a tree, sipping bottled vanilla milk noiselessly and played with the tiger mask. He stretched the elasticated mask up and down, fitted it into his face and then growled like a tiger. He took the mask off in a while.

As he swung left and right with his feet lightly stroking the ground… he glanced around at the vast Serengeti plains. It evoked in him a sense of wonder and profound respect for the animal kingdom. He reviewed the surroundings. The place made him wonder why animals are kept in zoo at all. It's so wrong to them.

Both the driver and guide accompanied them in the car ritually, stopping at places, chatting and showing them around. The big Toyota Cruiser had a pop up window at top. They could standup and see through it easily and it was quite exciting.

The going was slow over the long distances and often bumpy roads. The hot mid afternoon sun hung head on in the middle of the sky and got the temperature soaring to twenty eight degrees during the day.

'A little bit of patience will go a long way towards your enjoyment of this wondrous land!' the driver commented. The driver wore a cap, was average height and spoke good English. His forearm had a distinct tiger tattoo, his head endorsed a crew cut.

The guide reflected, 'Regardless of having a lot of animals the name Serengeti originates from maasai language "serengit". It means "endless open plains". The name was inspired by the wonderful large plain sights, hard to find elsewhere. It is truly a big prairie of rolling grassland.'

'What's your name and how long you work here?' asked Antorio.

'Siyabonga, sir I am into this activity for seventeen years now.'

'Which year was Serengeti established?' quizzed Antorio.

'Year 1951. It was done to protect the lions. The British colonial administration made a partial game reserve of 800 acres in this area in 1921. It laid the foundation for Serengeti National Park.'

Danh commented, 'Look! dikdiks eating the smallest leaves of the tree, elephant eating the leaves that are bigger and higher up, and giraffes eating leaves that are top most. Wildebeest eating only short grass and impala the taller grass. Looks like your height matter.'

'Which grass will you eat buddy? Have to get a medium size,' the guide chirruped sportingly and everyone laughed. He was a clever man with a whacky sense of humor.

The trio had had a great support in the guide, he knew all the spots so well and which places to stop at. The animals were just as mentioned in the safari brochure. The guides likewise radioed other vehicles routinely and got info on events going on in nearby locales.

With well trained zoom lens, the party could make out

subtle differences in size and coloration between individual animals and watch exactly what each one was doing closely. The two guides jabbered all along with each other, effortlessly dialogued and delivered full guidance to the trio as they shifted from one landscape to another.

Their shifting lenses caught in a lone Giraffe lying close to the edge of the tree, chewing cud. A couple of yards away, alongside a clump of an umbrella tree lay a huge buffalo, with a small calf relaxing close by. At the very back of the clearing, two vervet monkeys and olive baboons were seen hanging in trees. A sixth animal was feeding in the deep shadows. The rolling grassland was distinctively studded with isolated flat topped trees.

'Whir whir– click.' The cameras rolled in to rob in as many memories as could. The Land Cruiser rolled on and the binoculars re-focused from one spectacle to another with complete ease. The party observed vultures, many impalas, wildebeest being taken down by lions, female African leopard and her cub in a tree, grey crowned crane bird, herd of elephants, a starling bird.

Every morning they had two baby elephants just outside the Gontyp lodge, drinking out of the camp's water supply. They chilled out with their trunks in the tank making jovial trumpet sounds and sprinkled water into the trees. Many people splashed water over them and played with them. The two friendly babies were named Ale and Lacy by the lodge owners.

Danh said wistfully, 'This is my fairy land. I could live here forever.'

'I thought you didn't want to leave your home,' Zunu grinned.

'Oh, are we talking now?' Danh asked with a childish pout, jabbing Zunu with his finger.

Zunu straightened up and grinded his teeth at him.

The purpose built overland vehicle permitted fantastic viewing, and was furnished with large sliding windows. There was no cooling, so it got dusty and hot on occasions. They saw all the major groups of animals, up close and in chasing mode, feasting mode and resting mode. It was amazing to see so many, so close.

They spent most of their time in the northern Serengeti where they witnessed stuff like the river crossings. Had it been a different time of the year, they would've never got to see the crossings. Climate was by all accounts fairly predictable in that piece of Africa. At that moment was the dry season.

The guide briefed them about the migration. 'The wildebeest migration is throughout the year, as animals constantly seek ripe fresh graze and it's now thought for better quality water. It's a circular migration. It begins from southern plains of Ndutu and Kusini, in February each year. After calving in Ndutu as the rains start to get over in May, they move to western river Grumeti for fresher water. By the next month they cross over northern river Maasai Mara. It's almost suicide. Both the rivers are infested with crocodiles. Thousands of wildebeest and Zebra lurk around the bank for days till one animal takes a leap into the water and then suddenly the entire clan follows. Vultures feast on the remaining carcasses. Both the rivers are known as game reserves. When the short rains of November re-arrive in southern plains, the animals are back to it. They follow the thunder and clouds.'

The driver added up, 'End of November is the beginning of the rainy season with short rains. The only time visit not recommended is during the long rains of April and May when it pretty much rains non stop and roads in the park are pretty much impassible. We can hardly drive.'

'Thanks, now we understand the complete ecosystem,' said Antorio.

Zunu and Danh just sat wide eyed, speechless. Both the kids were unusually quiet, and totally consumed in the wild landscape.

..

Dinner was really good but huge portions. Danh remarked, 'They must think all tourists are fat! By the looks of people, seemingly it's also interpreted as not liking the food if you don't clear your plate. I had to really lick it clean as I was getting bad stares uncle. Most of the food is western taste. It's not bad, but it would've been nice to experience something more local like Vietnamese dishes too.'

'It's a different part of continent. The culture and food habits are bound to be different,' Antorio explained.

The driver opened the trunk of the car, pulled out a tent, sleeping bags and loaded it to the ground. Then he grabbed out a black duffle bag full of handy stuff and some extra clothes. They camped outdoors that night and all were was thrilled.

The Toyota land cruiser had a pop-up roof. Antorio slept on the roof and had a few couple of rocks to throw if jackals and hyenas got too pally. He didn't like being trapped in tents. It was cool at night but it got suffocating inside the tent.

In the western plains the reddening glowy dusk quietened into the belt of the dark clouds hushing the day, day after day. The nights saw deadly predators.

They had spent five entire days in the park - one evening, four full days, and then the next noon. They had low light binoculars and it exploited the first light and nightfall hours beautifully. That's when natural life was most dynamic, and generally most visible. The driver and guide cracked a chilled beer every night. Antorio and party carried a pitcher of freshly brewed ice tea in an ice box everywhere. Yum! Yum! Evening summers fun! They wore long pants and sleeves at night as there were swarms of tsetse flies and it did hurt like crazy when bitten.

Night drives were spectacular. Siyabonga was a smart guide with flaring eyes, just like two flashlights in the dark he would look around for special signs. That night he spotted some footprints alongside the road, as he looked in the development of close by birds and tuned in for animals sending cautioning signals. He called out to the party in excitement, and they quickly chased down the rough terrain. The way curved down, then turned rightwards into a narrower lane. Lots of trees, dark and thick clumps stood right above their head and moon light fell into the pale leaves glistening them. The headlights made the entire highway far and wide shimmer. The driver quietly dipped the headlights, switched off the engine and they all waited in silence. The air was warm and slow mild breeze blew carrying the clouds. At around seventy yards they spotted a beautiful female Cheetah. It was roosted on a tree at least seventy meters in the bush. As they drew nearer and nearer they realized that they had just meddled on its diner of an Oryx.

On another one occasion the vigilant eagle eyes of Siyabonga stopped the vehicle abruptly and had them look out into the bushes. The three of them clamored to make sense of what they were looking at. After some more direction from him they finally spotted a pride of lions, using binoculars no less.

This kept repeating on several occasions and even at night. Siyabonga's watchful eye was able to see, sense all that they were oblivious to. The driver too had permit to drive off road – a license that was available to only lodge drivers with appropriate vehicles and grants.

They also saw some hyena feeding on the remains of some poachers killed by the lions the other day. There were gunshots heard the other night.

..

Zunu and Danh picked up a small, thin leaflet brochure from the entrance desk that evening as they entered the lodge. It had pictures of balloon ride. They ran to Antorio and handed it over to him.

'Dad, Balloon ride please please!'

'An additional $500 per person,' the desk informed Antorio over the phone.

'Sir it's quite reasonable,' the man with short grizzled salt and pepper hair, magnificently white teeth flashed a smile as Antorio visited the desk.

'Sure, that's reasonable enough. Thanks.' Antorio made the payment without hesitancy.

The next day they drove to the dispatch site, a big green lush field at sharp 7 a.m. The site had a crew of twelve or so people to run it and one of their guys had stayed at the lodge overnight to drive them.

The only sound heard was the air blasting into the red yellow striped balloon, just above their heads as they entered it. The breeze was quiet and the air was superbly warm. As the balloon gradually turned in the sky, they saw the rosy sun peeking over the horizon. Its orchid glow spread across the sky. Danh kept thinking about how interesting the world must look from the eyes of a bird.

Danh screamed, 'I want to touch the sky…' Zunu held his shorts as he started jumping up and down.

'Can we go to your galaxy using this balloon?'

'Nopes.' Zunu swayed his head left – right.

'Oh nooo, my cap – it just flew off,' said Danh feeling his empty head in circles and looking down.

'You can pick it up later as we land,' said Antorio. 'Or maybe we'll get you another one, a nicer one!'

The balloon was now dropping to tree top heights and even brushed a few of the treetops which was kind of thrilling. The rocks in the stream were very up close. Zunu picked up leaves off the trees to add to his collection while Danh stayed busy touching the clouds.

Danh offered a banana to a primate monkey in trees, who grabbed it, stuck out it's tongue at him and then went hiding into the branches with his troupe. The snub nosed monkey's odd features made him look like a victim of plastic surgery. His troupe stared at them from their hideout for even more bananas. Then suddenly the gang jumped onto the balloon giving everyone a fright. They pounced upon the entire banana bunch and disappeared into the dense leaves with frantic quick moves.

'Danh, you always invite trouble,' said Zunu, terrified as the balloon wobbled and swithered unsteadily.

'Why? Poor monkey was so hungry, good I gave it food no.'

The basket threw them to the edges now as the balloon rocked insanely and uncertainly. It quietly resumed the balance back again.

'Ya, but it could have scratched our eyes out. You don't feed them this openly in the wilds,' Zunu shouted.

'You freak me out Danh!'

Danh ignored and looked around for more monkeys.

'Danh you need to learn a lot. Otherwise your fingers will be their next sausage!' Zunu pulled Danh's hair strand from behind and Danh let out a squeal. Next instant Danh busied himself humming and whistling a loud tune, still not looking at Zunu.

'Da da di da… Di da.'

Danh had his standpoint. He just hated over sermonization.

The balloon floated ahead peacefully… The party flew up for about sixty minutes. When they were brought down they were served a small breakfast picnic of hot sandwiches. A clown like man with black and white funny striped trousers walked up to them. He opened a diary and read out to them,

"The modern era of flight was inaugurated in 1783, when a sheep, a duck and a rooster boarded a prototype balloon and flew for some eight minutes before crashing to the ground. The king of France had proposed the use of prisoners as passengers, but the Montgolfier brothers, inventors and engineers of the balloon chose the animals, for what were considered logical reasons. It was believed that the psychology of sheep was similar to that humans, the high flying duck would not suffer from ill effects of the elevation and the rooster which can't fly, was a good way to measure the limits on the altitude."

'We share this knowledge with all our customers. Bye bye,' he grinned wide with empty pink toothless gums.

'So, animals were the first to fly, not humans,' grinned Danh.

It was an objective to at least see the big five and they were fortunate to have accomplished it. (They luckily saw the

Cheetah on the very last drive.)

Danh counted over his fingers, 'From memory I saw zebra, elephant, rhino, giraffe, lion, leopard, impala, hippo, hyena, crocodile, kudu, buffalo, mongoose and …. exxxotic birds! I can't really set a count! I'm sure if I try I would skip some.' Zunu laughed.

Final day the tours provided them souvenirs in their room. They were each given a pink mug with glittering animals embedded in it. The entire staff clicked a picture with them. It truly was the trip of a lifetime. They stood together silently in the balcony and watched the soft light from the sky as the sun rushed below the sapphire horizon. As minutes passed by the sun left behind a gorgeous bright hazy drop and a few clouds carried ruddy lines. Mild shadows set in the tree tops. The quiet savanna land was soon spilling with pale peach light and gold drops over the highway and parkway. Their last night.

Antorio scribbled a small note.
8th September 2019.
– safari through the savanna in search of stealthy predators! This kind of trip should be rewarding to those with a hunger for knowledge and a gratefulness for nature –
I am now readied for thrills, challenges and discovery on this amazing excursion of Planet E!

Antorio

CHAPTER FIFTEEN

The Odd Man

Zunu woke up early pre-morning hours and it was still dark. He went and sat over the car hood. Around him the quiet grass swayed in the sweet summer breeze. He noticed the beads of water over the wind screen. He drew with his finger a face with two eyes and wrote galaxy 1x below it. The dew soon smudged and washed away the drawing as morning drew closer. It was their last day at Serengeti. They had taken a lot of photographs as memoirs. The tour agency was very warm and friendly and asked them to be back again next season. They would wait for them to be back. It was a blistering cloudless day with sultry breeze.

Zunu stripped off his sandals and was just hanging around the lodge lazily with Antorio when he spotted a car stuck in middle of muddy fields... The wheels were spinning, but the car wasn't moving at all. The engine was still on and the car keys still in it.

'How did the car even end up so off track from the road, it isn't raining. It's kind of strange,' said Zunu as he moved his fingers through his hair with a confused face.

'Appears so that someone abandoned it in a hurry,' Antorio commented straining his neck to take a better look.

They went close by and checked the back seat, it was empty. They lifted the boot. There was a medium sized jute sack in it, the ends were roughly tied with a dry grass string. Antorio felt the bag, it was heavy. There were some blood stains over it. He untied the string and was alarmed to see rhino horn, a chainsaw and a gun in it.

They figured out instantly that the car belonged to the poachers and had skidded off the road possibly while attempting to flee and instead got caught in the soft wet mud.

They had a word with the lodge owner and three of them went again to take a good look at the car.

The worried lodge owner informed, 'Rhino horns are highly prized, estimated to fetch up to $60,000 per kilo on the international black market, much more than the price of gold or cocaine. It is composed mainly of keratin, the same component as in human nails. That's why it is used in traditional Chinese medicine too. It's usage as a status symbol is increasing now, just to display success and wealth. We have many killings every year.'

'Poachers are ruthless,' Antorio commented with disgust, hands firmly over his hips.

'What do we do now dad? Do we call the cops?' said Zunu.

'Yes, we will inform the control room, they will seek further action.'

They heard some unsettling disturbance and soft strides in the grass close by, and quietly tip toed to take cover behind the trees just fifteen feet away. From that point on they watched. Danh too came running seeing the chaos.

A tall thin dark brawny man in his thirty's emerged… black ruffled hair, and eyebrows like charcoal smudged across the brow. He started to look around nervously, his skin was bunching around the eyes. He raised his trembling big hand to shut off the motor quickly.

He had a pointed stick which he used to excavate all the mud from around the wheels. His head was tucked low which cocked every now and then at passersby in a sneaky way. He filled the rut quickly with dry material like gravel, rocks, sticks, foliage and levelled it down for a smooth transition in the surface.

Next, he took the car mat out and placed the tip of the mat right under the stuck tyre, while the rest of it lay at the front. He got back into the car, it briefly chortled and then came to life. He drove slowly forward to reach solid ground, his eyes cold and hard as desperate as those of an animal caught in a trap.

Antorio and gang immediately sped towards the ignited car, pounced over him, got him by his collar and hauled him right out of the running vehicle. The man got frightened.

'Hey! Where are you off to? You are going nowhere,' said Antorio.

Danh was so angry that he grabbed the stick lying next to the car and began beating the man.

'How dare you kill the animals! All animals have god in them. They have families too, you shameless man.'

'We should tie him to the tree trunk till the cops reach here,' Zunu suggested.

'I have informed the control room,' Mr. Antorio replied.

The man started to beg and plead literally in tears.

'Please let me go. I am just a driver and compelled by my boss to accompany for all kinds of jobs. I have never shot an animal in my life. Driving is my part time job. I work in gold mining industry in Sudan. My boss owns it.'

'Why should we believe you? How do we know you are not a poacher.'

'Sir, here is my driving permit. It has my name and photograph. I am not driving wrongfully and am not into any sort of illegal poaching activities.' He looked disturbed.

Antorio took a good look at his name, country and photo.

'You belong to Jordon?'

'Yes sir.'

'I am a simple man who works hard for a living. My name is Abed Haddad.' He was trembling now.

'I still find it hard to believe you. Why are you working with poachers?' Antorio said suspiciously.

'I am left with no alternative. My eleven year daughter Sana works in the slave market. I have to free her,' Abed said worried, his lips were quivering.

'My boss Denis Jordon owns a gold mine. That is my

permanent job. I have to listen to everything he says and follow it. Otherwise he will throw me out. I was asked to drive this vehicle.' He had tears in his eyes.

Antorio looked at him. The man appeared sincere. He didn't wish to throw an innocent person behind bars. He unfastened the ropes.

'I will hand over the Rhino horns to the control room. I will request them to track down the poachers. You could drive us out of this place, so that they don't suspect you. I will say, I called you up to drive us for the airport terminal.'

The man touched his feet, 'You are an exceptionally good man. Thank you. I will always remember this.'

'Do you have any idea who these poachers are?' Antorio quizzed.

'No sir. They are connected to Denis Jordon is all I know. He owns the Orwi gold mine in Sudan.'

The control room authorities arrived and Antorio handed over the Rhino horns and told them to track down the poachers.

'They couldn't be far,' he said with a grim look.

They gestured the frightened man inside the lodge and into the lobby sitting area where they offered him some tea and biscuits.

'Please relax now. In future I don't want you to be a part of such activities,' said Antorio.

'My daughter is in a trap,' Abed started to cry inconsolably.

Antorio was moved by his tears. He wanted to know his story.

'Would you not be willing to break a few laws if it made the difference between watching your children go hungry and feeding them? If you were led to believe that you could go to Africa and sell enough to send more money home to your starving kid, knowing you could never stay back and provide for them because there is no work at home, would you not do it?' said Abed.

'I would turn around and fight the system,' Antorio said nonchalant.

'Exactly!' Zunu replied and Danh gives a nod.

'The system is too complicated for us to fight as we are powerless. We are slaves and our passports are confiscated too,' Abed said with distressed blinking eyes.

'A man can change the world through awareness and learning,' Antorio said looking deep into his eyes.

'Vietnam too had a lot struggle but we built our life in a village without any facilities. Even now we don't have much money, but we stay happy. My dad taught me peace brings happiness,' Danh asserted proudly.

Antorio pushed the tea and biscuits plate towards Abed.

'Have it. You will feel better.'

'My story is different. I do not advocate any of malpractices. If you could put yourself in my position just for a moment you may not judge me so harshly. Perhaps you should try it. How long could your family survive with no money coming in? And then what? We are from Syria. We were living a better life than this in Syria but then the situation changed due to war, and now we are refugees in Jordon. Exactly, peace brings happiness and prosperity. But when it's lost to war, people suffer,' he gobbled up a whole biscuit. Sadness clouded his face.

'We owe the landlord in Jordon about four hundred dinar, an enormous sum. I couldn't find another job that could pay more. Of course, they are exploiting our circumstances, because they don't treat Jordanians the same. They place them in superior position. They only use us for odd jobs,' Abed paused and guzzled down one more biscuit.

He was very hungry and started sucking the hot tea in large gulps. Antorio watched with pity.

Abed continued, 'Of the fourteen lakh Syrians living in Jordan, about six lakh are displaced refugees. Approximately one lakh live in refugee camps, with the remainder living in mainly rented accommodation outside,' he stopped and swallowed hard...

'My eleven year old daughter is forced to sell fruits in a market and works twelve hours a day. I have to pay back my debt, only then my daughter will see freedom,' Abed was sweating profusely and appeared very upset.

'That's terrible for any child,' Antorio said sympathetically.

'People have a right to work as much as they want to and as much as they can. All of that being said, every single human being deserves food, medicine and shelter.'

'It's for her that I accept all jobs without asking questions. My boss runs a huge smuggling racket. He is a very powerful man with profound roots in Jordon and Sudan. Every week between sixty and hundred kilograms of extracted gold from Orwi is sent to Khartoum for black market sale and export. Seventy per cent of the gold extracted gets smuggled. It is being enabled by the inconsistency of policies regulating the sector, monetary policies, and corruption.

Antorio switched on the air conditioner as Abed was dripping sweat now.

'Thanks.' He dipped the biscuit in tea and continued, 'We poor people have no say at all. Due to huge debts we are their slaves and work in all kind of conditions. Nobody cares if we bite the dust. The government has tried to introduce regulations for the people employed in the industry. But most operations in Sudan are rudimentary and rely on purely traditional extraction methods. Mining accidents are common place. Sixty miners were killed in one accident last year when their tunnel collapsed.'

'It is specifically responsible for war crimes too in the country's south. Civilians living around the gold mine site have suffered killings, and the torching of their homes and fields at the hands of armed groups.' Antorio poured him some more tea.

'Until all people are treated equally none of us stands a chance,' Antorio remarked thoughtfully.

'I wish to meet your daughter.'

'But she stays in Jordon,' Abed replied.

'We can travel,' Antorio answered.

Zunu and Danh gave each other a high five! A thrilled elated Danh decided to place all his weight in excitement over Zunu and threatened to sit over him (almost) with a smashing notorious dimpled smile.

Halfway Zunu pushed him, 'Get off me, you mad elephant! You will crush me.'

'Oh... I grant you some pity,' Danh roared like a king.

Danh broke a huge slab of delicate milk chocolate and offered it to Zunu. He crumbled it into many pieces and then offered it to all of the staff as a parting gift and dropped a few in his short's pocket too for the journey. The irresistibly smooth milk truffle filling melted into their mouths as they left Serengeti. The strips of warm grass, the grasshoppers clicks and the chirp of crickets became a *memory*.

CHAPTER SIXTEEN

The slave market

Tanzania to Jordan was 6046 km. It took them around three days 18h to drive from Tanzania to Jordan capital Amman. Flight tickets were not available. Abed's boss was mad at him at the seizure of rhino horns by authorities. Abed was afraid to even face him.

A shy girl -dusky complexion, curly tangled and unkempt hair and twinkling dark innocent eyes smiled at them. She was selling fruits in the central market of Amman. Abed introduced her as Sana, his daughter.

'Hello, what's going on with you?' Antorio offered her a chocolate.

She nodded her head timidly as affirmation to his presence, extended her hand and reluctantly took the chocolate.

'For me?'

'Yes, your dad is our friend and so are you,' Antorio smiled.

She looked at her dad, who gestured her to accept the chocolate.

'Do you go to school Sana?' Antorio asked while Zunu and Danh gazed her with pity. Her clothes were old worn out and she looked tired and meek. Not the regular upbeat children.

'No, Dad doesn't stay here all time. I have to sell fruits otherwise we will lose the roof over our head.'

'I'll like you to go to school, take up education. When you grow up you can take up family responsibilities.'

'Would you like that too?'

'My mom died in Syria due to lack of medical facilities. It was her dream that I be a doctor someday and serve people. It was my dream too. But dreams are dreams and they don't always come true for us,' said Sana.

'I wish to help you materialize your dreams and for that I

need your support and courage,' Antorio said.

'My dad has taught me to be brave always,' Sana said upbeat.

'I will be filing a complain with Syria embassy that your passports are confiscated and they should be returned back to you right away. Child labor is a crime. Every child should remember that and know their rights too. You are being made to overwork and being paid very low.'

'I will have a word with your landlord and set you free. I have also spoken to a child welfare organization. You will be shortly moved to a proper shelter.'

'Will you support me in this fight Sana?' Antorio held her arms and sat down on his knees.

'Yes.'

'I am taking responsibility for you child, and will follow adopt a kid, a program the country validates, whereby I send dinar 200 a month, and it keeps a child in food, school, clothes and medical care. You can study and build a future,' he gave her a reassuring gaze and thumbs up.

'I don't believe it. Nobody has been so nice to me. Dad, who is this uncle?' The girl smiled radiantly, her diminished eyes livened up, suddenly showing up a lot of life and she jumped up energetically to hug Antorio in delightful amazement.

'He is our god, and has come from some other planet to save us,' Abed said laughingly.

Zunu and Danh exchanged stealthy glances, with stifled smiles, hands covering their mouth. Danh nudged Zunu.

'People realize there is something different about you. If we tell them they will put you up in a museum, that's what they do to aliens. he he.'

'Shut up, Danh,' Zunu giggled.

'The next time you stop me from talking, I will get you fixed in a glass museum,' Danh said bossily.

There were many kids selling fruits around Sana. They gathered around and began telling their stories to Antorio. They were thinking of him as a savior.

'I labor for twelve hours per day, everyday. And it's very hard work. What's more, you don't get a day off unless you ask for one and then they don't pay you,' said Hasan.

Fifteen year old Ala said, 'Strawberry picking is extremely labor intensive. You're bent over all day picking with a quota to meet. The season starts in the south and moves north, so do the laborers.'

'The problem with the agricultural sector is that the children work for really long hours, and under exceptionally terrible conditions in the sun. Some of them work for no money. They only work for shelter. The biggest one is thirteen years old and there are three year olds too,' Abed said wiping his sweaty nose with a tissue.

Antorio spoke to another fourteen year old boy Amir, who worked as a cleaner in a prominent business in the northern city of Zarqa for at least twelve hours a day, seven days a week. Many of them were working alongside their parents and siblings on farms near the Dead Sea.

Nasir earned just half a Jordanian dinar an hour; less than one US dollar. This was less than even half the minimum wage.

Lilah informed that farmers often kept the families of Syrian refugees separate from other farm workers, and that many were housed in tents.

Antorio promised them that he will put up all the issues with embassy and child welfare organizations and together they will find a solution. He was deeply moved to hear such traumatic inhuman living conditions.

Antorio made a quick dash to the embassy. At the embassy a disturbed Antorio told the poised stern looking secretary, 'Let's say it is modern slave labor. The conditions they are living in are horrible and they are accepting them because of their vulnerability.'

An authority on condition of anonymity squealed, 'Exploitation of child labor is rife throughout Jordan, approximately 46% of Syrian refugee boys and 14% of girls aged fourteen or over are working more than forty four hours a week. The legal age in Jordan is sixteen. The government has issued directives but they are not followed. People who are victimized rarely complain due to fear of loosing jobs,' he directed Antorio to another officer.

Antorio refused to budge and started shouting in the room with raised hands, rigid cords in neck, 'I'm starting to think about whether you have the boldness to be completely forthright. What number of you have illicit caretakers and maids? Have you checked the resident status of your gardener? What about the plumber? The guys that put a new rooftop on your home? Shouldn't something be said about the decent mother that does a car pool with your kids everyday?

Do you check the status of everybody you work with, or only those with accents? On the other hand, only those with a specific shading skin or hair? Where do you take a stand? Would it be a good idea for them to be treated as human beings or not? Do they deserve to be treated as slaves?'

A smartly dressed officer in two piece suit and tie showed up hearing the commotion.

'Sir, we understand. Please don't get angry,' the officer requested him to relax. He withdrew the cigarette from his mouth, billowing and puffing out a gust of dark charcoal smoke in the air and offered Antorio a glass of cold water. He rubbed his nose with shifty eyes, trying to project a calm demeanor.

'Are you not aware? Many growers don't pay overtime and withhold taxes too. Guy selling fruits on the street shouldn't be taxed at all, he is poor. Somewhere down the line, somebody is making plenty of money off this low level seller and not paying any tax. Likely the money is going into gang activity with funds. I'm certain a lot of that cash turns around and comes back to haunt back as unlawful activities,' Antorio spewed fury and barked at the wooden headed man angrily. The officer reclined into the feather filled red cushion chair uncomfortably.

'Sir, we do look into all complains and seek action against the proprietors. But when the moment comes for deportation, immigrants don't wish to go back. Rather they choose to suffer odd jobs. Jordon doesn't detain any immigrants who work illegally. Unfortunately, many don't come forward or complains are withdrawn with matters being solved on the table within days,' the authority replied fixing his tie and blazers, a bit nervous seeing an over charged Antorio. He held his cigarette with the lit end down, burned the stub off in a paper cup, meshed it and grinded it nervously.

He removed some files from the shelf in defense, and scattered them over the desk, his fingers swiftly flipped the pages as he scampered to show the number of cases solved. He tossed and swept through the documents, sucked his index finger in his mouth, swiped the wet edges of pages at quick pace, his lips pursed.

'Officials at the Jordanian Ministry of Labor did give the details of the hundreds of companies found to be exploiting children. A year ago, 214 companies were closed down. Please take a look at this. So far this year, 357 have been closed, and a further 794 employers received fines of between 250 and 500 Jordanian dinars.'

'We do seek action, but not many pursue complains,' he stuck out his tongue every now and then. His shining black waxed shoes were worked up too.

Antorio arched one eyebrow and banged his firm wrist very hard on the table, 'The files can do no justice. Their complains are quashed just like them. Many cases where migrant workers are not paid on time. Some are deceived by employers who guarantee to pay them toward the finish of a contracted period, but fail to do so.'

'Some lock their workers in the home, forcing them to work

up to twenty hours a day, seven days a week. Withholding passports and restricting movement are also common, according to advocacy groups.'

The ruffled and intimidated officers wheeled out of the room and glided back in with a signature form. He handed Antorio a pen.

'Sir, please complete the formalities. We'll take care of everything.'

Antorio added, 'I am ready to fund these kids' education and shelter till they are settled. Please find them a suitable place to live and take action against the owners.'

He handed over the names of Sana, Hasan, Ala, Amir, Nasir and Lilah to them. He signed up for support a kid program the country permits and put up the Vietnam address.

The officer promised him complete investigation and support into the matter. He shook hands with Antorio with a lackluster smile. When Antorio left he reclined into his chair with a huge sigh and relief, not soon enough his relief melted into horror.

The meshed stub still had some chinks of fire left in it. The ember was glowing and the paper cup suddenly caught fire. An alarm went off with dark smoke all around. The fire spread to the adjacent chair and to his precious laze 'the pebble fabric sofa too'.

The officer poured the cold glass of water lying on his desk over the fire and started beating the flames with the rough coir door mat. Finally, he disposed off the paper cup in the paper bin. The room was smelling foul with the lingering nicotine smell and damp smoke. He burnt another cigarette with a sigh of relief as he collapsed into the chair.

'C'mon in! It feels like some loony mad chimp just dug out my eyes and bit me hard, Owch!' He ruptured out to the secretary who was keeking surreptitiously through the door.

Back in the central market, all the kids were ecstatic with the news and promised to work hard.

'Danh and Zunu, you have a cool dad!' the kids screamed praises and danced around with joy. There were Antorio chants all around and joyous delicate laughters of children filled the otherwise sullen lanes that only stayed toasted and scalded in the sun. The streets were decorated like a birthday cake, using pinwheels made from scrap paper with whimsical accents and glitter balloons everywhere. Crate paper never looked better, the pink pieces were streaming throughout the fruit market.

Antorio smiled and felt it was the right thing to do for these kids. He felt a sense of peace.

Now they could just head back to Vietnam.

'Abed, it's time for us to take a leave. Danh and Zunu are tired of travelling. It's been long drives,' Antorio gestured.

'Sir, a small request. You have spoken for us but you have also aggravated our owners by setting us free. They might try harm you, it's not unusual here. You must leave quietly early morning via Saudi Arabian border. That's a safer route for you. I will personally drop you.'

Antorio scribbled a brief note that night:
I do not wish to change the said system, nor modify it, because of a feeling of guilt. I cannot change the whole world as per my views. I can't have those rights. I am alien.

..

The golden snail…

It was around four hours drive. City Amman of Jordon was roughly 360 km from the Haql city of Saudi Arabia.

'We have to reach the Durra Border Crossing مركز حدود الدرة. It is the border crossing between Aqaba in Jordan and Haql in Saudi Arabia. Once you have safely crossed the Durra border, you can catch a flight back to Vietnam,' Abed explained as he steered the wheel.

The car swiftly crossed the Amman city. Abed considered it his fortune to be able to drive them all to Saudi Arabia. After all that Antorio had done for him, he had only immense gratitude.

Zunu and Danh couldn't be happier. Absolutely every trip was a big reward, as both were bitten by the travelling bug. Every city was a spectacle in itself with different people, so many nationalities, and a diversity in nature and culture.

There was always a tiff as to who would take the window seat...

And finally, who dominated whom? Danh undoubtedly controlled and called the shots as against submissive Zunu who accepted situations... well... when blackmailed, "You are older to me... have some grace blah blah..."

Danh had all aces up his sleeves. He always managed his way by throwing tantrums. Zunu somehow liked to comply with it or simply call it selfless compromise. This time they had Sana and Abed for company. Sana sat in between the two. Danh sat to her right. Danh talked about Vietnam farming and Sana exhibited her marketing skills.

'How I hate golden apple snails! They eat young and emerging rice plants. They cut the rice stem at the base, destroying the whole plant. Earlier we never had them in a

Vietnam,' Danh said massaging between the eyebrows.

'Earlier you were grumpy of cows and now insects,' Zunu taunted Danh with a poker face.

'NO NO... Never without reason. One day-yy I saw something like strawberry and many-yy strawberries in the field...' Danh gulped, his eyes big now. 'I didn't know the golden apple snail had infested our field. Mistaking them for strawberries, I collected four baskets of snails in just an hour, thankfully I never ate them,' Danh twisted his mouth in disgust to one side.

Zunu laughed heartily, 'Good... you didn't eat them, but they can be controlled by pesticides easily.' Sana agreed to it.

'No... it's very difficult. The snails reproduce year round in the tropical region. It's able to eat water plants and multiply in rivers, canals, and drainage ditches and paddy fields are it's favorite place,' Danh threw both his hands in the air.

'Once when I bit an apple there was a maggot in it and I immediately spit out,' Sana added.

'I tell you it came from Vietnam,' Zunu said and Sana burst into peals of laughter.

'Why will it come from Vietnam? We don't alone host all such creatures,' Danh cringed his nose and made a face.

'My owner packs each and every peach, apple and grape from his backyard with plastic bags to protect from flies as soon as the fruit starts to grow from the stems, which in turn protect them from hosting maggots,' Sana said tossing her hair from her face. 'But once in a while the fruits do rot. The heat gets to them. My customers bring back the fruits and even scream at us. They are not so understanding. We have to take a lot care.'

Danh continued his whine, 'There was a time when the golden apple snail had become such a major enemy of rice, armies of golden apple snails were feasting on hundreds and hundreds of acres of rice, destroying the crop. This was when I was one year old.'

'You know on the surface everything seemed good – lush green paddy fields all around the village. But underneath was a huge concern for all villagers. Dad said the snails had destroyed more than five hundred acres of paddy, and nearly fifty acres of his own paddy fields. Danh shuffled and squeezed his buttocks uncomfortably, sandwiched between Sana and the car door.

'He then sought the help of the agriculture department in controlling the menace,' Danh added, now elbowing furiously for still more space.

'Will you stop pushing in Danh? I have my one leg squared over the other as it is,' Zunu said annoyed.

'Can't you use paddy dikes to pump out water. If the fields are not flooded, that should control the snail invasion too? These days we have many solutions. I have worked in so many fields,' Sana said with concern.

'Your fields seemed to be doing ok, when I last saw,' Zunu exclaimed.

'Yes. That's because they did give us a pesticide that can kill snails even when paddy fields have water. We tested it, and it worked,' Danh replied. 'Villagers whose paddy fields had already been damaged by the snails had no choice but to replant. Some people even ate the snails.'

Abed added up, 'The practice of eating snails spread to Asia from South America. They are well edible and are often considered a protein rich delicacy. Consuming these snails is an interesting option in the areas where they have become a pest and treat for the rice. Escargot is very much a delicious gourmet menu in French dishes.'

'Eeuks! Would you really eat it?' asked Zunu.

'When we have no food, man must learn to eat everything. Yes, I would,' replied Abed.

'So, it's not just Vietnam, even Jordon and France eat it,' Danh prodded Zunu and raised his eyebrows up and down playfully.

Antorio was listening to the conversations and thinking how quickly children grow up. Their curious talks suggested maturity far beyond years. They will grow up to be just fine intelligent youth one day. Antorio smiled to himself.

Ahead was a crossroad. As the car suddenly turned left, Sana slid to the right and had to hold on to the seat firmly to keep falling over Danh. Zunu giggled.

'Go ahead Sana. Grab the opportunity. Reduce him to pulp. Squash Squash! Look Danh is puking pizza! No sorry that looks to me golden snails!' said Zunu, while a much stunned Danh left speechless gave a continued dark stare to both. There were quite a few left turns ahead, and Sana kept up Zunu's words.

CHAPTER SEVENTEEN

The Bedouin Life

They were at the head of *gulf of Aqaba* inching slowly towards *Haql* (the brow of the Levant). The dry wind was loaded with torrid warmth. Twenty seven dry miles isolated Aqaba of

Jordan from Haql of Saudi Arabia. *Durra* pass was a pretty ordinary border crossing with a lot of truck of supplies. They stopped at a gas station over the highway. The air smelled distinctively of petrol, gas, oil and burnt tyres. There was a white square store in the premises. They purchased a few drinks and moved away.

Their on and off fuel was small bottles of orange juice and potato chips. Drive was quite scenic with a view of gritty and stinging sand, sand, and more sand…The sun beam beat down through cloudless skies and baked the land. The ground heated the air so much that the air ascended in waves, they could actually see it. Those gleaming waves befuddled the eye, into seeing distorted images.

At a point, after a few miles drive they waited a signal for the traffic to clear, Abed pulled out his right arm and swung it up and down to a lorry behind. He took a right turn, slowed down the car and then stopped at a road corner.

They had reached Hejaz, probably better known for the Islamic holy cities of Mecca and Medina. Strolling through the Hejaz was a fantasy. The manifestation of modern desert architecture unbared how design and material could battle the challenging climatic conditions of arid environment of a backward society into a maze of buildings.

It was a blazing day. Salty sweat rolled off their noses and stung their eyes, their clothes were overwhelmingly hot and sticky. The beast and the bird were not too enamored of it's heat and as soon as the sun was high in the sky they looked for spread in the gulches; but for all that the chief glory and wonder of the desert was still its broad blast of ubiquitous light. Daring dancing lizards popped out from under the rocks, they quickly lifted one leg at a time off the hot desert sand and then another… Antorio liked them but they kind of freaked Zunu, Sana and Danh out.

'I hate lizards,' Danh said biting his nails.

'These days you seem to hate all animals,' said Zunu ironically drumming his fingers with a clever face.

Danh looked for chocolate in his pocket and ignored Zunu. The chocolate was sticky and already melted, it stuck to Danh's fingers like thick glue. Danh opened the wrapper and dropped it into his mouth and then licked it off his three fingers and thumb.

They ran into a well and looked for rest from the harsh sun in the branches of shade thrown by the surrounding thorn trees. Water held in the underground well slowly trickled down from a stone built aqueduct that supplied water to the nearby village and smaller wadis. They were tired and rested till evening, the heat was unbearable.

Dusk continued to mask the land and the sky, when they heard faint distant voices and the squawking of a bird.

He was a rough faced, graybeard, heavy long moustache, large and well armed man. He wore a traditional ankle length - long sleeve cotton garment, called *thawb. He* tickled the neck of his camel with his toes, and his sandals hung on the side of the saddle. A rein of sorts was attached to the camel's nostril passing under the muzzle. The camel lowered itself, the man got down and wore his sandals after slapping the sand off them. He held the camel rein loosely as he looked on *steadily*. A pretty gallant brown falcon sat arrogantly over his shoulder goggling hard.

He then spread open a white sheet and poured ancient artifacts, rapier, cold steel knives, dry fruits, hard bread, shimmering jewels and glittering metals in it.

The man gestured with his hands, 'Looking for treasure?'

Antorio gestured back with hands, 'NO.'

'Then what are you doing in this scorching heat?'

The man could tell they obviously weren't here to buy a falcon which many do and walk around with on their arm, but still he was eager to show his bird.

'Her name is Kivu,' he came across as chatty, friendly, and curious.

'Helloooo Kivu,' Antorio tapped her head softly with forefinger entranced by her looks.

She went, 'keka k kukkkkkk.'

Antorio put on a glove, and fed Kivu. When he looked into her large beaded round and black eyes, he felt like she was surveying his spirit profoundly. Her large brown wings opened, as though asking him if he would like to ride with her to the skies, tossing a test at him and judging all that he'd done at any point. Like no species he'd experienced at any point, nothing of past, present or future got by the careful vigilant falcon. She glanced through him.

'Look at these!' the man said. He displayed a vintage cuff link, a camel faced stone dagger and a Saudi Arabian old nickel coin.

'Do you wish to buy?'

'How old are these things?' Antorio questioned.

The man didn't know. 'la yujad fikra,' he shrugged, no idea.

'It could be *19th* century,' Abed picked up the dagger and tried to analyze it.

At a short distance they could see tents anchored with ropes and nails pegged into the sand. Tent walls were made of thick, sturdy cloth that kept out the sand and dust, and also allowed cool breezes to comfortably blow through.

The man beckoned them just outside of the tent. There was a "dallah" brass coffee pot holding dark, rich coffee. It sat on an exquisitely structured wooden cut table enriched with small intricate carvings of vine leaves and grapes. Three veiled hejazi women refilled tiny cups with coffee non-stop. Possibly his wives. Most Saudi nomads did have more than one wife. They didn't question as it appears intrusive. All women had a full face veil, wore long black robes, and hands covered.

The camel guy invited them in his tent house where they sat down to chat. It was surprisingly well structured, chic, and global with stylistic theme. He introduced himself as Aafiya Harb.

They could see just outside the tent, a cook stove over open flame and numerous men laughing. Bedouin men sat on kilims and carpets around a hearth outside the front of the tent drinking coffee, tea and eating sweets. The most important and the oldest guest was served first, by filling a fourth of the cup, which was then refilled time to time.

They were recounting old stories, smoking hookah, lying on their elbows, and sipping tea. There were discussions of falconry, the Arabian horses, and the saluki dogs - all animals that bedouins credited with raising; swords and tribal wars were other issues of significance for the clan.

One of the men recited poetry and sang. Two other men played the oud and drummed; while another moved, clapped, and danced. For a goat herder he had had quite incredible moves. Everyone joined them in.

Danh, Sana and Zunu formed a circle, threw their hands up in the air, swayed and danced. Sana lead the moves, with snake like funny movement of hands. To mark the end of the meetup, the host burnt incense in a mabkhara (incense burner) passing it to each of his guests to inhale in and then fan their garments with.

'What does bedouin community imply?' asked Antorio.

One of the elderly men explained, 'Bedouin means "desert people". In1950, roughly fifty percent of the population was bedouin nomadic and lived in tents. They moved with herds of camels, sheep, and goats to seasonal pastures and for access to water. It was a fun and simple life.'

He crushed some tobacco in his palms and shoved it into his mouth, his broken dark stained colorless teeth chewed it with great ease.

'So, breeding was the means of your livelihood?'

'Yes. We adjusted to traveling desert life by breeding camels, Arabian horses, and sheeps. We also grew date palms and other harvest, for the most part hiring others to perform agricultural work. Traditionally, finding grazing and water were the primary worries for us, in addition to raids, to seize horses and camels,' he added spitting tobacco in a brass pot which already had many red stains.

'I see you do have a lot of modernization, new setup and buildings now… has it brought about positive changes?' Antorio questioned again.

Aafiya Harb was quick to reply, 'Oh yes. Modernization has brought much change, especially for bedouins. Many have moved to urban regions, and the number of purely nomadic people is now only a small proportion. But some disappoints have come in along too… These days young city people indulge in extravagances and waste a lot of food. We elderly people remember meals of the past as simple but adequate, without a morsel wasted,' he said adding some coal to his hookah and puffing hard.

'Can't we visit Mecca and Medina…' said Danh.

'No… you won't get entry,' the elderly raised his two hands in a cross gesture and offered Danh dry fruits in a platter lovingly.

'Thanks.' Danh picked carefully a roasted cashewnut, and dropped it in his mouth.

'Unfortunately, it's true. You all could have visited the holy cities Mecca and Medina but it's not open to foreigners, only Muslims. Howsoever I'll pray for you. "Barak allah fik" - God bless you,' said Aafiya Harb.

At a distance, on the loudspeakers an Imam sang the crowd into prayer. Everyone knelt in front of the meal, prayed and underneath the searing dark sky, ate in tender silence.

Night swallowed the desert. It came out of the blue, in purple. Free air, the static stars and the silver moon penetrated down out of the sky and soaked the desert in a pale white mist.

Any astute watcher would say it is in the deserts and high puts that beliefs are produced. Those beliefs and faith make the journey of the mystical desert meaningful in its own way.

They said goodbye to Aafiya, his friends and family, who would remain friends for life. They had almost forgotten they had a flight from city Tabuk to Hanoi (Vietnam) after one day.

They retired to their camp tents, the little wind was raising puffs of dust at their feet. Next day they had to move to city Tabuk. It lay at the junction of Hejaz mountain range.

Early morning was a high point to get the first shaft of the sun. Rapidly the light spread descending, until the entire tent was tinged by it, and then suddenly sides of porphyry just outside the tent started to gleam in the rays. It hit Sana's eye. She got up and strolled out.

'What's this red boulder? So unique!' Sana shouted out caressing the smooth stone. Danh quickly fetched his camera and clicked it.

'I have seen this type back home,' Zunu remarked.

The two local men guarding the tent walked up to them. They had swords hanging from their scabbards and wore white robes with rings over their head cloth. 'It's an Imperial porphyry, a red purple stone from the volcanoes actually found only in the Egypt. No one has idea how it landed here.'

The other man added, 'Some historians had claimed this

rock was the hardest known in classical times. It was used for monuments and building projects in roman empire era and meant only for the Imperial family. It was also used for the very famous blocks of the Column of Constantine in Istanbul with statue of Constantine at top.'

Abed joined in. 'In cold countries cars have studded winter tyres. It is common to see highways paved with porphyry aggregate. It makes the road withstand the extra wear from the spiked tyres. It's really very strong.'

They retired back to the tent for morning tea.

It wasn't some time before incredible shafts of light, now rotating and alternating with shadows, stretched down the plains in front of them. The sun was gushing and spilling through the highest points of the eastern mountains and the sharp pointed apex peaks were cutting long shadows in the wide light.

They sat in the car and Abed sang out loud with light taps at the steering: 'That beam of light! Was there anything ever so much delight!'

'Oh! How it flashes its color through the shadows,' Sana added clicking her fingers.

'How it gilds the tops of the mountains and gleams white on the dunes of the desert!' Antorio added whistling.

'In any land is there more than the magnificence of sunlight!' Zunu added clapping.

'Glorious than any other light!' Danh added with a smile tapping his foot!

They hummed their way to the city Tabuk— Not really

noticing the linnets and kestrels that build nests in the cereus, and finches that sang from the astounding point of the saguaro.

Indeed, there is animal and bird life here though it is not always obvious unless you look for it. The golden sun climbed higher and higher. The car turned around, convoluted, paced, halted, then moved on– screeching the unfriendly disagreeable sand. The wells in the transit cheerfully allowed them a pail of water that they drank turn by turn. The wells longed for travelers in quiet solace. The pulleys were waiting to be rolled in and the creaky rusted hinges rejoiced as they were of some use now. The hot sun shone in the water adding a sparkle to the still bucket, to the sky and to the parched dry roads.

The cottony bordered heaps of puffy clouds, and the tongues of flame twisting each and every thin wispy cloudy strand, awaited in the southern sky as the car paced along the straight road towards the southeast.

..

Out somewhere in the middle of ocean, in a different continent a young boy was traveling in a boat to the middle East. Lost in thoughts he spilled tea over his blue shirt and grey trousers. The book lying over the floor plank got stained too. He wiped himself clean and then cleaned up the book.

He lay comfortably in the boat and sang a song!

Oh! When I sing to the sea
The adorable sea sings back to me!
The fishes jump up and down
They tell their little secrets to me

and quietly splash the water all over me!
I dream, they dream with me
I love the sea, the sea loves me
The stars shine so bright
I feel I need no brighter light
No ghost to be scared
Though shadows from the water always chase meeee!

Far off I see the land
My hopes and my dreams
Yet I travel in the seas
Forever the ocean beckons me... la la lalala la

Soon I'll go home
Someone waits for meeee! la lalalala

He whistled, looked at the mighty sky and soon fell asleep. The boat moved quietly in the ocean, as though it was furiously predetermined to reach the shores as soon as possible.

Morning sun brushed the young boy's eyes and he woke up. He realized he was very close to the shore. He had a very huge bag of spices to unload. A lot of work to do. He had a small bag pack with some money, documents, sharp knife, rope, tooth brush and some eatables still left in it.

He jumped up to drop an anchor in water, so that it was deep enough to keep the boat floating at low tide and used a loop to back it into the shore. He quickly unloaded his bag and then pulled the boat back to where it was, anchoring the line to keep her in place. After a few attempts, he thought he got the distance right.

He had pulled her out to safe waters…

And there she sat happily… till the tide suddenly went down… and down… and down… and she dried on the reef.

'ARGH!' He knew how big the spring tides were, but had miscalculated just how far out from shore the boat would need to be. Although he'd anchored in a good three meters of water when the tide wasn't completely high, he could still walk to pickup the anchor off the reef rubble without getting the feet wet.

He called out to the fishermen, 'Help me please,' and gestured towards the restless boat.

Fishermen came running and gladly helped him anchor, this wasn't the first time it happened.

All done he hired a cycle from beach premises, put on his cap, picked up his bag of spices and pedaled towards the market place greeting people along the way.

CHAPTER EIGHTEEN

The Book Lane

Tabuk city...

It was a crazy 'another' day. The party rounded through an

alley, into a narrow passageway. It had tiny grass growing in cracks of the stones and wriggled into congested lanes and endless by lanes…

Three storeyed neat old houses were packed on both sides painted in burnt orange, evoking vision of flames. The plaster chipping off the red brick walls had the raw cement exposed. Such homes ran in between, and behind many more buildings in the older part of city.

They saw women drying clothes on compact shriveled terraces, gently wringing and shoving the water off with tight jerks and shakes before pinning them to wired lines and then running hands down the edges to ensure wrinkle free hanging square. The sweet smelling clothes opened, billowed and swayed with the wind gently, secured tightly by metal pins.

Danh could feel the water tricklets into his face carried through the warm breeze every few steps they took and hear the cloth wimp. He stuck his nose in the air, and looked up, his eyes widened at the sight of shimmering water droplets escaping into the air… The sun bursts the drops into multiple pearls that disappeared into the atmosphere in no time, it was pure rainbow time in desert. Indeed refreshing! With his face up towards the sky, he was now ambling and dawdling behind and quickly moved his pair of feet to catch up pace with others.

Various little shops were numbered to identify them with ease and were stretching over a narrow path just outside of the homes. Sheets of green canvas at top and numbers, secured and verified the shops. They added a cool green glimmer to the dainty paths that were left for people to walk by on foot. The tight pavement was flooded with books, spilling one over another irregularly.

There was a heap of small second hand stores stretching all through the confused complicated path loaded with years of wistfulness. The smell of earthy, nutty coffee was so conspicuous every where, Arabians love coffee!.. but books? All believed the country was closed culture, not so accepting towards others. This impression was validated by Sana, the marketing genius, wordly wise and well read, always with many tales to tell – No less than Danh at chatting. Just this time her information was not so updated with Arabia.

Abed exclaimed, 'I'm surprised at the variety of books. I believed Arabian countries only permitted religious books.' Sana was surprised too.

A book seller was brewing coffee in the sand. Looked like he had a tiring day, he had prominent lines in between the eyebrows, face was covered with beads, his light hazel eyes were droopy with dark circles. He was sitting cross legged waiting for customers –talking to them, showing them new books and trying to make sales.

"As-salam alaykom." Antorio said politely.

"Wa Alykom As-salam." the book seller smiled, "May peace be upon you."

'Do you have some interesting books?'

'Sir, living with the demands of current age is quite a test on me. Yes, I have some good books,' he said with a degree of confidence.

His attention then turned towards his coffee brewing strongly in a pan, filled with sand over an open flame. The cezve appeared warm. The coffee foamed to the top almost immediately. He removed the cezve and swirled it in the sand three to four times and then served it in a small cup. The coffee ground quickly settled to the bottom making for a strong, thick cup of coffee.

'My grandfather was an educated proud man from Turkey, and that's where I learnt the art from. While this may not be your go to brewing method for early mornings, but this brewing method is the real deal and might be the most authentic way to get a cup of Turkish coffee,' said the book seller.

He sipped his thick and frothy coffee and offered them too. They declined politely as having too much coffee was giving headaches already.

'Thanks, but not used to insane amounts of consumption till it's truly a stress filled day,' said Antorio.

'We might just gulp it down regardless of whether it's coffee, water or sharbat…' said the book seller.

Zunu and Danh hadn't slept at night, they showed perfect caffeine insomnia symptoms with extra alert minds and hadn't let others sleep either.

A respectable moderately aged woman who had all the earmarks of being an old client, wanted to purchase a duplicate of 'The lost tomb' by R.R.Y. Tunkin. She discovered one in great condition. The book seller approaches her for 8.20 Saudi riyal after bargaining but the woman had just 4.37 SAR on her.

'You can store 3.28 SAR and hold the book,' said the book seller.

The woman didn't have a hankering for it. 'I am an old client. You simply don't give discounts the manner in which you used to,' she whinged.

'I need to make sensible deals,' the bookseller said with a helpless frown.

'You just don't care if we read your books anymore.'

The miserly annoyed customer left grumbling still arguing about her unrivaled rights as she was an older customer. She felt she wasn't treated fair… and the book seller had to let go of what might have been his solitary deal in the entire day. Antorio went through some of the old books. They had a written note that described back to a record of its own. The ex- library books conveyed a type of check mark, that demonstrated the name of library that had previously owned it. They were in the form of a stamp, a standardized bar code mark, and a 'old school' pocket for the checkout card. They also had all kinds of stamps bearing the word "discarded", "withdrawn", and the bar code tag had been darkened with a pen. These second hand books appeared exhausted, torn, each with a pale wrinkled page and fraying spine.

'In Africa, as a kid I did almost certainly find a modest duplicate of a book even if it was scarce and costly, be it a recent edition. Even today, I can buy five old books for the price of a new one. That is correctly why the presence of the book shops shrivels, just why will anyone spend over a new book?' Abed dwelled.

The book seller agreed and said he does long for more clients.

'About thirty years ago, when I opened my stall, I took in 32.78 SAR a day simply by crediting books to readers. That meant a lot, I was doing well. In today's date, I don't hit as much the 5.46 SAR mark daily, and that too only if I sell a book. Nobody wants to borrow or share anymore, nobody is interested in reading.'

He then sluggishly communicated, 'I would like to have a noteworthy big library, the size of a building someday…'

'Are you interested in international hits, meaning how long a book has been in publication, or simply raw sales?'

'Any readable interesting stuff will do,' replied Antorio.

'Which is awesome, but are sales what you're looking for? If so, "The Bible" is in a category by itself. It's sold more copies than any other book but is often printed and distributed for free. So many copies are bought by churches around the world.'

'Bible is based on god?' Antorio questioned and called upon Danh to take a look at it. He knew Danh had a great deal of interest in religion.

Danh gives a positive nod, 'Thank you Uncle Antorio.'

'How much for it? I will buy it.'

'18.18 SAR. But I give you a concession of 1.61 SAR as you are my first customers for the day.' He clasped the round knob and shoved open the creaky drawer of the broken dingy table and tugged out a calculator. He moved his index finger over minus sign and started his calculation. 'That's 16.57 SAR only.'

'Listen, you said we are your first customers. We are very impressed with your books and your dedication towards literature. I will be giving you extra 1875 SAR so that you can fix your shop. Then I can come down to buy more books and you can maintain a better collection. It's just a small amount as a token of our love,' Antorio smiled and pushed the riyal down his pocket before he could react or utter a word.

'Thank you, sir. Only once in a while I get customers who are passionate and helpful. If all customers took interest in my books, I should be able to stay afloat and go back to my glorious days,' he smiled showing his crooked set of teeth.

Then he complained angrily, 'A few big libraries don't have the facility to find recyclers for their books. These libraries simply discard books to people who reuse them, and there are also people who sell them online for their own profits. We lose there. People who once used to turn up with large carton boxes full of books to donate, come almost empty handed now.

'Do you read English books or just Arabic...' Abed inquired curiously.

'I understood English by reading books over a period of time. I never gave up and it only got better with everyday reading. It took me about four months to finish "Just Hundred Years of misery" by Goncho Barcilla and "A life of Prejudice" by Dickson Joyce is my favorite.'

'Don't mind it. I found them boring. Not up to my taste. I mean... they maybe great but I like a bit of thrillers not just histrionics. Isn't it correctly said that books are like people, we meet many but fall in love very seldom,' said Abed with a grin.

'Then maybe those in that shelf are the ones I believe have had a worldwide impact and resonance, not necessary in that order. For sure all of them are worth reading at least a couple of times if not more !' He pointed towards the old rack lying in the corner.

Zunu, Danh and Sana rushed towards the rack to find books on witch craft, fairy tales and adventures. They looked completely lost in reading the previews, description, rating and stars.

'Children will always be children,' Antorio commented.

'Look, Fairy Tales - Snow White...' Sana pointed out.

'I have read that one,' said Danh.

'Me too, but I can read it a hundred more times,' Sana said wide eyed with excitement and rushed to her dad with the book tucked under her left arm. Her yellow striped sneakers curled down from the front, almost knocking her down.

'Dad!' she pushed the book onto him.

Abed slid his hand in his trouser, popped out a brown wallet, and happily bought it for her. His look saddened as he saw his wife's old picture in the wallet, smiling and holding two year Sana in her arms, chestnut hair blowing in the wind. He placed the wallet back in the left pocket. His daughter and her wishes meant the world to him.

'How do you feel about the way technology is now shaping the readership?' Abed inquired.

'Although I like going along with the times, I believe that no e-reader can replace the vibe of an actual book in your hand. When I was younger, I only wanted to spend my time reading classic novels. Nowadays, all of teenagers only want to read romance crap. Disgraceful "poo" in right words,' he frowned.

'I swore never to read another romantic book after one shitty read. I could never figure out why trash sells. I was forced to comply with times and maintains all kinds though. See that corner? Its full of it.'

The road was getting unfilled at this point. Numerous peddlers were abandoning, it was late in the evening.

Twelve miles away the sand spun.

They could see the wind moving gradually over the sand beds in tall sections three thousand feet high and sparkling like shafts of marble in the evening light.

The bookseller pointed at it, 'There will soon be a sandstorm.'

They all looked in the direction. How grandly the winds moved, their feet upon earth, their heads transcending into the sky!

'Are you afraid of it?' Abed asked.

'No. We are desert people with hearts of steel. It is just god's wrath towards us. It will subside down as we offer our prayers.'

The bookseller packed up all of his books, covered them with neat sheets of green canvas. He tied the entire thing with ropes from one end to another. He was done for the day... but not quite yet with his grumbling, while his hands tied the knots into double knots around the corners of the wrinkled tarpaulin and properly stretched the sheet after beating out the air with thumps, he grimaced, 'The sand storm will ruin the books too. Usually I leave them open even at night. Nobody steals. Should I be happy or sad. Speaks on our changing culture.'

'Stalls selling garments and merchandise on this stretch have about multiplied, but bookstalls have stayed unaltered in number,' he cribbed as he packed up slowly.

Antorio agreed that the future looked bleak. The book seller interrupted his faltering thoughts with the snap of a finger...

'There is still fairly left for you to see,' he dug out a few books and showed him some pages loaded up with content in Arabic that he had written.

'This is about health. This one about power of mind, and this one about unconditional love.'

He turned over the pale white pages of the note book that had light blue horizontal lines one after another. His interest in reading had led him to write. Below every write, he had closed down as 'Eymen Yilmaz' and explained the meaning of each letter in unique style. 'The meaning of Eymen itself is "lucky and fortunate",' he explained.

'E is for easy going, no ruffles here.

Y is for yes, always open to new outcomes.

M is for mighty, your inner strength.

E is for enchant, for enchanting your will.

N is for notable, distinguished are your feat.'

The scribbles were inked proudly in a befuddling, naïve and running tilted text, some of the extra ink from pen had leaked onto the paper making all letters look 'double' and fat. He turned the pages one by one...

'I have a new born child and I've dedicated it to her, she is my inspiration,' he said with pride. His adam apple protruding out.

'That's cool and so inspiring,' Antorio replied inflating the man and adding a blush to his cheeks.

The book seller rattled, 'I admire the book characters such as Four French by A'gtanan, The pushback by Ruberg and Pary in Lost now. These days I am investing time in reading the Quotations from the works of Maose e-gunf.'

His camel sat there waiting patiently looking as beautiful, and bashful as a newly wed bride, decorated with colorful tassels, beads and mirrors. Even the tail was a sight to see.

The man loaded his stuff sack and the goat skin water bag onto it, then threw his leg from one side over the middle of hump, and quickly mounted it. He leaned backward as the camel stood up, then finally forward as it got onto the front leg. He instructed his camel with the sound, "hut hut hut". The wind rippled past his jacket as he turned around to say a good bye. He threw a book at them and said it's a free gift from his side. Sana caught it with a smile. They all waved at him..

"Wadaeaan." "Good bye." …he waved back to them and left.

The sun threw elongated shadows of the camel against the neighboring dune, making it all look a like giant riding trained dinosaur and the lumbering UFO spies from the skies.

Just behind the shop was a very old structured broken wall

that appeared to belong nowhere. It had tiny unrepaired cracks with green moss running through.

Antorio saw a dusty write up over it by a modern Arabic calligraphy artist. He had taken lines from famous Arabic, Turkish, and Persian poems and scribbled them in the most delicate and beautiful font after translating them to English. Antorio swept his hand over the wall, and wiped the dust to read the faded write up…

"Traveling— it gives you home in thousand strange places, then leaves you a stranger in your own land."

— Ibn Battuta

The quote really stood out, and had a great meaning for him. It gave him a connection to the place that he wouldn't long forget.

The party turned around and walked…

On the route to the desert camp where they'd be spending the night. Led by two locals who looked like twins; silent and stoic figures alongside their steeds, both draped in ash blue and crowned with turbans, they gradually gained ground. But every shifting minute on the dunes was a minute too long… the desert winds raised now furious billows of sand! All the air shone like gold dust and the drowning round sun turned enormous blood red at the skyline.

'O! Such a smothering sulphureous air!' Abed shouted taking a deep breath, 'must be much fresher at heights.'

'Sir, the gigantic winds and skies are indicators of omens,' one of the twins replied nervously, 'could be a good or negative sign for us. We must appease the storm god Quzah through prayers and pray for forgiveness. We must accede to their demands.'

'And what is that they demand?' asked Antorio.

'Commitment to fight against the evil forces. If even one sins from the tribe the entire tribe must pay. Only the moon god can calm Quzah. Whenever Quzah god is angry he hides the moon too with dusty skies. But as we pray the moon god shows up and Quzah recedes into a calm,' the other twin said.

The first twin added, 'Our family lived close to the mountain valley of Jizan, a region totally crushed by hurricane Dukahm. Just prior to the storm, our father had been reading the holy book as part of his devotional time. On Saturday night when the storm reached a noteworthy force, we realized that the red water sea was getting close to our tent. When my father went out to move our camel, ram and mule to safer land; he recollected moon god's immense sway and power as revealed in the book he read and decided to draw an imaginary line in the sand in front of the tent praying, 'O moon god, I ask you that you permit this far, yet no further; that the water may come till here before 'the arrogance of Quzah must be stopped.'

The other twin remarked, 'Fifty birds died. Flooding drowned three hundred of date palms trees and flooded two valleys. Winds wrecked many homes. Miraculously, when we went out the next morning to see the desolates of the storm, we saw that the seawater had come up, but did not cross the line drawn outside our home. God had given us a promise, he kept us through the storm and he answered our prayers! He is dependable and his word is real, solid and true!'

'Our neighborhood was crushed but we know moon god looked after us and spared our home to be used for others in times as this. God is almighty and always, always so kind.'

The horses couldn't be made to confront the approaching storm. They turned their backs to the breeze and balanced their heads between their fore feet. What's more, the breeze thundered and whistled through the slender date palm plantations. The fragile growths bent and bowed in the effect, the sand heaped high on the trunks; and only the strong tap roots shielded them from being torqued from the earth. As they struggled to walk further, Sana passed on the 'packaged' book in her hand to Zunu and locked her hands firmly at the waist. Zunu in turn tossed it to Danh who swiftly got it in his hands. He opened the brown package that was loosely clipped with two stapler pins and then screamed in delight. He started jumping up and down with squeals, too choked to speak – completely restless.

'Call him back! Someone call him back…!' Danh screamed loud.

'Call who?' Antorio questioned.

'Oh! the seller… the book seller….'

'What's wrong?' Antorio was puzzled seeing such hyper activity and over excitement. Did Danh have coffee again… Danh almost jumped over Zunu's foot who yelled in pain and let out a howling scream.

'Danh gone maddd again.'

'Yes! I am mad, you will go mad too….!

Just see this?' Danh started to dance and circle around

Zunu!

'Dad…! ….OMG! Callout for the book seller please…'

Sana looked on trying to understand the event of such celebration utterly confused.

'Please somebody – explain?'

Antorio turned around, ran backwards… his quick paced feet throwing the sand behind into the now duskier desert and into his face, little did he care… he could still see the pale bleak figure far off at the horizon amidst the strong sand storm brewing in, hitting his eyes… the driving particles of sand cut the face and his hands like blizzard snow.

He screamed….'Hoooooo!!!!! Please wait….. Please wait tttt…'

His high pitched voice repeatedly echoed silently and endlessly in the desert but didn't turn back around to answer him… he ran further… then fell down on his knees… breathless, waiting a moment – he drew a deep breath. He took the book around his mouth and quickly rolled it into a tunnel structure.. then screamed out again the loudest he could, the voice amplified reamplified furiously… as he looked down exasperated…!

— A faint low voice from very far screamed back, 'Are you in some trouble.'

Immediately Antorio questioned him, 'Where did u find the book that you just gave us….?'

'Please repeat… can't hear you.'

'Who gave you this book? Where did u find it?'

'The book. Oh... There was a guy who was heading to Mecca - Medina for prayers, he stopped by me and said he had an English book on him which he can't carry to Medina - as they don't allow foreign language stuff and it might be offensive to the holy place. He asked me to keep it.'

'What was his name? Who was he?'

'I don't know.... a young boy wearing blue shirt, grey trousers...'

'Is that all?' the book seller screamed back... 'I leave now ?...'

'Ya... that's all... Thanks! Many thanks!'

Antorio watched the shadow of camel faintly dipping into the dark horizon line... he was gone. Antorio walked back a mile...

Zunu and Danh maintained a stoic silence.

'Dad, we can go back home now. We have 'The Guide Book.'

At the seashore, the guy in blue shirt and grey trousers whistled silently as he lowered his boat into the waters.

'How was your trip to Mecca?' the friendly fisherman recognized him and quickly gave a helping hand.

'Success. I prayed for my five sisters, my dad and mom.'

He knelt down, looked towards the sky, recited a prayer.... said 'Ameen'. The boat rushed into the waters ready to face any turbulence.

Sprawled in his tiny boat, he again sang to the stars:

  I go back home

home calls me....

But the lovely seas, they never do forget me

....dadada -dd- da...

and splashed water. The tiny colorful fishes played in his palm as he caressed the sea and the dark friendly waves pushed him further and further.... far away from the Arabian dreams. Not many knew who he was, yet the ocean could guess him.

CHAPTER NINETEEN

Home

The storm was calmer in an hour. Abed said he and Sana must take a leave now. 'I have work to attend and Sana must start preparing for school.'

Antorio shook hands with him, 'You have been a great help to us and left us safe across the border, I cannot thank you enough. I hope we get to see you in future too.'

'Sure. It's never the end…' Abed broke into a smile. They stepped outside the camping tent.

Sana, Zunu and Danh too were having their conference.

'So, Sana, you leave now,' said Zunu sadly.

'Yes, I have to leave, but I have two new friends now.'

'Don't talk like you are leaving forever, when you become a doctor you must treat me free,' Danh said trying to get not too emotional and hugged her. He already had a tear that was at the brink of falling down his cheek.

'That's too far off. Byes aren't forever. We are all friends now. I am sure Sana can make it for summer holidays and mail us once in a while,' Zunu added quickly lightening up the heavy mood.

Danh quickly removed a piece of paper, 'Antorio uncle, can I have your pen please?'

'Ya sure,' he fidgeted his left pocket, then right and pulled out a blue ball point pen that was always handy on him.

Danh took it and started scribbling his address…

Mr. Nguyen.
Na Rang village, Ha Giang Province
Vietnam

'Ask any of the locals. It should be easy to find.'

'–And Zunu? Where do you stay?'

Zunu scratched his head, raised his eyebrow in a slant, eye balls popping out not knowing what to say –he looked at Danh through the corner of eye.

'Sana, Zunu doesn't stay here…' Danh quietly whispered in Sana's ears.

And Sana exclaimed: 'Where then! Another planet!'

'Yes. Exactly… out of the world.'

'Oh, you mean some place like Mauritius, Harbour Island, Bahamas…Horseshoe Bay, Bermuda triangle, Seven Mile Beach, Grand Cayman, Cayman Islands…?'

'No, he is from another planet. Don't tell anyone or else they will museum him,' Danh stood on his pointed toes, shoe crimped. He placed one hand upon Sana's ear to speak very softly such that nobody hears.

'Really, that sure is funny and myself from Abra ca Dabra, no maybe land of ghost!'

Zunu scratched his thick black hair giving a funny look to Danh, 'She won't understand, forget it. Will explain later.'

'Zunu and Danh, I look forward to seeing you soon. Take care. It was a lot of fun. I will miss you guys. Please don't forget me,' she and Abed opened the car door and got seated.

'You must come down to my place in summers. It's always fresh in the fields. You will like it. Bye Sana.'

'Please give our regards to all your friends – Hasan, Ala, Amir, Nasir and Lilah,' Zunu said.

Danh peeped into the car window for a last look and started to cry, he raised his arm to wipe the streaming tears. His pale yellow shirt sleeves were wet as he murmured, 'I want to go home too...'

Zunu held his hand and said to him, 'Me too,' and they would be home soon.

Abed fitted in the car's keys, the car made a roaring start sound, and then slowly started pulling away leaving a trail of sandy tracks behind. Sana jumped up halfway through the window and turned back to say her final bye with flying kisses. She looked at them for a long time, waving her hands side to side in the warm breeze. Inching back to her seat, she looked into the side rear view mirror, it was grimy. She removed the glass cleaner from the deck and squeezed some liquid into a tissue paper. She rubbed the mirror with it to wipe the blind spots and the dirt.

The corner of her left lip twitched slightly as she turned around once again sentimental eyed. She continuously watched the mirror and saw the land fall back.

After her mom's demise, she was a strong girl and tears weren't easy with all the hardships she had to face in her life. She remembered her mom's words, 'Never cry and accept the life's flow, it's just one precious life, make the most of it. It's a part of growing up and responsible behavior.'

Abed turned around and told Sana, 'That's my strong girl.'

She smiled at him, her eyes stronger now, still absorbed in the flitting mirror and the reflecting landscapes as she fell asleep telling herself, 'I will see them all soon.'

Antorio asked both the kids to head inside the camping tent, it was late and they needed to eat and then sleep. They had an early morning flight to Vietnam next day.

Both Zunu and Danh barely ate some rice and chicken gravy. The excitement of the day had kept them too occupied and on their toes with all the discussions and the ongoing events, thus sparing food. They were now a bit bogged down with lapse of energy. The shining line was the 'Guide Book' that they didn't discuss at all, it was too much of a shock that'd brought about a silence. Antorio didn't know what was to come and if he could be home.

Antorio sat on the black asphalt road tasting on a jug of

lemon cumin drink that he'd obtained from a tiny store. He observed the traffic go by… women and men drove past as though he didn't exist, traffic lights blinked into his eyes and gradually faded. The antiquated hushes of the wells, their old dust laden ropes, the silent sand and his journey to Earth had ended with the now found 'guidebook.'

He thought Serengeti was so vivid and live as compared to the desert that was so mystique. His purpose was accomplished. His mission ended. But how will they ever return back home with the guidebook… There was no passage, no way. They were stuck on Earth.

He took another sip with a deep furrow in his forehead. The sweet salty drink was so ordinary but it would go on to be his last memory as he turns around at the fading wells lost in time. They will call out to him always… to rediscover the place! The emptiness and mystique. Utilized or not, the wells will remain. In their cellars sparkled circles of pale sky—and perhaps a part of his home… his galaxy 1x… as he raised his head towards the sky. Each twinkling star spoke of a universe far far ahead. A stark kingdom shut to the world.

They were just pioneers through earth. Drifters through time and space.

A hand swiftly turned him around.

'Dad! You must sleep now.'

Antorio looked down at the sand coating his shoes and said, 'Yes.'

He dropped a tiny sharp stone into a well as they strode by. It hit the bottom with a thunk, and a clonk. He screamed into the empty well. 'Next time we come this stone will be a reminder that we must refill you, Bye!' The empty sound of the stone travelled back to the surface giving him a tight invisible hug. Antorio felt the ghostly touch and flinched a second.

Antorio threw his one arm around Zunu.

"Zunu, the distance the stone falls is given by:

$$d=1/2gt^2$$

We know that average speed = distance travelled / time taken.

If we are given the speed of sound as 343 secs then

$$d=343 \times t2$$

Say:

$$t1 + t2 = 3.2s$$

It's easy to find t2 if t1 value is calculated. Seconds multiplied by time give us the distance."

'Zunu, the particles are a lot nearer together in water than in air. They can rapidly transmit vibrational energy starting with one molecule and then onto the next,' Antorio connected his finger points together to display it. 'It means the sound waves in water can travel faster than in air, and around four times faster actually, but it takes a lot of energy to begin these vibration.'

'Sound in air travels at approximately 332 meters per second... that is fast but not nearly as fast as light which travels at 300000 kilometers per second....'

Antorio's "classroom" went on as they headed for the tent...!!! He rubbed his shoes at the back of his trousers and cleared the tiny sand that grazed the vamp. The sand blew away softly, carrying with it the last footprints too.

Zunu and Antorio lay still in the tent. The orange hued desert moon; how large it looked that night. And how it warmed up the East southeast sky. Pale, milky glowing light... Under it miles and miles of prickly cactus - half revealed, half covered; and far away against the dim mountains the dunes of the desert shimmered white. Undoubtedly in the desert, where it fell savage and hot as a downpour of meteors, it was the preeminent supreme excellence to which all things still paid allegiance and devotion to. Be that as it may; far away the universe had its standards, dictates and concurs too.

A little planet crossed its direction. The moon cautiously and daintily leaned aside. With a bit of ovalish squeeze in itself for a second, it let the quiet cosmic system cruise by. And that night the unfamiliar unknown galaxy 1x passed by swiftly.

–Still inconspicuous and mighty insignificant to Earth's wisdom.

CHAPTER TWENTY

The Unseen Gift

They reached Vietnam in evening. Na Rang village lanes were hustling and bustling with gossips and activity.

As they cruised by, a woman chewing betelnut gossiped, her shoulders pulled low as she clutched her pale dress with fingers, twirling it nervously at her knees.

'I saw a shadow last night under the banyan tree. It disap..peared.'

'Guess... me too... Suddenly the curtain of my window flew in a rage as though it was hit by some unseen object,' said the other lady as she pulled over her cashmere cotton shawl across the shoulder.

'But yesterday…no wind. then how it happen ya?' the betelnut lady's stained teeth were bursting with stories to tell.

' — I know. That's what nooo,' said the other lady holding her shawl closer and tighter now.

The air was full of gossips. The betelnut lady breathed into every ear she could.

'Dogs too were wailing so bad – wonder why?'

'— I tell only you. Black cat crossed my rooftop yesterday.'

'It's the monk. His own didn't give him a proper funeral. His spirit is now haunting,' another rosebud lipped auburn haired old woman uttered as she spit betelnut out. She replayed the event over and over with a shaky voice. Her one eye twitched repeatedly.

'My stove caught fire yesterday. I had to throw sand over it. Some unhappy person is haunting the village,' a small built restless woman with fuzzy hair and long bermuda pants stated gnawing her nails as she edged closer to other ladies with distrusting eyes... Looking behind again and again for shadows in daytime.

'I TELL YOU – It's him.'

'My son had fever yesterday. — You are right. His ghost is surely back,' said another.

The village appeared obsessed with the ghost theory. A rooster exploded amidst the evening session tiring it out and interrupted the gossips of the dusty lanes...

Kookdokooo. Kookduko.

Ladies retired to their homes as Zunu passed by with deadpan expression. As they walked the old lanes Danh couldn't be happier. In the plane and throughout the bus journey to Na Rang from Ha Giang province, he was staring out of the window just dying to be back home. How he hopped up at the sight of the white screwy board with a green fat bolt mark pointing straight ahead to 'Na Rang'. Coconut trees looped their length towards the sky and their pinnate leaves danced with the familiar winds.

Danh ran towards his home as it came in sight and Zunu right behind him. Bambi's thin neck and round eyes looked on curiously from across the fence with a rippling bleat 'meehhhhh'.

'Danh, you will rip your pants. He he! slow down,' Zunu shouted out.

Danh turned around and stuck out his tongue at him, adjusting the midline of shorts that was pinching him.

'Mami! dadaa. Mami!' Danh screamed. Mr. and Mrs. Nguyen were already waiting for him outside the compound. They embraced him tightly.

'Dad! It was a wonderful trip. I saw all animals I have never seen and as much heard of,' Danh was breathless.

They all walked towards the house. Zunu was silent for two seconds and looked at his dad. Only they were not back home. Their home Galaxy 1x.

Antorio read the silence.

'Zunu, one journey is over. We did find the Guidebook. I am sure the second will begin too.'

Zunu tried to smile but his lips were not willing to part.

Danh was jumping around, showing photos of their journey and spoke non stop about Serengeti, Jordan and Saudi Arabia.

'Dad, I have invited Sana home, she write to us.'

'Ok ok… Good. You have many friends now,' Mr. Nguyen said and silent Mrs. Nguyen looked on affectionately at Danh rubbing his hair. The apple of her eye was back.

'Dad, we have to gift the laptop to Danh.'

'Yes, it's the right time for him to make use of it.'

Suddenly anxious troublesome restless 'mooing' sounds were heard right inside the courtyard. They all rushed out. 'moo' had chosen their courtyard for birth. She was pacing around, getting up and laying down repeatedly. She was looking at them for help.

She has been in that position likely for the last hour or two, and hadn't advanced any further. Mr. Nguyen rushed inside to find a pair of gloves. He used some lubricant on the gloves, reached inside the cow to see how the calf was positioned.

'Be careful. She appears a bit cranky. Sometimes cow's hormones are going so wacky that she may decide you to be the source to vent out frustration,' Mrs. Nguyen cautioned while everyone held up a decent thirty minutes…

'That happened to me already,' Danh said it loud and stared accusingly at the cow without flickering his Chinese beady eyes, his jaw stuck open at the event.

As she came very close, a water sac was seen hanging from the vulva, a yellowish spherical sac. Soon both the front feet showed up, followed by the nose. The tender infant calf was having the base of it's feet pointing to the ground. Mr. Nguyen pulled it out and fell flat over his back as the calf came out and landed on top of him.

He cleaned out the calf's nose quickly with his fingers to get all the amniotic fluid out as everyone watches in fascination. He tickled its nose with a clean piece of hay, put some water in its ears to make it shake its head, and performed artificial respiration to get the calf going. The calf started to breath within thirty to sixty seconds.

Moo looked pleased and thankful and she quietened down. Danh and Zunu looked on with crazy eyes. Days had passed by with absolute outright insane episodes.

Mrs. Nguyen ensured there was some feed and water for the cow to keep her upbeat while she got to know her new youngster. She even helped the calf suckle the cow as it was experiencing difficulty. She held up the young close to the cow and guided the teat into the mouth of the calf.

'This first meal is very significant for the health of the calf and should be taken within five hours of birth,' she remarked.

They left the cow and her newborn calf alone for a while to allow the cow to mother up to the calf, and encourage her to begin nursing.

They walked back to the kitchen area and got seated over the hand woven mats. Zunu went inside the other room and pulled out the gift for Danh from his bag.

The kitchen was flooded with the smell of grounded, crushed starchy grains and chopped spring onion porridge bubbling over a wooden fire with rapid charcoal exhaust which

Mrs. Nguyen fanned away.

Zunu tiptoed back in behind Danh and said, 'Stretch out your hands and close your eyes.'

'Why?' asked Danh.

Zunu quickly shut his eyes with his one hand and placed the package in his hands.

There was an unexplainable pleasure, amusement, and fulfillment that Zunu felt after he saw Danh's bewildered face as he started opening the gift with big eyes.

There was a small card at the top attached with tape. Printed over it were tiny yellow flowers. It read:

To my sweet friend Danh,

'My friend is the one that brings out the best in me. You are a blessing in my life!'

with love Zunu.

Danh read it loud with pride. He swept his hand along the length of it, stroking it lovingly. The glossy paper wrapper made little sharp crackly noises in the silent room. Then Danh cut the ribbon and unwrapped the transparent cellophane wrap film paper.

He was so upbeat doing it that Zunu felt like that was the most perfect gift ever. He felt sure, he would not have felt the same pleasure giving him some other gift. Danh had been longing to own a laptop and after receiving it from Zunu, he hugged him and screamed.

'I thought of clothes, books, perfumes, shoes, household appliances, and bags, but then this was of better utility to you,' said Zunu.

'It's awesome. I can access net easily now,' Danh opened the dark 20" laptop and ran his fingers over the keyboard.

'Wowww,' he exclaimed with lost words and a twinkle in his eyes as he stared down at the laptop screen.

'Da, see this! My dream.'

Mr. Nguyen looked at Zunu with deep set gratitude.

'I will teach you how to operate it,' smiled Zunu.

Danh rushed inside and returned back with an envelope.

'Zunu, when you go back to Galaxy 1x you must open this. Ok…?'

Zunu nodded… 'Okk.'

At night Zunu and Antorio pulled over the mattresses close to the window for some air. They lay down. There was a flash of forked lightening and streaked thunder followed by sweeping rains that thrashed the roof top.

Zunu stared out of the small window at the hazy Sequin silver stars that winked at him. Once again, he missed his home. How he wished to be home again.

He couldn't sleep. A radiant moonbeam was slanting through a gap in the dark trees. A tiny spot was shining right on his chin and on the floor. All others in the family had been asleep for a while now.

Zunu shut his eyes and lay onto one side. He made a decent attempt to doze off, changing sides. There were flashes. Flashes of his cousin Baggy thumping his back telling him, 'Bro the moon will bring you luck. It will direct you.'

Tiny Drinkiwell showing him the moon in the sky. His thin voice telling him, 'It will console you when your heart is sad. Whenever your heart wavers it will give you courage. With every heart beat it will remind you who you are. Whenever you loose powers it will empower you back. The moon will look after you. Cause this moon is a blend of Grewins precious tears.'

His cousin Lavender's voice resonated, 'We are aware you will have no powers over planet Earth. Ever feel lonely, look towards the sky. And you will be back home soon with moon luck on your side.'

The man in the desert, his words echoed, 'Whenever Quzah god is angry he hides the moon too with dusty skies. But as we pray the moon god shows up and Quzah recedes into a calm, God had given us a promise, he kept us through the storm and he answered our prayers!'

The moonbeam was like a white spear cutting through the window onto his face as he opened his eyes. He twisted and turned around. The house was totally muffled, 'Not even Danh's ancestors appear alive today,' Zunu thought to himself. No footsteps came up from anywhere, there was just no sound.

The window behind the curtain was a bit open, nobody was strolling on the footway outside. The moon looked to be a quarter full. Hung above like some silver inverted bowl. Tall and small shadows of still houses lay unmoved far and wide in the silent criss cross lanes. Shadows of the trees fell in the empty streets making them eerie. Not a teensy weensy sound from anywhere and not a cloud moved.

The moonbeam was smiling more than ever on Zunu's face, playing with him. He got out of bed, took a long look at the moon, it seemed so magical. Then he squeezed tight the gap in curtains —only to reopen it again the next second. He gazed up once more longingly for the times he'd spent with his cousins.

Soon it was a dark and blustery night and the downpour fell in deluges except for infrequent interims when it was checked by a violent wave of wind. It cleared up the boulevards and rattled along the thatched rooftop. It fiercely and savagely, agitated the scanty piffling flame of the lamp that battled against the haziness. Water was dripping from the leaked roof into a small bucket. Plop plop...

Soon Zunu fell asleep and dreamt....

The guide book was calling out to him. He was standing in a deep dark sandy alley. It was raining sand and thick layers of sand stood over quiver trees. The book grew hundred times it's size... It kept growing. Its pages were flipping open one by one and the book was whispering to Zunu...

'Zunuuu....'

"The day you stepped outside of galaxy 1x, was the day you paved your way back too.

He who has a heart, he who is true, One with valour, One who is noble, One who has spirits, One who has courage to do the right thing, he who has humanity will find their way to galaxy 1x.

You carved your way back already when you first made the effort and sacrifice to go hunt me. I was waiting for you.

I shower my respect and blessings to all those who endeavour valorously in every battlefield, who do not need any saviour, who have discovered something that matters more than fear & who exhibit great enthusiasm, commitment & are ready to spend themselves for the noble cause.

Hardship, hesitation, uncertainty, fear, sickness & disappointments can make anybody quit but letting your judgement, instincts & willingness overcome every obstacle makes you win & succeed in life. Find your amazing strength & become mindful to utilize it to accomplish anything even surprisingly ordinary.

Stay Blessed Zunu! I bless you."

Zunu raised his head and stared wide eyed at the enlarged book pages printed in rose gold blushes and pinks. They were richly decorated with curly vintage floral border with a white background and gold headings.

The letters flipped and rolled from one corner to another. They turned, swiveled, bent and made living eerie 'type writer' sounds. They wore frilly flip flops with slumping ankle length socks and slid down the pages like roller coaster rides. They walked towards Zunu and danced around him merrily singing –

"We cause gladness and tender feelings
We make you think a lot about a subject
We give you a delightful story
We offer you three hankies – boo-hooer

We give you index, glossary and append
So who are we?
We are the letters series
Bold, thin italic and fat!"

They had egg shaped white eyes with yellow arc running at top in one eye, at the bottom in another. Tiny blue balls inside, that rolled all around like dice. Wire like brown brows, and eyes that never blinked. A flat button nose, heart shaped lips. A round face that bobbed over a white thread.

The letter C held Zunu's hand with care
The letter H gave him a hug
The letter P pampered him with pastries
The letter J gave him a friendly jerk

They picked up the sand in their thick gloved woollen hands and threw it naughtily in the air, it fell all over Zunu. Zunu looked down and there was a mark in the sand that spelled Galaxy 1x.

They zig zagged and squiggled back into the book, bashing each other to get in with tiny squeals.

An abrupt resound silence was followed by,

"ZUNU ZUNU ZUNU Zunu Zunu Zunu..." the murmurs roared... deeper and more profound...

Zunu woke up startled out of sudden emptiness. All the darkness and haziness surrounding him suddenly lightened up. He rubbed his eyes. His head was over his dad's shoulder who was awake and smiling.

The wooden cable car had stopped at the 'Planoi station' of layer 2…. it started inching its way towards layer 1.

'Dad! am I dreaming?' Zunu rubbed his eyes, lifted his eyebrows and fluttered his lashes. With his mouth open he got Antorio with both his hands and shook him… 'Please pinch me. IS THIS REAL DAD!!!!'

'Yes Zunu… I woke up an hour back to find myself at station Planoi level 3.'

Zunu hopped close to the window, rubbed a patch clean and stared out with his nose stuck at it. He could see sand. Lots of sand. Indeed, it was Galaxy 1x. The cable car made 'zhuck zhuck' sounds as it picked up speed. The cable car had services to provide you with paid tea, magazines and other entertainment. A man was busy taking request from people, pushing a small trolley serving cart with a generous smile.

'Magazine sir?' he stopped and inquired with Antorio.

Antorio picked up a magazine, "Galaxy 1x New Invents".

'Welcome sir.'

'Oh! I could do with the Tarot Cards too.' He paid 3-3/4 Sanddunes, the currency od Galaxy 1x. It was a metal coin with a sand tower and skyline -/°\\- .

'Dad, why these tarot cards? Do you have faith in this stuff?'

'Hmm, someone revealed to me that color blue is fortunate for me, and so it was. Ha ha,' he giggled a healthy chuckle not giving any further clarification or explanation as he himself was left so confused with the events.

The cable car began creeping its way into layer 1. It passed by the Pinea town and Pinea library and stopped once again. Zunu saw numerous passengers get down. The back of a tall man clad in a flowing attire caught his attention... Vaguely familiar— Zunu immediately headed out of the compartment, into the passageway aisle towards the entrance of the cable car...

'Hey... hey there...!' Zunu shouted stepping down.

The man didn't turn around. Something rolled out of the man's bag through a tiny hole. Just then the cable car fired the alert ringer and started to close its entry door.

Zunu sprinted and bent low to pick up the fallen object and then pranced back into the cable car on his one foot as the cable moved ahead in pace. He stared at the object long....

It was a round white translucent pebble. A pebble he'd seen before... He tightened his fingers around it and held it close to his chest, frozen.

It'd belonged to him. He had gifted it to someone special. He pushed it back into his pocket with a slight smile. While he stood there dazed, still staring at the back of the man, his palms flattened upon the closed door to catch his last glimpse, the cable moved 'zhush zhush' horizontally now as it picked up speed through the sand hills towards home... Zunu's home... A board said:

Obere Tuftra, Plot no 12, Pinea town.

Tropical rainforest green plant wallpaper finishing brought beauty and a relaxing environment to Zunu's room, opening up the boundaries between the home and the outdoors.

He stared at his room as though he was seeing it for the first time in his life. The atmosphere was fresh and alive as it ever had been… it was like he had never left it. Antorio was busy unlocking the doors and windows and Plastica was helping in dusting the house spic and span.

Zunu could hear some voices downstairs. He peeped out of the bedroom door. It was granny. She had seen their windows open and had come down to greet them with Tibby. Tibby looked pretty healthy and well fed.

Granny was standing under an umbrella double her size with her niece too under it. Of course, it wasn't raining. The umbrella had special multichromatic light at its boundaries so whatever colors she wore were noticeable loud and clear to everyone. Zunu could see her round beaded necklace dangling over her bulging stomach, she hadn't changed a bit.

Her ten year old grand-daughter Smasha visited her often. Huge purple butterfly crystal sunglasses double her face, she recoiled her nose often and looked upstairs to smile at Zunu with brace laden teeth as she clutched onto her silver purse dearly. The whole family was a bit funny. She adorned a hat with a tiny brinjal hanging from one side and a brinjal pattern pleated frock.

'Zunu, would you like to race with me. I'm a champion and just came first in school,' Smasha yelled out to him proudly.

'Err… No… I'm -m sure to lose. I am panting already.'

'Oh! baffling. Everyone is so scared of me.'

Granny looked at her proudly.

'Grandma, they are all jealous of me,' she said as she doffed her hat in her left hand twirling her auburn hair, her head tilted to one side. Then with a bark of silly laughter that suggested victory, she held granny's hand tightly.

'I know, I understand… sweetie!'

Just then Mr. Antorio showed up. The trio engaged in routine conversation.

Zunu shut back the door of his room, slammed his eyes shut and heaved a sigh of relief. 'What a stupid girl,' he told himself. 'No idea, how dad tolerates them - Really!'

He sat over his bed, opened his bag to find the sealed envelope by Danh. Danh had asked him to open it once he reached galaxy 1x. It was a simple post card with scribblings from Danh.

Zunu,

May all your dreams come true.

It is not very expensive but keep it with you as my memory. I had no previous preparation for buying a gift.

With good wishes and cordial love.

Danh

CHAPTER TWENTY ONE

The Letter

Dear Danh,

I would like to tell you your dream of orange trees was as real as my dream of being back home! No superstition. I am back home.

You were right... Dreams do come true.

Also I met the great man... only this time I didn't follow him. But I know he is here to stay... and he is one of us.

Zunu.

Zunu beamed the letter to Danh. Danh had a tiring day searching all over for Zunu. He was glad to receive a message from him. He quickly twigged him a signal… Zunu received it.

'Zunu, where in the world are you? Whatever did happen, how did you suddenly go away without as much informing me?'

'Don't know… I had a dream. The dream just came true. It brought us back.'

'I looked for you all over the village. I thought someone museumed you. he he!'

'No, no one museumed me. I am truly back home. I am in Galaxy 1x.'

'That's great. I am very happy about it. Though I will miss you very much,' Danh remarked. 'I told you dreams do come true, didn't I?'

Zunu acknowledged it, 'Yes. You were right and you know,

you should visit me in the multichromatic season. It should be fun Danh.'

'Multichromatic… What's dat…?'

'Oh! That's when Galaxy 1x is full of colours and special privileges. It's only December to April when we get to see all colours.'

'Oh! I understand. You will beam me up?'

'Yes. Whenever you are prepared.'

'During holidays. I look forward to seeing you again!' Danh said excitedly.

'Me too.'

'By the way, whom did you meet? Which man…?'

Zunu clutched the stone tightly to his heart… and showed it to Danh…

'What! You mean, the great man? He is aliveee??' Danh screamed seeing the beamed print of the stone over his floor.

'I have no idea… what he was doing over planet Earth and who he is… What connection I have with him. But I felt I knew him. Time will tell. I hope I get to see him again. I have so many questions.'

'I do as well, Zunu!' said a stunned Danh. 'By the way, I switched on the laptop. It's windows 27. How do we print what we write?'

'Press ctrl P,' Zunu said.

'See this Zuny… he he.'

'And how is moo doing ?' asked Zunu.

'Moo…moo has dirtied th…'

'Stop it Danh,' shouted Zunu.

Meanwhile Antorio was busy discussing Tarot reading. Granny and her grand-daughter were occupied with him giving him their opinions and advice.

'ONLY I can give best predictions, everybody says,' Smasha exerted snootily, shaking her red white floral printed two velcro strapped leather sneakers to and fro, with a silly chuckle.

Plastica looked on, 'You are a show off S-M-A-S-H-A. Do not defy nature with iffy predictions….012 012..'

MORE BOOKS

AVAILABLE PART 2 - VERY SOON

Alongside a novella!

To all the wonderful readers,

If dreams indeed come true….
I want 500 million people to read this. It's my dream too ;)
Do suggest the book to your associates if you like it.
Do share the link to 100 more.

Follow on Twitter and Pinterest for updates :
@Friko_MS

ABOUT THE AUTHOR

M.S. Friko is the pen name of the author. The author holds a diploma in jewellery designing. A useless engineering degree, is a writer and illustrator out of choice and spends time in a number of hobbies. The author keeps out of social site chaos, although maintains a digital presence where needed. We stay who we are, but the different energies and billion souls will interpret you differently person to person. So, we realise it and stop the complexities towards better visions. The book is written, designed, illustrated, and formatted by the author.